SILK AND SWORD

P.S. SCOTT

CONTENTS

ONE

PETRONILLA

It was hate at first sight.

The minute Lieutenant General Petronilla laid eyes on Acelina, she knew the woman was up to no good. Clad in an off-the-shoulder mint-green kimono that showed off her creamy skin, she flittered over General Darius, plying him with drinks and fake smiles. She hated how her body responded to the wicked woman's wiles. It was hate, she told herself. Pure, undiluted hate. Acelina left no stone unturned when it came to furthering her business. She gave her patrons everything that they desired. That's why Duality, Acelina's pleasure house, was the most exclusive destination in the red-light district.

Acelina turned her eyes to her, fluttering her sooty eyelashes. Petronilla snorted and turned the other way. She didn't know why she'd taken such an instant dislike to Acelina, just that she had. Maybe it was something to do with the fact that she hated people who sold innocent women for sex. Acelina might look like a siren, but she was a monster.

They'd met for the first time three years ago when Petronilla visited Duality because she was suspicious of a criminal hiding on their premises. A battle was underway back then, but that didn't stop Acelina from barring her entry.

"I can't let you disrupt my business," she'd said in her cutting, professional tone. As the proprietress of the most famous pleasure house in Inferno, Acelina was a legend. She didn't care who her customers were, only that they paid. Her job was to make money, and she considered it her right to use any means necessary to achieve her goal.

"This is a matter of national importance," Petronilla countered, proceeding to knock down the door. That had resulted in a long bill for damages being sent to her general, which was ultimately footed by the crown. It hadn't affected her standing, but it had been an embarrassing incident that had planted the seed for their acrimonious relationship. Ever since, they'd met several times, mostly because General Darius, her superior, liked to spend his time here.

"Do you want anything?" Acelina's sickly sweet voice asked. Her obsidian gaze met Petronilla's in a direct challenge, unlike the subservient escort she was supposed to be. Toward people who she didn't consider 'customers', her demeanor was icy.

"No, thank you." Petronilla turned to her food. She pretended to eat but nothing went down her throat. Fresh flowers arranged in lacquered porcelain vases – roses and lilies- scented the room. But it couldn't completely wash away the scent of liquor and sex that permeated these walls.

Coughing, she looked up at General Darius who shifted on the mat next to her. Their team— thirty of them— were crowded around a lacquered wooden table in the VIP room of Duality to celebrate another successful year of winning battles. It had been a relatively peaceful year, which is why they were at Duality, not on a battlefield. Duality was a Japanese-style house with low tables and bamboo mats where patrons sat.

Darius held up a glass of liquor and smiled at her, his clear green eyes filled with mirth. His black wings dropped behind his muscular build, dark stubble forming on his angular jaw. He squinted at the food in front of them then said to Acelina, "The food is delicious, as always."

"Thank you." She bowed as gracefully as a swan. Frowning, Petronilla picked up a glass of water and held it up.

General Darius was an angel, though he'd been living in Inferno for a long time. Their continent of Atea was divided into four nations- Elysium, Terra, Inferno and Escayton. Elysium was the country of angels. It was also the only country that didn't have a monarchy and had a heavenly hall of nominated angels and deities instead. Unlike Inferno, the sun always shone up there and the waters were clear and blue. The weather was pleasant, free from the oppressive heat of summer and the biting cold of winter.

Petronilla, who was originally from Terra, was human. Unlike the demons who lived in Inferno, and the angels in Elysium, humans had a finite life span. Terra was also the only country in Atea that experienced four seasons. Summers were sweltering hot and winters were freezing cold.

Escayton was an ancient country with many mystical

practices. It bordered Elysium to the north and Inferno to the south. Of the four countries, it was the smallest, but abundant in natural resources. It had days and nights like Terra, but the weather was mostly warm. People from Escayton looked human but possessed magical healing powers. King Delton of Inferno was married to Princess Xara of Escayton, which technically meant Escayton was now part of Inferno.

Inferno was where they all lived now. It was open to immigrants who could prove their worth to the king. Originally home to immortal creatures with demonic power, it was now mostly occupied by half-humans thanks to the liberal immigration policy. Angels rarely came to Inferno, the weather a threat to their health. Inferno was eternally hot, with a powerful monarchy. King Delton was always looking to conquer more land in Atea, which is how the infamous Millennium War with Elysium had begun. However, Inferno was also the only country in Atea where relationships between members of the same sex were permitted. Terra had liberalized its policy six years ago, but the effects were yet to be seen.

"Did you know he's a fallen angel?" Hadda, one of the newer female recruits, whispered to Petronilla, pointing to Darius' black wings. She wore her black hair in a ponytail and her amber eyes twinkled with suppressed gossip. "I heard he betrayed Elysium in the Millennium War—"

"Cheers," Petronilla announced loudly before Darius could announce a toast and swallowed a glass full of water. Darius blinked, then nodded. Petronilla's voice was lost among the clinking of glasses, ribald laughing of courtesans and the sound of rice wine being poured in crystal goblets.

She was tired of hearing of the Millennium War that had taken place a century ago, long before she was born. She knew it was the reason Darius now resided in Inferno and had such a strong friendship with the king. The Millennium War had sealed the hostile fate of Inferno and Elysium. Though a peace treaty had been signed after the war, she knew King Delton would never give up on conquering the realm of angels.

"Next time, let me defend myself," Darius whispered.

She looked to him, her eyes wide.

"You heard her?" Abandoning the empty glass of water, Petronilla watched General Darius' unperturbed expression.

"It's the truth," he shrugged. "I did betray Elysium during the war."

"I don't like anyone bad mouthing you," she said. He was her mentor and guide. He'd rescued her from a horrible fate, and for that, she'd always be grateful to him. Before she could voice her objections, Acelina appeared before her.

"I'll take that." She bent down and picked up the empty glass. Her eyes were obsidian, reflecting Petronilla's hate. Acelina was half-human. The demon half of her blood had unfortunately not been expressed as much as the human half, so she wasn't immortal. Half-humans never were. But she had a long life span and her dark eyes sometimes shone red, like devil eyes did. Petronilla always thought the demon side of her showed her true colors.

"I'm so glad you decided to bring your comrades here, General," she said to General Darius, who was laughing again.

"I wanted them to have fun. And Duality is the best there

is," he said. Acelina preened at the praise, making her want to throw up. Then, turning to Petronilla, he lowered his voice to a whisper, "Are you doing okay?"

No. I'd rather be in hell.

"Yes." She looked out of the window at the trees and the row of gaudy red lanterns that decorated the red-light district, while distractedly nibbling on some fried potatoes. The number of red and pink lanterns hung outside each pleasure house door showed how many male and female escorts they had available. The whole set-up was repulsive to her, so she continued to focus on the food. Square paper lamps with red and green ink paintings were fitted in every corner of the room.

Petronilla felt nauseous. Though the Duality was supposed to be a classy establishment, it was a pleasure house nevertheless, and all pleasure houses reminded her of her past- a past in which she had been desperate and powerless. As she watched the escorts, dressed in fine clothing parading around like peacocks, the sense of hatred ballooned. Two decades ago, she had been one of them— eager to please, and always falling short.

"I didn't want to leave you out, but if you're uncomfort-able—" General Darius' face tensed with concern, his lips thinning to a line. His dark brown hair was a contrast to the paleness of his face. It was like he could read her thoughts.

Returning to the present, she shook her head, obligated to display strength before her mentor. "I want to be here."

General Darius moved his hand over the table as if feeling for a glass. His hand slipped over the smooth ebony surface, cutting the glass from underneath.

"Watch out—"

Before Petronilla could finish her sentence, he'd accidentally knocked a glass of liquor, sending liquid spilling down the table.

"I'm sorry." He shook his head upon feeling the wet liquid seep into his trousers. Petronilla heard a note of despair in the upbeat general's voice. Darius loved drinking and was well-known to spend his free hours in the arms of courtesans. In that, he was the exact opposite of her, but then again, you'd never guess how much he drank from the way he looked. "Looks like the alcohol went straight to my head."

"Marie, get more food," Acelina ordered, inserting herself between Petronilla and Darius to mop up the alcohol. "Don't worry about it, General."

"Thank you, Acelina. What would I do without you?" Darius' voice was light, but his eyebrows knit in a frown. She smiled at him, showing the better half of her two-faced self.

Then she glared at Petronilla, signaling her to move and give Acelina space. When she didn't comply, Acelina crowded her space, her silk kimono brushing Petronilla's arms — a deliberate attempt at provocation. She mopped under her crossed knee, hitting it with deliberate nudges.

So, the hate was mutual.

The poor maid entered and immediately averted her gaze. Dressed in Duality's beige uniform, she wore her hair back to keep it from falling.

"Marie, clean this up." Acelina left the maid to it, who bent down and got to work, afraid to meet Acelina's sharp eyes. She'd just finished delivering heavy plates of food, but Acelina didn't cut her any slack.

Petronilla's fist tightened, and sharp words lingered at the edge of her tongue. Acelina looked up, the light sliding over her perfectly formed cupid's bow and luscious pink lips. She was the worst sort of criminal- the kind that sold people's innocence for living.

She knew the power she had. Yet, she abused it.

Acelina reminded her so much of the cruel madame from her childhood. She bound girls who could've chosen something different to this honor-less life. She knew how much misery those smiles hid better than anyone else. Though their clothes were luxurious, and faces painted with beauty, their souls were ravaged.

Just like hers.

"More of this good liquor," Larian called out, holding up an empty white bottle, oblivious to the tension crackling in the atmosphere. His blonde hair had turned a shade darker thanks to the heat and sweating.

"You should stop," Petronilla said in a low voice.

"Right away." A maid plucked the bottle from his hand, her warning ignored.

"You're not eating anything," Hadda remarked. Her amber eyes gazed down at Petronilla's untouched plate of fried food and full liquor glass. Ever since Petronilla had become Lieutenant General, more women joined the army. Her heart filled with pride, knowing her work inspired others to choose a life of honor, instead of one of obligation.

"I'm not hungry," Petronilla said. She wanted the party to end as soon as possible. If Darius hadn't been the general of Inferno's army and her mentor, she wouldn't have come. She always found excuses to avoid the year-end gathering at pleasure houses. But Darius had roped her in today, and she was trapped.

"I think I'll leave in a bit," General Darius said, rubbing his eyes. "But not before we play a game."

"A game?" Acelina flitted from one soldier to another, like a pollinating bee. Larian laughed, entranced by her charms, and whatever meager wit she spouted. Her gaze met Petronilla's from across the table, questioning and challenging. Her gut reacted on instinct, and she turned away, heartbeat flooding her ears. Larian's blonde brow rose in question, noticing the tense exchange between the two women.

"Would you like something to drink?" one of the female escorts, Jasmine, asked, her large brown eyes fluttering. Petronilla cringed.

"I don't drink," she said, holding a hand over her cup. "Would you like me to entertain you, then?" she asked, the sexual innuendo unmistakable.

"No. Go away." Petronilla frowned, taking another bite of food. She couldn't taste it, living in the land of her memories. Two decades hadn't been enough to forget the pain.

Her profession meant the world to her. She'd carved out a path for herself, who had been a human without any blood-lines or future. Pride rose in her chest every time she thought of how far she'd come. Whatever the future brought, she'd face it with honor.

"It's your turn, Lieutenant General," one of the girls said. "What?" Engrossed in her thoughts, she'd lost track of the game they were playing. A silver spoon pointed at her, gleaming under the lights.

"The game," Darius reminded her. Petronilla hadn't realized they'd started.

"Truth or Dare?" Larian asked, from across the table. Acelina's hands reached into his open shirt, stroking an expanse of curling golden hair before reaching further down. She turned away, in disgust, aware of Acelina's eyes on her.

"Dare." The words were out of her mouth before she knew it.

"I told you she'd pick that," General Darius laughed. "Well, I have one."

For all that he looked like an angel, he had the heart of the devil. Being the leader of Inferno's army required devious tactics and Petronilla had the feeling he had decided to turn those tactics on her.

"I wanted to-" Larian said, throwing his hands up in the air.

The escort's arms fell to her sides, eyes fixed on Petronilla. "I'm sure the General has a better one."

"Oh, you won't be disappointed," Darius said, setting aside the arm of the male escort holding him. His eyes glinted with wicked humor.

"What's my dare?" she asked, putting her cutlery down. The sooner this ended, the sooner she could go home. Darius' finger ticked on his chin, deep in thought. Acelina whispered something into his ear, which made his eyes light with mirth.

"No, I had something else in mind," he said, almost standing up. A silent moment passed, in which Petronilla heard her heartbeat. "I dare you to spend a night with any escort in this room."

"What?" Petronilla spluttered, her eyes narrowing on the

escort whose gaze was diverted. She'd moved on to the next person, pouring him drinks. The whole room burst into a cheer.

"Good one," one of the other boys said— Damen. The rest of them burst out into hoots and cheers. She could feel the embarrassment washing her like unexpected summer rain. "I couldn't have come up with a better dare."

The sound of cheers filled her panicked ears. Darius' eyes held her in a steady gaze, challenging her. Of all the people in the world, he was the only one that knew about her past.

"General—" Petronilla lost her voice. She never thought Darius would be the one to push her into the abyss from which she had just emerged.

"I never thought I'd live to see this day," Hadda laughed, oblivious to the silent conversation taking place between them. "General Petronilla is as strait-laced as they come."

If only they knew.

Petronilla clicked her tongue. "No."

"A dare is a dare," Darius intoned, still watching her. He took a few steps closer and then whispered, "I think you'll enjoy this more than you think."

"But–" Petronilla paused as he backed away. Just the thought of going back into one of those rooms made all the hairs on her arms rise. In each of those, she saw remnants of the past.

"You can never outrun your past," Darius whispered from behind her. "I think it's time you faced it."

Only he could deliver philosophy in a pleasure house. As his protege, she understood his motives. But as a person, she hated him at that moment.

"Let's get our best staff lined up for the Lieutenant General," Acelina said, snapping her fingers vigorously at a prospective business opportunity. The wooden door slid open and a few more men and women came in. Dressed in silks, perfumed and painted, they stood like the colors of a rainbow rising in a beige sky. At the end of the line, Acelina stood in green, as fresh as mint with alert, dark eyes. Something about that cool confidence irritated her. Petronilla ground her teeth, surveying the escorts buzzing around the room.

"Stand in line," Acelina ordered. "Let's help the customer choose."

With her arms crossed over her chest, she inspected the escorts who huddled closer to each other, forming a line next to the wall.

"This is everybody." She pointed her long fingernails, painted in red. "They are our best. Take your pick."

The escorts shifted from one leg to another, some winking at her, some casting sexual glances, while others were so nervous, they looked at the floor like their lives depended on it.

"Take the guys out," Larian said. "Our lieutenant general prefers women."

Acelina shot her a sharp look. Petronilla had never been secretive about her preference for women, though she'd never acted on it either. Acelina merely nodded and waved away all the boys. Six girls remained, including Jasmine, the escort who had sat beside her. They batted their eyelashes, wondering who was going to have the lucky opportunity to break open the reclusive lieutenant general. The escorts were all very different- some tall, some petite, some dark, and some not- but all of them beautiful.

Larian whistled. "What a stroke of luck." A slur revealed his drunken state. "We get to see our prudish lieutenant general break out of her shell, at last."

Prudish?

Petronilla wanted to laugh.

"Take your pick." Acelina flashed a large smile, like a fox awaiting its dinner. No doubt, she was eager to make some money off Petronilla, who'd been her source of annoyance for the last three years. However, she would be sorely disappointed tonight.

Petronilla's gaze traveled over the escorts vying for her attention, as Acelina watched on. Her luxurious mint-green kimono was a cut above the rest. With her hair artfully arranged up in curls to reveal the slope of her neck, Acelina looked more promising than any escort. If Darius was to be believed, she still took clients occasionally. Their eyes met across the room, and her mind was made. She knew she was playing with fire, but Petronilla could handle it.

A satisfied smirk spread across her face. If General Darius was going to challenge her, then she'd rise to the challenge. "Have you made your choice?" Darius asked, waving a hand.

"Yes," Petronilla said, taking a step towards the escorts who started fidgeting. They all smiled at her, standing in attention. She walked by the line of courtesans, pausing at the end. Acelina looked up, her chin sharp enough to cut glass.

"Who did you choose?" Acelina asked, schooling her impatience into neutrality.

"You," she said, pointing at Acelina, whose gaze sharpened like a dagger. "I choose you."

Silence descended on the room. Everyone was too shocked to react. She wasn't even in the race, but Petronilla only wanted her. Tonight, she was going to teach the proprietress a lesson she wouldn't forget.

"Try walking in the shoes of those you control," she thought.

Larian whistled. "Petronilla has fine tastes," he jested, followed by a wave of laughter. Darius' mouth quirked up in a smile as if impressed by her challenge.

"Well done," he said.

With a formal bow, Acelina recovered composure. The flush was gone from her magnolia skin. "I'm sorry, but I'm not available." Fluttering her eyelashes at Darius, she continued, "But we have many other beautiful escorts."

"Name your price," Petronilla challenged, tapping her fingers impatiently. Their eyes warred, heating the air several degrees. "Everyone has a price."

Darius' eyes swung like a pendulum from Petronilla to Acelina. The air crackled with antipathy.

"I'm sorry," she bowed, feeling no remorse. "Choose anybody else. We'll give you a discount—"

"I don't want a discount. I want you," Petronilla declared. Now that it had taken root, the idea was rapidly growing on her. She had to make Acelina realize what she was doing to the others. Now that she finally had the power, she wanted to show this arrogant woman how the powerless people who worked for her felt. "Or there's going to be no dare." She slammed her hand on the table, rattling all the dishes. Acelina's eyes met her in a direct gaze instead of a deferential bow. An eyebrow rose, her teeth grinding in frustration. The cogs of her twisted brain turned.

"Come on, Lieutenant General, choose someone else," one of the drunk boys said— Aidan. "There are so many other pretty women."

"You said I could have any escort of my choosing. I want her." Then, turning to Acelina, "What? You don't do women?"

"It's not that—" Acelina looked away, her tiny nose silhouetted against the plain wall.

"Then, what's the problem? Are you going to deny a customer's request? I thought you ran the best establishment in the city." She raised her eyebrows to stress her point. It was a direct challenge to the proprietress' professionalism. Her gaze was unflinching, as usual, which irritated her.

The other escorts stood in line, twitching and shifting their weight from one foot to another. Their collective gazes were fixed on their mistress, who looked graceful as a swan, but Petronilla was sure she was sweating under that impenetrable facade.

"Please oblige our lieutenant general," Darius cut in, amused at how interesting this game had turned out to be. "She rarely chooses anyone, and I'd hate to miss this."

"I agree," Hadda joined in. "I never thought she'd show an interest in... anyone, really."

"But-" Acelina paused. General Darius was her most prized customer. She weighed her options, as the pair settled into silence. "If that's what you desire-"

"Thank you," Darius said, fixing her with one of his dazzling white smiles. "You're the best."

"Good. It's done then." Petronilla felt a smug sense of satisfaction at having Acelina brought down a notch. An involuntary smile tugged at her lips, heart lighting at the small feat. "I'll see you in a few minutes. Choose any room you want."

She brushed her fingers, dismissing the courtesan. "Jasmine here will guide you to a changing room,"

Acelina went on, her tone curt and business-like. "I'll see you in a bit."

Petronilla didn't miss the loud noise the door made when it slid shut, or the frown lines in Acelina's forehead as she exited. The line of escorts merely blinked, a smile tugging at Darius' lips.

"I think I've had my share of fun for the evening," he announced.

"But," Hadda paused. "Shouldn't someone stay and check if Petronilla fulfilled her end of the bargain?"

"She will." Darius smiled. "I trust her."

"We'll hang on a little longer," Larian suggested, inviting eager nods from the rest of the team. They were like wolves waiting to see Petronilla fail. "The night is still young."

"You should," Darius said. "I fear I'm getting old."

"Good night, General." Petronilla's voice was a gentle whisper.

"I'll see you all tomorrow morning." He stumbled to the entrance with uncharacteristic hesitation. "Turstin, come guide me to the door."

A male escort followed him obediently, leaving the rest of

them inside. He was a young man, not more than twenty-two by Petronilla's estimation with curly brown hair and dark eyes. She also saw that he was human like her.

"We'll have a few more drinks and leave." Larian's eyes glinted.

"Don't do anything stupid," Petronilla said.

"Don't worry," Hadda offered, her voice an octave too high. They were all enjoying this. But Petronilla didn't mind. The tables had turned. She was in the position of power now. And she was going to make Acelina see the error of her ways.

TWO

ACELINA

Acelina stormed out, pissed and ready to breathe fire. How dare the arrogant woman cut her off in her establishment? This was her house, her kingdom, her domain. If General Darius hadn't asked her to accommodate his colleagues, she'd never have agreed to this idiocy. A strand of hair fell from her tightly knotted bun, her golden hairpin askew.

She had no idea why Lieutenant General Petronilla hated her so much, only that the hate was mutual. It had started three years ago when she had denied Petronilla entry to protect one of her customers. From then on, Petronilla had become a regular annoyance in her serene life. She liked Darius as a patron but hated the fact that his visits implied that Petronilla wasn't too far away. The lieutenant general never missed an opportunity to look down on her. Last winter Petronilla criticized her poor taste in flowers. The year before that, it had been the taste of the finest wine she served, and before that one of her courtesans. Every time she visited to retrieve Darius, she'd find yet another thing to find fault with. Despite her numerous visits, she never once came as a customer, always leaving with General Darius when he was done. Thankfully, she'd stopped coming a month ago.

Until today, that is.

Acelina wound through the wooden hallways of Duality, rushing along the maze-like arrangement of rooms. The hallway smelled of freshly cut flowers, which her staff placed every morning. Taking a right at the end, she emerged at the back door. Impatiently twisting the doorknob, she found herself outside, staring at the gardens. Warm air teased her skin. Even the air was boiling, sparked by her anger. The gardens were decorated with trees cut in geometric shapes, flowering bushes, large gray stepping stones, and her favorite — a pond filled with clear water. Goldfish swam in the pond, leaves and cherry blossoms shedding into the lake. Acelina made a mental note to get the pond cleaned.

"Madam?" the maid's voice filled her ears. "Which room should I clean?"

Acelina sighed, looking into the night. She hadn't taken a customer in ages. Most of the rooms were occupied tonight, which left only a few choices.

"The creme room?" the maid suggested, but the gears of Acelina's mind were turning. The creme room was clean and unscented. It was tasteful and neutral—the way Petronilla seemed to prefer things. However, Acelina wasn't in the mood to please. It seemed that irritation provided a fertile ground for ideas.

"No. I want the red room," she said, a sly smile lighting

her up from the inside. If the arrogant lieutenant general wanted the best, she'd give her the best. At a huge price. General Darius would have to be extra-generous to foot this bill, and knowing how Petronilla idolized him, she'd never let him pay.

Taken aback, the maid opened and closed her chocolate brown eyes rapidly. "A...are you sure?" stammering, she went on. "N-nobody books that room. It's expensive—"

And very dangerous.

"We'll use it tonight." Acelina stood with her back straight as a rod, her regal posture demanding to be served. She was the best courtesan in the city, and damn Petronilla if she thought she could get away with treating her like some common maid. Acelina hadn't come this far in life to be ordered around by the likes of her. She'd show Petronilla what dangers awaited anyone who messed with a courtesan.

"Yes, ma'am," she complied, bowing. With reluctance etched on her face, she left to clean the room.

Knowing it would take a while for the maid to clean, Acelina sat on a bench overlooking the pond. The party was loud, joined by more shouts from neighboring rooms. A shadow, General Darius, left as Turstin bade him goodbye. Turstin was a new addition to Duality, and he was doing well from the looks of it. But Turstin could never own Darius' heart. Nobody could. In her opinion, his heart already belonged to someone else, but she'd never managed to figure out who. Turstin walked back after seeing the general off and Acelina took a moment to admire the beautiful building she now called her own.

This was her life, and she was proud of it. Despite having

no parents or connections, she'd risen in the world, purely based on hard work. Sure, she hadn't had the best start, sold into prostitution before birth, but she wouldn't have her life any other way. She had worked in the kitchens and scrubbed floors until she was old enough to service patrons. In the beginning, she had hated being passed on from one person to another, but this was her path in life. There was nothing she was good at except pleasing people. Her personality and body had been crafted to please, trained in the art of seduction from a young age.

She liked it. She liked sex, the feel of skin on skin, the pleasure it gave her, and most of all, she liked the chase. Getting the client to open up to her was as rewarding as an orgasm. When they went away pleased, faces aglow with pleasure, hearts lightened, she knew she'd done her job well. Life was transient, and free will was a myth if anything. Her job allowed people to steal a moment of happiness from their dreary lives. That's what made it all worth it.

However, it had been a while since she'd entertained a client herself. Ever since opening Duality, she'd become more of a manager and less of an active participant. She only saw clients that interested her, having the luxury to pass on the ones she didn't feel any attraction for. Until tonight, that is.

It was a full moon night. Acelina saw her reflection in the moving water, disrupted by goldfish.

"I've never seen anyone so beautiful," the madame who taught her the trade had once told her. She had gentle brown eyes, and a large smile. "You could have anyone's heart in your palm."

Over the years, many men and women had asked Acelina

to come with them, to be their eternal companion, but she didn't want to lose this freedom. Duality was the only thing she cared about, her only true love. The love of human beings was transient, but this structure of brick and wood would stand the test of time. It would reward her with money, freedom, and progress.

The first madame Acelina worked for said that marriage had an inverted graph. "It never gets better than when you started. Everybody starts deeply in love, but as the years go by, only a figment of that passion remains, and that too, if you're lucky."

One's career, however, only grew with age. Though it might begin with hardship and effort, it rewarded you with money and power when everything else was gone.

Today, the face she saw in the pond was aged. She was thirty-six, not young by a courtesan's standards. This profession aged people very quickly. Soon, her days of glory would be over, and she'd have to content herself with long, lonely nights. But she had prepared for it. Duality was her life's work and the key to a secure retirement. Though she didn't regret what she'd given up, Acelina sometimes wondered how it would be to have love and money. But she was just being greedy.

She pulled herself away, knowing such destructive thoughts led nowhere. She had more freedom than women tied to one person did. And she planned to enjoy that freedom. Lieutenant General Petronilla was a minor irritant in the scheme of her life. And she handled pests very well.

"The room is ready, ma'am." The maid had returned.

"I'll be there," she said, bidding the fishes goodbye. She had a difficult customer to please tonight, and she was looking forward to that challenge.

THREE

PETRONILLA

PETRONILLA ENTERED THE ROOM SCENTED WITH ROSE petals and cringed. Everything in sight was red, from the curtains flowing down the bed frame to the carpet to the rose petals floating in a tub of water. The lamps were red too, casting a gaudy red light on the large bed. The color made her stomach curdle. Pleasure houses preferred red because they had a way of stimulating the senses. In her days as an escort, she had lain in numerous red rooms, each memory more horrible than the other. But this was the worst of all. Handcuffs, ropes and a host of other equipment lay on a black velvet shelf. She'd heard what could be done with those things, but never actually used them.

"I hate roses." She glared at Acelina, who merely bowed.

"And the color red."

Everything Acelina wore— from her nail paint to lipstick was red. No doubt another ploy designed to irk her.

"You should've let me know in advance," the courtesan said, inwardly pleased.

"Isn't that why you chose this room?" Petronilla challenged.

"This is our best room." She maintained a poker-face. No doubt, she was enjoying charging Petronilla extravagantly for such an ugly-looking room.

"Your best room, huh?" she remarked, leaving her shoes outside. The velvet red carpet felt divine under her feet, but she wasn't going to say that. "You have appallingly bad taste."

Something like hurt flitted over Acelina's face, instantly masked by a smile. Petronilla cringed on the inside, instantly regretting her callous remark. She recognized the reaction all too well, having hidden her hurt the same way many times. But this woman didn't deserve sympathy.

Stay strong.

Being cruel was the only way to pull this off. People like Acelina derived power from exploiting the helpless, and she was about to give her a taste of her own poison.

"I welcome feedback." Acelina recovered from her insult, moving to the drawer of horrors. "Is there a particular item you prefer?"

"I don't prefer any of them." Petronilla continued to walk around the room, looking down her nose at the bathtub. A white bathtub lay on one side of the room, rose petals floating on the warm water. "What's this for?"

"In case you want to take a bath. I'll get it removed if you don't—"

"Take it away," she said. "And get rid of the toys while you're at it."

Acelina went to pull the bell for a maid, but Petronilla stopped her. She pulled her hand back as if struck by fire. "Don't call a maid. I want you to get rid of it."

"Excuse me?"

"Carry it out," Petronilla explained. "Do what the maid would do."

"It's not my job to carry things," Acelina explained, drawing in a steadying breath. "A maid will be quicker. And it'll give you more time with me."

"No." Petronilla shook her head. "It gives me great pleasure to watch you do the work. Isn't it your job to ensure I'm happy?"

"Y-yes, but..." Acelina's breath was unsteady. "Get on with it, then."

"Fine." She hurried to her side, catching the coat falling off her shoulders. It slipped through her fingers, leading her to grind her teeth in frustration. Acelina began pouring water from the bath down the drain and pulled the heavy tub towards the door. When the door didn't open, she ground her teeth in frustration.

"Did you just grind your teeth in front of me?" she asked.

Acelina didn't reply, irritation twitching in her temple.

"No," Acelina lied straight out. Petronilla suppressed her smile. She had gotten under Acelina's skin. That meant success.

"Get this done quickly," she ordered.

"Why? I thought you loved watching me suffer." The work hadn't blunted her tongue, apparently. Acelina was now shutting the cupboards filled with objects, chains, and ropes.

"Do you speak like this to all your customers?"

There was no answer to that except the sound of the bathtub skidding across the floor. It was finally out of the room. A soft thud that signaled the closing of the door followed.

Petronilla sat on the bed fitted with plush silk cushions and duvets and examined the material.

"Is there a problem?" Acelina asked, bolting the door behind her.

"I've changed my mind about the silk ropes," Petronilla said, taking long strides towards the closed cupboards. "We should use them, after all."

"I'll get them out." Acelina rushed to her side, covering Petronilla's fingers with hers. Petronilla jumped back but Acelina didn't let go of her hand. Every brush of her fingers against her skin sent electric sparks exploding in her nerves. Her body tingled with sensation, warming to an uncomfortably high temperature. "I'll do it. You're the guest, you should rest." Her eyes shone with an evil gleam as if she understood what caused that reaction.

A black silk rope emerged from the tiny opening in the cupboard. Acelina let go of her hand, handing her the rope. Petronilla's heart beat a little too erratically as she took it.

"Would you be requiring any food tonight?" Acelina asked, moving to the candles. The light flickered on her perfect, pale skin, bringing out the smooth, untarnished curves.

"No." Petronilla moved towards the bed. She thought of tying Acelina to the bed with the rope and running away, but she had a dare to fulfill.

"Should I turn down the candles?" Acelina asked, being a

busybody. "Some people like the dark. I think you're one of them."

How did she know?

Petronilla's mind cataloged all the imperfections that covered her body. There was a cut on her right arm where she'd been stabbed in a battle. That had taken weeks to heal. The others were smaller, with a large one running down her belly, and her thighs. There was a large black scar on her knee, which made her wince. She'd gotten it after she slipped on the road and scratched her knee. The stupid scar had never faded. Her body was a diary of all her mistakes, experiences and sufferings. And right now, she hated all those mistakes.

"Do whatever you want." Petronilla waved her hand dismissively, breath hitching. She secretly hoped Acelina would extinguish the candles, but no such luck was to befall her tonight. She moved to the bed and sat on it, the candle-light closing in on her.

"I'd like to leave it burning, then." Acelina gave up on putting out candles.

Of course, she would say that.

"How am I supposed to sleep with so much light?" Petronilla complained.

"You're not supposed to sleep," Acelina reminded her, moving to her side. "It's my job to make sure you stay awake screaming all night." A small hand, with long, manicured fingers came to rest on her shoulder.

Petronilla doubted the kind of screaming Acelina had in mind was sexual. But that didn't stop her heart from thudding as fast as a racehorse. When she'd signed up for this, she had no idea her body would react so violently to the escort's touches. However, it was too late to turn back.

"I'd like you to put out the lights." Petronilla grasped at straws to delay the inevitable.

"As you wish." Acelina moved away from her, blowing out candles one by one.

"How old are you?" she asked, out of the blue. Maybe the conversation would distract her from this pesky attraction she was feeling.

"Excuse me?" "Can't you hear?"

Her eyes shuttered her emotions, turning cold. "Thirty-six in human years," she whispered.

Human years were used as a reference so that humans could understand immortal ages. Acelina, being a half-demon could've easily been alive for fifty or more years, but thirty-six was her reference age.

"You're ancient," Petronilla scoffed, splashing water everywhere on the wooden floor. "I should've chosen someone younger."

"You're free to choose again," Acelina said. This had to be annoying her. How was she managing to stay calm? If it were Petronilla, she'd have flipped the candles. Then again, she'd never made a good whore with her willful nature.

"No. You'll do. I hope you live up to your fame."

"I'll try my best to please you," she said, her lips quirking. "May I ask how old you are?"

Thirty-five.

"No, you may not," she said. "I don't like the smell. Is there any way you can get rid of it?"

"I could bring in some flowers. Do you have a preference?"

"No. I don't think flowers will do. This awful perfume clings to the walls and seeps through the bedsheets."

"Do you want me to air out the room?"

"That's a good idea."

"Do you want me to scrub the floors and wash the curtains while I'm at it?" Acelina asked, the sarcasm obvious.

"Even better," Petronilla said, suppressing a smile. "But it'd take you all night to do that."

"It would be worth it since you derive so much pleasure from watching me work." She emphasized the word 'pleasure'. "Some of our patrons have kinks like that."

She had no such kinks, but her attempts to postpone the inevitable were edging close to an end. "No, just leave the windows open."

Acelina complied, lighting a candle first, then drawing curtains over the open window. "The odor will be gone in a few minutes."

Once she finished her task, she came to sit next to Petronilla and put her hand on her shoulders.

"What are you doing?" Petronilla sat up straight, her heart beating wildly. Acelina's silk kimono brushed her, except for where it bared her shoulders. Her black hair was tied back in a bun inserted with a golden hairpin. A few blotches of rouge and lipstick lined her face, contrasting her porcelain skin. Petronilla touched her cheek and a smudge of rouge transferred onto her finger.

"Wash your face. I don't want that stuff getting on me," she instructed. Acelina's breath was unsteady as if she were trying to sigh out the frustration. She closed her eyes and took a deep breath.

She slid off the bed and left the room. Petronilla studied the gaudy room for a moment, wondering how she could prolong the torture. When Acelina returned a minute later with her face devoid of makeup, whatever imperfection Petronilla hoped to find under the paint didn't surface. Her skin looked soft like a baby's, the natural rawness bringing out the color of her eyes. She felt as though a noose was tightening around her throat.

"Should I massage your shoulders? You look tense," Acelina offered.

"Yes." Her voice was hoarse.

Acelina positioned herself behind Petronilla. Petronilla felt her presence like a warm ember spreading through her back. Within seconds, fingers were massaging her shoulders, kneading loose the tension she didn't know she had.

"That feels good," she said involuntarily and imagined Acelina grinning. Acelina's fingers hooked at the edge of her shirt, massaging lower to reach the opening.

"It'll feel better once I get your shirt off," she said. "I can't get all your muscles through the cloth."

"No, leave it on." she said. The massaging went on a few more seconds after which Acelina yawned. She rolled off the bed and stood, signaling it was time to move on from shoulder massages to something more intimate.

"Would you like anything to drink?" she asked, all politeness. There was some water on the nightstand.

"No," Petronilla said. The proprietress continued standing, waiting for permission to sit. Suddenly, it dawned on

Petronilla that sex was part of the dare. She couldn't just order her around and get away. The thought of sleeping with someone made her skin prickle with fear.

Memories of those torturous nights with a host of random men passed over her eyes, intensifying the goosebumps. They grabbed her and shoved their dicks into her, never thinking about the pain she felt. They thought only of their pleasure and took it until she was sore and aching. There was no pleasure in it for her, because she wasn't attracted to men. Since Terra's laws forbade same-sex relationships back then, she'd been forced to take on only male clients. Her throat burned, eyes pooling with unshed tears.

"Are you okay?" Acelina asked, passing her a glass of water. The reflection showed her wide, unfocused eyes seized with fear. She inhaled sharply, pushing the horror back.

"Fine." She drank the entire glass in a gulp. "Sit down." The proprietress sat next to her, her clothes brushing Petronilla's covered thighs. This was a dangerous game she was playing. While Petronilla had spent half her life being celibate, Acelina was a master in seduction. Her every move was designed to illicit pleasure, from the seductive flutter of her eyelashes to calculated touches.

The thought of exposing her body to someone, especially this someone, made her break out in cold sweat. It had been so long since she'd been with someone, and the only experiences she'd had, had been paid for. Now, their roles were reversed. She wasn't a powerless prostitute anymore. She held this woman's life, pleasure, and happiness in her hand. And she was coming to realize it was a bigger responsibility than she thought.

Petronilla roughly pulled the golden pin from the courtesan's hair, sending a silky mass of black hair cascading over her porcelain white shoulders. The contrast, coupled with her luscious lips and intense black eyes, made her look every bit the legendary beauty she was. Acelina's breath hitched in her throat. She shoved away one end of the kimono roughly, as the courtesan looked on silently. When she reached for the other side, her hands stopped.

This wasn't going to be as easy as she thought. In every touch, she saw her old self, fervently hoping somebody would treat her with kindness. How could she do this to someone else when all she'd wanted for so many years was a kind touch?

"Undress," she ordered, sparing herself some misery. Acelina blinked, and then, in a few efficient movements, got rid of her mint green kimono. The garment gathered at her feet, leaving her entire body exposed. Petronilla inhaled sharply, heat pooling in her belly.

Acelina was magnificent.

She'd never seen a body so beautiful in her entire life. Her breasts were small, but firm, ending in rosy, taut nipples. They'd fill her palms just right. The creamy skin spread down, widening at her hips, and then tapering down her legs. She had long legs for someone so small. Fat gave her skin a luminous glow. There wasn't a single scar or blemish to be seen, each feature carved to perfection. A triangle of black hair hid her sex, contrasting the paleness of her body. There was no way anyone could look at her and not feel dizzy with lust. Beauty like hers existed only in dreams, and Petronilla realized her dream had come true. If only it had been someone else—

"You're pretty flat for an escort," she said, feeling like a moron almost immediately. Where had that come from?

Self-conscious, Acelina looked down, turning an inch to hide them, making Petronilla feel like a monster. What kind of person said things like that, even to a whore? She believed herself better than that. But when she saw Acelina, cruel words just seemed to pour out of her mouth.

"I'm sorry if I don't please you." Those obsidian eyes betrayed no hurt, but guilt tightened harder around Petronilla's heart. She moved closer, wanting to apologize, but the words didn't come out.

"There's nothing you can do about it," she offered. "Let's get on with it, then."

"What would you like me to do?"

Swallowing, Petronilla said, "I don't know. Do your thing." She waved her hand.

"Do I have free rein?" Acelina asked, moving her very distracting naked body.

"Yes. I'll tell you if something is wrong," Petronilla said.

"I won't hurt you." Acelina bowed, and the next minute her fingers were on her skin, nudging her shirt from her shoulder. Butterflies fluttered in Petronilla's stomach, her core heating.

Despite her composure, she was rattled. Acelina sensed it in the quivering of her skin, gently brushing away goosebumps from her arms. The kind gesture made her heart leap, her body wet and hungry for more. Compared to the gorgeous escort, she felt like dust. Petronilla should bring out the silk rope now and tie the courtesan's treacherous hands, but she didn't want her to break contact.

That was when the door rattled. At first, Acelina ignored it.

"Madam," a sharp voice came from the other side.

Acelina slid off her, pulling out a robe from the cupboard and wrapping herself with it.

"What's the matter?" she asked, standing behind the door.

"The party has left." A maid's head poked in. Petronilla vaguely saw a homely pale face with small hazel eyes. "The maids are cleaning up."

"Good." Acelina opened the door. "We don't want to be disturbed."

"Larian asked me to pass on a message," the maid went on. Petronilla saw her round face, dotted with freckles and carrot-red hair. "He considers the dare honored as long as you manage to stay in the same room past midnight."

"Really?" Petronilla got off the bed, releasing a breath she didn't know she'd been holding. Buttoning her shirt, she told Acelina, "We're done for tonight, then."

"But you already paid for the room," the maid said. "You can use it to sleep."

"Sleep..." That's when Petronilla realized how exhausted she'd been. It was a stupid idea to say the least, because one brush of Acelina's fingers ignited her desires. "I'm going to sleep."

The bed, despite its gaudy color, was warm and inviting and if she was going to pay a fortune, she might as well sleep in it. She laid herself on the plush mattress and shut her eyes.

"I will leave you to sleep, then," Acelina said, amused. "Should I close the window?"

"You can't leave!" Petronilla called out, nearly falling off the bed.

"Why not?"

"The bet was to spend the night with an escort. The night isn't over yet."

"But I don't sleep with customers after my work is done. Unless you want—"

"Then what good are you?" Petronilla went on. "I paid for a night, didn't I?"

"A night of lovemaking, not sleeping," Acelina argued. Irritation flared.

"It's going to be a night of whatever I want, and I want you to sleep in this room," Petronilla said.

"I'm sorry but—"

"Turn the lights off." With that, she turned the other way, pulling the bedsheets to herself.

Darkness descended in a second as Acelina blew off the candle that the maid had brought in. She kept her eyes closed, tense. However, a few seconds later, the stubborn escort joined her in bed, tucking her body swathed in silk clothes under the covers. She stared blankly at the ceiling, aware of the warm body nestled next to hers.

"Having second thoughts?" Acelina's voice chimed. "Good night. We still have the silk rope and all these

interesting objects. I could show you how to use a few of them," she bit out, turning the other way and pulling the blanket over her face.

Mid-way through the night, Petronilla woke up, thanks to

Acelina's snoring. For someone so small, she snored like a boar.

"Stop this infernal snoring!" she bellowed, waking her up with a jolt. Even in her sleep, the woman was determined to irritate her. Acelina's eyes opened ever so slightly, taking in light. Her body moved, making Petronilla's respond instantly.

"Who are you?" she asked, half-asleep.

"Your customer," Petronilla replied. It was dark enough now, and the sounds in their neighboring rooms had died down. It was past midnight. Petronilla had officially completed her dare. "You can go back to your room now. I'm done with you."

Acelina merely turned the other way, sleepy.

"I said you may go back to your room," Petronilla repeated right into her ears. That made her sit upright, flashing with irritation. She rubbed her eyes and swayed side to side sleepily.

Her expression changed the instant she realized where she was. Picking herself up, she stepped on the floor and disappeared from the room with minimal movement. As she watched her leave, Petronilla's heart was seized with guilt. It felt a lot like throwing out somebody in the middle of the night. Why did she care what happened to this vile woman who exploited others to make a living?

Petronilla stared at the ceiling wondering why she didn't feel any better after having exacted her revenge.

She fell asleep, dreaming of those nights when she'd cried with hunger and pain, the moon her only companion. Then, she dreamed of Acelina, of kissing every inch of her body, especially those rosebud lips, and woke up bleary-eyed and aroused.

Sunlight broke through the dark, spreading quickly. Petronilla emptied her pockets, leaving a whole stack of notes on the table. For the worst night of her life, it was an exorbitant price to pay.

FOUR

ACELINA

Last night had been a nightmare. There was no other way to describe it.

As Acelina counted the stack of notes left on the dresser, she wondered what had prompted Petronilla to leave her such a generous tip. Maybe the arrogant lieutenant general couldn't count. That had to be it.

The window was shut, red velvet curtains hanging over it. She sat in her private room, looking at account books. It was her sanctuary and she retired here when work was done. A large bed with silk sheets sat behind her. She liked it because she'd never shared that bed with anyone. This was where she could be herself.

From the moment she had entered the room, Lieutenant General Petronilla had nothing but complaints. It was how she typically acted in Acelina's presence. For some unknown reason, the woman hated her. She'd even called her breasts small, criticizing everything from the drapery to the rose-scented water. Never in her life had she met such an unpleasant customer. Even the men who had forced her in her youth were entranced by her beauty.

But not Petronilla.

All she wanted was to torment Acelina for some unknown reason.

Pocketing the money, Acelina prayed she'd never have to see her again

"How was last night?" Turstin asked, helping the maids clean. The maids listened, pretending to brush the porcelain clean, but their ears were glued to gossip. Too bad the paper and wood sliding doors didn't offer much of a barrier to prying ears. Since coming here, he'd become a favorite among the women, who watched over him like mother hens. In exchange, he helped them with their chores.

"You're up early," Acelina remarked, exiting the room. It was already afternoon- time to prepare for another night of debauchery. The maids cleaned every surface meticulously while the courtesans were still sleeping. She treated her girls like precious jewels, and precious jewels needed their beauty sleep.

"I was worried about you," he said, following on her heels.

"Worried about me!?" Acelina couldn't believe her ears. "I can worry about myself thank you very much."

I'm ss-sorry," Turstin said. "It's just that...you haven't taken customers in a long time." His brown eyes looked up, hopeful. "You are angry today."

"I couldn't sleep last night," Acelina said, rubbing her red eyes. "Never in my entire career have I met someone so disagreeable."

After booting her out, Petronilla must've slept soundly. Acelina however, hadn't been able to get a wink of sleep, tossing and turning all night. Her body thrummed with exhaustion.

"Well, don't worry. We won't be seeing her again," she said, snapping her hands at the maids to resume working. The maids' curious gazes lingered on her. "That's all I want to say about last night."

FIVE

PETRONILLA

INFERNO WAS HOT, AS ALWAYS. THE FACT THAT IT WAS hot and humid was just her luck. Beads of sweat condensed on Petronilla's face during her short walk to the palace. In all the years she'd lived here, she'd only seen rain twice. The underground kingdom had hellish weather that ran from hot to hotter until the heat scalded skin. People born here had thicker skin than her, but she'd survived. Unlike the angels or the demons born here, she'd age and die someday. But until that day, she was going to dedicate herself to serving the king.

The red blood moon lit the sky, cloaking the country in never-ending darkness. The sun never rose in Inferno, as it had in Terra. But the moon's light was reflected in the darkness. It wasn't a real moon, of course, which is why it was red. Sometimes, they even got to see reflections of stars from Terra. There was no day here, only eternal night. The palace, a magnificent gothic structure, stood proudly in the distance, its spires rising like claws from a mist of smoke. The palace was opposite a row of shops that sold the finest clothes, houseware, and food in Inferno. Her quarters, as well as those of high-ranking military officials, were just beyond that crescent of luxury shops.

The streetlamps were on, as they always were in this country. Workshops and factories belched smoke in the distance. As she walked towards the entrance, the palace guards nodded their heads in recognition, opening the tall iron gates to let her through. Unlike the rest of the palace, the gates were golden, the pollution still not having leached at the gold. They were polished every day, Petronilla guessed.

"Good morning," one of the guards said to her and she reciprocated with a nod.

The familiar high walls of Inferno's palace stretched over Petronilla's head. There were murals of past kings on ceilings, following depictions of the conspiracies and bloodshed that had been used to dethrone them. As someone from Terra, she'd never understood the people's love of bloodshed and revenge. The paintings were graphic and Petronilla didn't care much for revenge. As Darius always said, resentment was like poison. Forgiveness was the cure. Too bad she didn't follow her own advice.

She traversed long, ornate corridors, wondering why the king had summoned her so early this morning. King Delton had a weird taste when it came to artifacts. The hallway was lined with skulls, animal skins, gifts from neighboring kingdoms that usually included daggers, swords, and once, even a live animal. The caged parrot sang in the corridor, calling her name, "Petronilla!"

The parrot had been a gift from the King of Terra, and

since Petronilla was the only human in the palace, the parrot remembered only her name. It annoyed the king to no end. Petronilla was surprised he hadn't killed the bird yet.

She saw her reflection in the mirror that followed, the one she covertly checked during her visits. Her muddy, dark hair was pulled back in a ponytail, her warm chocolate eyes red thanks to not sleeping well last night. She wore a deep red military coat, decorated with gold buttons on both ends, denoting her rank. Her pants were a matching dark red, ending in black boots. She was tall, at five feet and eleven inches, and though she had well-developed muscles, she sometimes looked like a pole. Her skin was golden, tending towards olive thanks to all the practice she'd put in the past week. Her face was neither angular nor soft. Most of her fat was stored on her cheeks. There was a faded scar on her broad forehead. Unbidden, memories of last night flashed in her mind, reminding her of how smooth and perfect Acelina's skin had been. There was not a scar to be seen anywhere. She was whole as Petronilla never could be.

With those thoughts, she proceeded down the corridor. "Good morning." General Darius stood at the end of it, dressed in a coat of green with golden buttons that brought out his eyes. His disheveled brown hair was combed back today, and he wore a wide smile, looking pleased. Stubble was beginning to grow on his sharp jaw, the effects of last night's drinking no doubt.

Petronilla wasn't attracted to men, but she'd thought him handsome the minute he walked into her brothel room in Terra nineteen years ago. He'd smiled at her as if he saw her for who she was, not what she could do for him. Unfortunately, that wasn't enough to save him from her teenage anger. She'd tried to stab him with a fruit knife in return, and he had laughed, dodging her, and slightly twisting her arm.

"You're feisty," he said, pinning her down. "Are all escorts in Terra like you?"

"I hate you," she'd spat, despite never having seen him before. She charged at him again, determined to channel all her anger and frustration into that strike. If she managed to kill him, she might be taken away to prison and finally be free of this place. She hated her life, she hated never being able to meet men's standards and she hated herself for having failed to escape twice. The knife she held had been stolen from the kitchen this morning after days of planning.

He dodged effortlessly, not a hair out of place, and seized her arms from behind, pushing the knife to the ground. Even at sixteen, she was tall at five feet and eight inches, but he towered over her, pulling her off the ground like she was a bag of potatoes.

"Let me go!" She kicked his shin. Doubling back with pain, he released her, and she spat. They stood on opposite ends of the room, eyes locked fiercely.

"I don't want to sleep with you. I'm not attracted to women. I just needed a place to sleep for the night and all the inns were full," he said, rubbing his knee, hopping towards her on one leg.

"Who comes to a brothel for that reason?" She thought he'd been lying. Aggressively, she bit his hand.

"Ouch!" He let her go, but as soon as she turned, he grabbed her with his good hand, twisting an arm.

"What are you doing?" She felt pain shoot up her

shoulder.

"I have a lot of enemies," he said. "But I don't remember offending you. I don't even remember ever seeing you."

"I will kill you. I will kill anyone that lays a finger on me. I'll kill everyone in this damned place," she said, eyes blazing with determination and hands reaching for the dagger. He moved like lightning and kicked it away before she could lay a finger on it.

"How old are you?" he asked, picking up the dagger and pointing it at her. Dread seeped through her veins, suffocating courage.

"None of your business." She circled him like prey, looking for open spots.

"You look young," he said. "I can't understand why you'd want to kill me."

Petronilla ignored his questions and tried to punch him in a spot he'd left open. Before she could hit him, he grabbed her arm and caged her. "If you're going to fight, learn the right way to do it."

"And where in a brothel would I learn that?" she hissed. "If you didn't want to entertain me tonight, you could've

just said no, you know. I prefer guys, anyway. I was going to tell you that," he said. His grip was strong, and Petronilla found herself unable to break it no matter how hard she tried.

Embarrassment washed through her body, but she didn't give up trying, flailing her legs.

"I hate you," she reiterated. "All of you." Her voice broke, and she realized a sob had emerged from her throat. "You ruined my life. I wish you'd die! I wish you'd all die!"

Her words took Darius by surprise, and he let go of her.

Finding her balance, Petronilla swirled back, reaching for her knife in his hand.

"You don't hate me," he said, holding the knife out of reach. "You hate yourself."

Petronilla was shocked. His words were so true they had pierced her heart.

"And, how do you know that?"

"You hate yourself for not being able to save yourself," he said. "I've seen people like you." Then, in a lower voice. "I used to be one of them."

Petronilla didn't know when it happened, but tears slid down her face. The sobs grew more and more uncontrollable until the salty liquid stained her cheap blue dress. Its luster was captured by the bright candlelight that flickered in the silence. The only sound was her sniffling. Darius' breathing had slowed down, and he now watched her with under-standing.

'Shut up, Petronilla,' her mind commanded. 'Don't you dare cry in front of this man.'

But she was too far gone to stop. Tears blurred her vision, and she kneeled on the ground crying. In those salty tears, she tasted years of frustration and rejection. And she hated herself for being a prisoner in this filthy place. For being powerless.

"Why did you try to kill me?" he asked, kneeling next to her, having pocketed her knife. His voice was soothing like he knew what she needed in this bleak moment.

"I...I...wanted...to...go...to....p-prison," she choked out between sobs. "I...hate it here."

"You didn't want to become a..." He trailed off, unable to

think of a euphemism to describe her profession. She nodded, wiping tears off her face. "Well, have you tried escaping?"

"I failed. Twice," she sniffed. Never had she felt so pathetic in her life, not even on the day she was abandoned outside the madame's door by her father.

"How old are you?" he asked, stepping away. "Sixteen."

"Hmmm..." He stood up, examining her from top to bottom. "Your punches were quite energetic, even if unfocused."

She brushed away the remaining tears from her face, baffled. "Huh?"

He gave her another moment to cry in which she saw him nodding to himself. He'd made up his mind about something. Maybe he wanted to help her go to prison by reporting her. Or maybe he'd just kill her and put her out of her misery.

"I want to take you to Inferno," he said, surprising her. "Would you like to come with me?" He was sitting next to her now, eyeing her with compassion. She felt odd at being seen as a human being.

"What?"

"Come to Inferno with me. It's a much better place."

"Why? Have you lost your heart to me?" she asked, clicking her tongue in disbelief. She'd heard several men claim such things to other prostitutes and then disappear without a trace.

"No. My heart already belongs to someone else. I couldn't lose it to you, even if I wanted," he said, a wistful expression crossing his face. "Have you ever thought of joining the army?"

For a minute, she thought he'd lost his mind, but he looked dead serious. "You're kidding me," she said, forgetting the tears. "Women don't join the army."

"Who said that?" he challenged. "We have a few women in Inferno's army."

She snorted.

Yeah, right.

"You don't believe me?" Darius stood up.

"Who would have me?" she asked, now long past crying. The cogs of her brain turned, and for a second, she believed it might be possible to change her life. "I'm not much good at fighting."

"You're built like a fighter. You could learn," he said. "I'll teach you."

"They'd never accept me. I'm someone who has-" unable to say the words, she hung her head low. "A past."

"There are no limits except the ones you place on yourself," he said, sounding rather philosophical. He had always been good at seeing through life.

"Do you say that to every escort you meet?" She crinkled her nose.

"No," he said. "But you're too young to throw your life away." He sat on the bed and looked down on her. "I'm a general in Inferno's army. If I put in a word, they'll recruit you."

"How can I trust you?" she asked, but her mind was already calculating. "For all I know, you're going to take me to some other horrible place and abandon me."

"Wherever I take you can't be worse than here," he said. "What do you have to lose?"

He was right, of course. He knew her desperate straits, but something told Petronilla that despite his debonair facade, he was a man of honor.

"The madame would never allow it," she said. "She always rejects the men who ask her to free her girls."

"I won't ask," he said, winking at her. "I've got a better plan."

The plan had worked, and she was in Inferno now. "Petronilla!" General Darius called out, voice echoing through the long corridor. Petronilla's steps hastened in a hurry to reach him. He was talking to one of the maids who was busy dusting a cage made of bones that housed a viper. King Delton's fondness for the slithering, venomous creatures was well-known.

"General." She bowed, feeling a surge of gratitude. If it hadn't been for him, she wouldn't know what she'd have done.

He raked a hand through his brunette hair. "Last night's drinks took a toll on me. I'm getting too old for this," he confessed. When he looked up, Petronilla saw a haunted expression on his face. He would be around forty in human years, and he looked like a thirty-two-year-old human. Angels were beautiful, and they never aged. "Are you here for a private meeting with the king?"

Petronilla stepped back, surprised. "Yes."

"Looks like Felix will be joining the two of us," he said. "Do you know what this is about? Things have been peaceful for some time." "We'll find out soon."

They both stared at the gold paneled door that stood between them and the king's chamber.

"So, how was last night?" he asked, shifting his weight from one leg to another. "Larian said you fulfilled your dare." There was a wicked gleam in his eye that made Petronilla's cheeks heat.

"I did..." she said, blushing like a beet. Heated images of Acelina's naked body flashed in her mind. Then, she remembered her own words, *"You're pretty flat for an escort,"* and cringed. She had wanted to apologize, but she didn't know where to start.

"To be honest, I didn't expect you to choose Acelina," he said. "I thought you'd forfeit."

"That was an option?"

He laughed. "Not for you."

"I'm hoping you had a reason for making me go through with the dare."

"I told you. You can never outrun your past," he explained. "When I brought you to Inferno, I thought you'd be able to heal and make peace with your past eventually, but you've stored it in a dark corner of your mind and forgotten about it."

"What's wrong with that?"

"You can't neatly file things in the brain without having resolved them first. Resentment will poison you—" he began.

"Forgiveness is the cure, I know." she said, having heard him say that before.

"Have you forgiven yourself for what happened to you?" he asked.

At that, the door opened. Three ministers spilled out, dressed in dark silks embroidered with silver thread.

"Good morning, general," one of them greeted Darius,

who flashed a pleasant smile in return. Petronilla, being lower in rank, bowed to them and followed Darius inside.

The king's chamber had golden walls studded with emeralds, rubies, and diamonds. How the metals hadn't melted in this heat, she'd never know. It struck her as impractical to have a room made of gold in this climate, but what did she know?

King Delton sat on an equally opulent throne made of bones, wrapped in sapphires, rubies, and diamonds. She'd never quite understood the design, but few things in the palace were practical. Wearing a crown made of sharp, silver spokes with a ruby in the center, King Delton looked every bit the red-eyed demon that he was. A bolt of grey hair ran through his long, curly mass of black. Just like angels, the demons never aged. He must be around the same age as General Darius, possibly a little older. The streak of grey hair wasn't a result of age, Darius had explained to her once, but was a unique feature. One of his ears was pierced with several silver rings and his signature floor-length black coat was embroidered in gold. Black was the color of royalty in Inferno, but the king was the only one that wore the royal insignia embroidered on his coats.

"General Darius." The king's resonant voice wrapped around them. When Petronilla first heard him, she thought he'd gargled nails. Now, she recognized it as his voice.

"Your majesty." Darius and Petronilla bowed, getting on their feet. His glacial silver eyes examined them, flickering from one to another.

"I have a mission for you," he said, getting straight to the point. Petronilla glanced back to make sure the door was closed.

"Yes, your majesty." Petronilla was the first to speak.

"I want you to find someone for me," he went on, eyes fixed on Petronilla. "A thief escaped from Terra carrying personal letters written by the king last night. We have reason to believe he is in Inferno."

Petronilla's head snapped up, filled with interest. As an officer in the army, it wasn't her job to find thieves.

"Are the royal guards not doing their job?" Darius was her senior and was more comfortable speaking to the king. If stories were to be believed, he'd allied with the king during the Millennium War between Elysium and Inferno and betrayed his own country.

"I don't want to get the royal guards involved," King Delton said, playing with the silver rings that adorned his sharp fingers. "This is a sensitive matter." He leaned in, and Darius joined him. "The letters contain information about the king's plans for the army."

"Sensitive information, indeed," Darius said. "And he trusts us with it?"

"Better than a thief," King Delton scoffed. "Terra is our ally. They always have been. Therefore, it's my job to make sure the matter is taken care of as soon as possible."

"I understand," Petronilla said. "Should we get one of the lower-ranking captains to handle it?"

"I want you to personally handle it," King Delton told Petronilla. "The matter is sensitive as the thief in question happens to be your father."

"What!?" Petronilla saw spots of light dance before her

eyes, feeling light-headed. That was a word she hadn't heard in a lifetime, not since he had sold her to a brothel at twelve. Before she could summon a coherent response, the king snapped his fingers and someone else stepped in.

The leader of the secret service, Felix, bowed to them.

Acelina nodded in recognition. Felix was a demon and the only one that seemed to age. His salt-and-pepper hair was tied into a small ponytail at the nape of his neck, leaving his squarish face clear. His build was on the smaller side, but his wiry frame easily merged with any setting, and his unremarkable face made a good disguise for a secret agent. He had a friendly grin and, despite the small frame, an air of authority about him. Petronilla had seen him once or twice when the military and the secret service collaborated.

"The secret service has been gathering information on him," the king declared in a raspy voice that carried, despite the weight. His hands prominently displayed bone despite a large amount of muscle that made his massive frame. "What have you found?"

"From what we found, he has connections in the red-light district," Felix said. "He was seen there twice in the past forty-eight hours if accounts are to be believed."

At that, Darius and Petronilla looked at each other.

"The red-light district is a hotbed of crime," Darius acknowledged. "Do you think we should be watching important places?"

"Yes," Felix nodded. "This is a delicate matter. If we go after him, he might flee or get rid of the letters. On the other hand, we can't find out more about him without attracting attention."

"If he's a thief, he'll want to sell the letters," Petronilla suggested. "We should look for possible buyers."

"I considered that," Felix said, looking to the king. "That's why we came up with a plan."

"Only an insider could get access to information about potential buyers," the king said. "The red-light district is full of secrets and they don't share it with outsiders."

Darius nodded, seconding the opinion. "Therefore, you must become one of them."

"Exactly," Felix said.

"An undercover mission." Petronilla's voice was airy. "The best way to gain access to information is to become a thief or a courtesan." Darius looked at Petronilla nervously, and that made her stomach turn. "Gaining the trust of thieves takes a long time and they don't talk so much, anyway. So, I suggest the second option."

All eyes were on Petronilla. The uncomfortable feeling transformed into full-blown panic. Memories from the past surfaced— sticky, sweaty hands clamping her mouth shut while her body was violated. She closed her stinging eyes. "You want me to go," she surmised.

"Yes," Felix said. "I'm too old to pose as a courtesan and General Darius here is well...he has other things to take care of..."

Felix turned helplessly to the king.

"I thought you should undertake this mission," Darius told Petronilla. "He's your father, after all. He might have some tender feelings for you."

"He doesn't," Petronilla assured, anger boiling in her veins. "He's not capable of tender feelings."

"Be that as it may, you're the only one that fits the description required for this undercover mission. I know you've been on one before."

That was a long time ago, but Petronilla realized she was trapped without any possibility of escape. She cast General Darius a sidelong glance, seeing his discomfort.

"Our guards would put him on edge, but he trusts you," Felix went on. "You'd be the easiest to get in and out of a pleasure house without arousing suspicion."

Of course, she wouldn't arouse suspicion. She'd been in this profession two decades ago.

"I promised the King of Terra this matter would be taken care of quickly and efficiently." The king's voice was a distant echo in her chaotic mind. "I trust you."

Petronilla grasped for something to hold, but her hands met only air. Just thinking of her father made her blood boil. She ground her teeth, racking her brain for excuses but none were forthcoming. When she escaped the brothel, she swore to herself that she'd kill her father if she ever saw his face again. It was because of him that she'd been born to endure a life of misery. Darius was right. You could never outrun your past. It was time she faced hers.

"I'll go," she said with steely resolve. "Really?" Darius asked, surprised.

"I'll do it," she said, meeting the monarch's eyes. "I'll bring back the letters."

Duty came first. No matter how much she hated her

father, if the king wanted her to find him, that's what she'd do. She couldn't put her feelings over her duty.

"I knew you'd come around," the king said, his smile

widening.

"But I have a condition." "Go on."

"I want to kill him," she said, fury tearing through her veins. "Once I'm done making him talk, I'm going to kill him."

Felix's eyes widened.

The king laughed, a sinister, excited laugh. "There's nothing I love more than bloodshed. But don't kill him before we get the letters."

"Yes, your majesty." She bowed, lighting up at the thought of revenge at last.

With that, he let them go to discuss particulars. Darius and Petronilla followed Felix to the secret service headquarters, which was down the street. It was a rectangular building made of cream-colored stone, lit with streetlamps all around. She stepped inside, engulfed by the sounds of pen scratching paper, a cacophony of voices meshing with chiming bell sounds. She smelled paper, ink, wood, and iron. They walked up the marble stairs carpeted in royal blue to reach Felix's office on the third floor. Being the head of the Sapphire Serpent, Inferno's secret service, he had the largest room in the building, but it was a complete mess. Papers, globes, ink, and feathers were scattered on his desk, making it unfit for work.

"Sit down." He pointed to two chairs cluttered with books. Petronilla and Darius both remained standing.

"Here's the plan," Felix said, gathering up papers. "As you know, we'll have you pose as a courtesan. You'll watch the patrons that visit at night and go out and talk to other people in the morning. Someone's bound to know something."

"Where will I be staying?" she asked.

"Acelina has very graciously volunteered to take you in–" Darius began.

"What!?" The shock was palpable. It took her a minute to digest that information. "That's why you took us there last night?"

"I had to prime her first."

Petronilla was already regretting agreeing to this mission. There was no way she could breathe the same air as that woman and not break out into a fight.

She wasn't going back there. And that was final. "No way!"

Both men stared at her, bewildered.

"Is there an issue?" Felix asked. Darius appeared tense as if he'd never expected her to rebuke his choice after last night. But he had no idea what went on behind closed doors.

"It's going to be different," he said. "Acelina is my friend,

and she won't force you to do anything. You're on official duty–"

"No," Petronilla cut in, sounding irrational even to her ears. "I'm not going back there. Choose some other place."

"Duality is the most famous pleasure house, as you know." Felix's thinly veiled irritation was masked by forced patience. "It's at the center of the red-light district's information chain. Someone there is bound to know about your father."

"He's not my father!" Petronilla snapped. Her emotions were getting the better of her, coursing through her like a wildfire. Felix's irritation went up another notch.

"The thief is likely to visit Duality at some point, which is why it was chosen as an ideal hiding spot. All the people with power exchange secrets there, and that's where you need to be," Felix finished through gritted teeth.

Darius moved closer to her, worried. She hated that she worried him, but the thought of returning to a pleasure house, especially that one, was repugnant. How was she going to face Acelina? The thought disgusted her. She'd never permit that heartless woman to be her keeper.

"You've never expressed such strong reservations before," Darius maneuvered diplomatically. If this were somebody else, they'd have been dismissed, but decades of hard work had earned Petronilla his trust. "Is there a reason you're reluctant to go?"

Petronilla pressed her lips together, unable to summon a rational response. There was no way she could tell him about the events of last night or their mutual dislike of each other. "No."

"I'll inform Acelina, then," Darius said. "Make sure she treats you well."

Right. Fat chance.

"General Darius will help you, and you'll report directly to me," Felix said. "I'll have members of the secret service posted at other places."

Petronilla mutely nodded, recognizing there was no way out of this situation. General Darius was sympathetic to her, but Felix had no obligation to be lenient.

"I'll report tomorrow morning," Petronilla said, not looking forward to this mission one bit.

SIX

ACELINA

It was another Monday evening at Duality, and all rooms were occupied. Acelina passed through the corridors, checking on her escorts and patrons with businesslike efficiency, correcting a crooked painting or an out-of-place flower here and there.

"Good evening," Lily, the first courtesan she'd ever hired said, her youthful features matured by age. Lily was human and she aged like humans. Where her cheeks had once been perky and red, they now sagged. Nevertheless, dressed in a crimson silk dress embroidered with flowers and trees, she wore her glossy brown hair down, moving with natural grace.

"Good evening, Lily," Acelina examined the age lines that were beginning to appear on her face. In a few years, she'd have to let her go. She'd saved up a decent retirement allowance for her, should things come to that. The least she could do was send Lily away with her best wishes and a comfortable pension. "I thought you had a client today."

"He's running late," Lily stretched her legs. Despite her age, she had the maturity of a sixteen-year-old, which is how old she'd been when Acelina had hired her. "I'm hungry. What's cooking today?"

"Ask Rose," she said, signaling to the kitchen. "And don't eat too much."

"Yes, ma'am," Lily waved, leaving.

Acelina had started the pleasure house fifteen hundred years ago, after having saved enough money to run away from the place house she worked for. With her savings, she'd begun life anew in the city, taking in clients of her choice. Slowly, her clientele had grown, and she'd rented a space. From the beginning, Acelina had known she wanted only the best, even if getting there took time. Her wines were the finest, as was her choice of staff, and the premise was cleaned several times a day. She only took healthy, willing women, who were reliable and paid them well to make sure they stayed.

"Turstin, have you eaten?" she asked the male escort who was rapidly gaining popularity. Unlike her and Lily, he was young and would be in the prime of his youth for quite some time. He'd started tight as a bowstring, but frequent visits by Darius had loosened him up. Now, he enjoyed his newfound fame, as they all did.

"General Darius is here to see you," he said, smiling. Darius had been requesting him frequently, and for his sake, Acelina hoped he didn't develop any feelings for Darius. In the years she'd known Darius, he'd never formed an attachment to anyone. She always suspected his heart already belonged to another, but there was no proof to validate her theory. "I saw him waiting at the door earlier."

"Darius?" she asked, surprised.

"He brought someone else along," Turstin said, an impish gleam in his eye. "Thought you'd want to know."

"Who?"

"Madame," one of the maids rushed in. "General Darius is here-"

"I know," she said, leading the way out. The warm summer breeze brushed her face. Her skin still smelled of the soap she'd used to wash an hour ago. Today, she wore a bright orange silk dress, one that covered her shoulders, but had a deep neck. It was embroidered with a yellow sunrise, pink butterflies, and green leaves. She'd had it custom-made.

Acelina wasn't happy to see her at all. If Darius weren't standing next to her, pleading, she would've kicked Petronilla out right away. After last night, she wasn't inclined to mercy.

Crossing her arms over her chest, she looked down on the frowning lieutenant general, dressed in uniform today. Reluctantly, Acelina admitted Petronilla looked extremely attractive in that red double-breasted jacket decorated with golden pins and buttons. Her short hair was pulled back in a low ponytail, chocolate brown eyes glaring. Yesterday, Acelina hadn't noticed the long dark lashes that fanned her cheek. But today, they made an electric shock run through her spine. A picture of feminine strength, Lieutenant General Petronilla was her brand of beauty.

If only she weren't so annoying.

"Good to see you again, General," Acelina purposely avoided looking at Petronilla. She pasted on a smile and turned to Darius. After last night, she wasn't confident in her ability to stay calm. Though she was a courtesan, she admired people who lived celibate, sober lives. It took extraordinary willpower to live that way. However, Petronilla's strong will was a handicap more than an advantage. The lieutenant general had so much ego, it was more blinding than the sun. "What can I do for you today? The VIP room is—"

"I'm here on business," Darius said, his moss-green eyes directed at her. "Do you remember what we spoke about last night?" He looked at Turstin and Lily. Acelina waved them away.

"You said you needed my help," Acelina recalled.

"Yes, you have a brilliant memory," Darius beamed. "Do you have a room I could borrow?"

"Of course. Anything for you," Acelina smiled, one of the dazzling smiles she gave the most favored patrons. Darius had been a regular since the day she began, and she owed him a lot of referrals. Renting out a room at Duality to one of his colleagues for a mission was no hardship.

"I need you to house one of our soldiers. Don't ask me why," he said.

Acelina crossed her hands over her chest and gave Petronilla a discerning glance. "When will the soldier be arriving?"

"I knew I could count on you," Darius shook her hand, pleased. "I'll recommend Duality to everyone in the army. This is a matter of national importance, so I ask you to keep our soldier's stay a secret."

"My lips are sealed." She bowed, nauseous, all of a sudden.

"Anything you can do to help her integrate is appreciated. We don't want anybody to know I will be watching this place. I'm sure that would make your patrons uncomfortable."

"That's very considerate of you," her tone was clipped. The horror increased. "May I know I am housing? Is it Larian?" As Acelina looked at Petronilla, dread pooling in her belly, she wondered how she'd not seen this coming.

He scratched his head absently, turning to the woman next to him. "It's going to be Lieutenant General Petronilla."

Acelina's face displayed the shock too clearly.

Petronilla looked just as unhappy, which was a little comfort. But that wasn't enough.

No, she didn't want to be part of this scheme.

"Thank you, Acelina. I owe you one." Darius was already stepping back as Petronilla stood, her foot glued to the stone pathway. Trees lined the perimeter of Duality, with strings of colored paper lanterns hanging on them. The summer breeze rattled the metallic chimes at the entrance, as fishes swam quietly in the pond. The serene picture should've calmed her heart, but there was no facing this situation calmly.

Suddenly, an idea entered her mind. "I have the perfect room in mind for our lieutenant general," she said, her red lips curling up. "I'll make sure she is very comfortable."

"There's no need to go out of your way," Darius said. "Any room would do."

"It's no inconvenience," she said, concocting the perfect revenge in her head. It was time to show Petronilla her place. Now that the Lieutenant-General was at her mercy, she'd make sure Petronilla understood how revenge worked.

"Follow me," she told Petronilla. Her heart lit up with a mischievous smile.

* * *

Hours later, the remnants of a candle flickered next to the

bed, painting her arms and shoulders in fiery orange light. She sat overlooking a warm body, naked. After last night's frustration, she'd broken her dry spell and started taking on clients. It was a reckless move, but Acelina needed release. She needed to channel all this frustration somewhere. Sleeping next to Petronilla without touching her had left her unfulfilled.

"You're worth the money." her client said, appreciatively glancing at Acelina's body. His curly charcoal hair was pasted on a mocha face, his black eyes drunk with lust. He rested his head against the pillows, done for the night.

"I'm happy you're pleased," she said, dipping her head low to cover her breasts. Why was she feeling self-conscious all of a sudden?

"Haven't done anything this vigorous in a long time," he closed his eyes, turning the other way.

Acelina stood up and began to dress.

"If you need anything, ring the bell," she said, pulling the silk covers over her patron. He'd leave in a while, and she'd send Marie to clean the room. As Acelina traced her way to the door, she caught a glimpse of her client's clothes hung up.

Acelina didn't know why she couldn't get the image of Petronilla in uniform out of her head. Being around the woman made her blood heat with irritation. Despite the attempts to hide her femininity, Petronilla's body had more curves than Acelina's. She summoned last night's criticisms to her mind, but they weren't nearly enough to wipe the image of Petronilla's chocolate-brown eyes assessing her. Never in her entire career had she felt so naked as she had last night. Every move of hers had been fraught with hesitation, bracing for a retort. She never wanted to live through that hell again.

Sliding the door closed in light movements, she followed the corridor down to her room. Lamps lit the corridor that smelled of the lilies she had bought that morning. The florist had made a beautiful arrangement of roses and lilies, scenting the air. The carpet was clean, as she liked it, and the wooden floor beyond it waxed to perfection. She caught a glimpse of her reflection as she passed.

Acelina's room was beyond the main building. The night was warm, as always, but she liked taking in the fresh air. She stepped on a wooden stair, ascending two stairs to the staff's quarters. Unlike the main building, their quarters had no flower arrangements or lanterns. A solitary candle provided light, guiding her down the corridor. Her room was the only one in the hallway, nestled at the far end of the white cement building. She slid the door open, placing the lantern she was carrying on her desk. Only when she was in, with the door closed did she feel comfortable. Letting her kimono fall to the floor, she sat in front of her dresser, lighting another candle.

She pulled out a fresh change of clothing from her wardrobe, eager to replace the smell of her patron with talc. She washed with a damp cloth, getting rid of the smell to the best of her abilities, and applied some perfume and powder. Following the dry cleaning, she changed into blue silk. As she sat on the floor, looking over the papers piling on her low desk, her eyes inevitably turned to the mirror. The skin around her eyes was beginning to sag, the perfection of her skin marred by growing fine lines. She was half-human and unfortunately, that meant she was prone to aging. As she parted the front of her kimono, she saw her breasts, which weren't as firm as they used to be.

'You're pretty flat for an escort.'

She remembered Petronilla's harsh words from last night. They had cut her deep, spilling out insecurities she kept hidden behind beautiful clothes and makeup. Under that facade, she was an ordinary girl, without birth or breeding. On top of that, she was aging.

"You're ancient."

Another one of Petronilla's remarks flashed through her brain, submerging her in disillusionment.

Aceilna had cut down on the number of clients she entertained several years ago, mostly because she wanted to focus on running the business side of things. But she'd always prided herself on being the most desirable courtesan in the red-light district. Her beauty and ability to please were part of her identity. How long could she keep going before people started noticing the things Petronilla did?

Acelina heard another knock on her door. Before she could open her mouth, it slid open and a frantic Lily stood on the other side, half-naked, covering her mouth in horror.

"What happened?' Acelina immediately got to her feet.

"There you are!" she shrieked. "Lieutenant General Petronilla is turning the place upside-down-"

Acelina shot out before Lily could finish. She hurriedly tucked her kimono back on the way to the VIP room. However, before she got there, she caught sight of Lieutenant General Petronilla, kicking open another room.

"Where is Acelina?" she bellowed.

"Here," Acelina called out, her eyebrows knitting with annoyance. "Why are you disrupting my business?"

Petronilla stalked towards her, irritated. "We need to talk."

Acelina grabbed her hand, taking her by surprise. Their eyes locked in an intense display of hatred.

"Follow me," she said, dragging her through the corridor, and to the staff's quarters. She signaled Lily to continue, pulling Petronilla into her room before sliding the door shut. She reached for a cigarette and placed it at the end of a long, straight pipe, lighting the end with a candle. Acelina exhaled jagged puffs of smoke trying to calm herself.

"Can you explain what you were trying to do?" she asked, regaining a modicum of composure.

"A thief is running around in the red-light district," she said, carelessly. "I thought one of your patrons was suspicious."

"Do you have any proof he was the thief you were looking for?"

"You came in before I found any proof."

"You can't find proof by turning my establishment upside down. You should've come to me first." She let out another puff of smoke, the nicotine only making her jumpier.

"I don't take orders from you. I'll do this however I want to."

Shoving the pipe aside, she pulled herself up to her full length and looked Petronilla in the eye. "You're annoying me, lieutenant general," she said. "I let you stay even though I didn't want to."

"I'm not thrilled about living with someone like you either."

"Someone like me?" Acelina's temper was getting the better of her, but she'd had a long day and she was in no mood to put up with insults. The smoke made the room oppressive, making it hard to breathe.

"You sell other people's bodies for money," Petronilla looked at her like she was dirt. "There is no nobility or honor in your actions."

Okay, she'd had it. Acelina wasn't going to let this go.

"My profession might not be as noble as yours, but it's my pride and joy. I give people a glimpse of bliss in their dreary lives. Don't put us all in one category so that your prejudiced mind can be at ease!"

"You're bartering people's innocence for money," Petronilla said. "You use them and throw them away. I can't put a positive spin on it."

"My escorts participate willingly." Acelina glowered.

"Is that what you tell yourself when you can't sleep at night?" Petronilla scoffed. "They do it because they are afraid and powerless. Nobody with a choice would end up in this profession."

Acelina paused, "I've made the best of the chances that life has given me," she said. "That's more of a reason to be respectful, don't you think?"

For a moment, Petronilla went still, memories washing over her. Her mouth went slack as if she was contemplating. Acelina knew her words had struck a chord. Acelina set her pipe down and moved closer, her eyes narrowing.

"You were abused," she surmised. She had no clue about

Petronilla's past, but abuse would go a long way toward explaining her chronic hatred of courtesans. Acelina moved closer, as Petronilla uncomfortably writhed under her gaze. Her lips wouldn't move. "Is that why you hate me? Because I remind you of...of what?"

"It doesn't change what you do," She countered in a weak voice. "Those women could've had different lives, better lives, but you took away their free will."

"Free will?" Petronilla scoffed. "Come on, even you can't be that idealistic. Free will is as mythical as world peace. Destiny chooses our path, and we walk it, willingly or not. If you think I control their destinies, you are exaggerating. I'm not god."

"You're selling their bodies, their souls, every night for a few coins," Petronilla sputtered. "And you do all this consciously. Nothing you say can justify that."

"You sell your body, your strength to the country for a few coins too!" she retorted. "We're not all that different."

"We're completely different. I have honor," Petronilla said, but her eyes were hollow. It seemed this argument had a personal effect on her.

"Like that makes any difference," Acelina countered. "You're in no position to judge me." She now stood only an inch from Petronilla, those mahogany eyes boring into hers. In their depths, she saw anger. Her blood heated at the proximity, but she wasn't going to back off. "Next time, I'd like to know what you're doing before you do something that could disrupt my business."

"I'm not going to report to you." Petronilla backed off, reaching for the door.

In a small voice, Acelina asked, "What happened?"

She was referencing the mysterious past Petronilla was hiding. Acelina sometimes didn't understand why Petronilla hated her so so much. But there had to be a reason. She'd sensed it tonight.

It was a whisper, but she saw gooseflesh rise on Petronilla's skin. Her hands froze on the door frame, the candlelight washing her back. She wore only her white shirt now, the outline of her feminine form a welcome sight. No matter how hard she tried to hide, she was all woman.

"Good night," Petronilla said abruptly, shutting the door with a thud.

It looked like honesty wasn't the best strategy to deal with Petronilla. She hoped her other strategy would work better.

SEVEN

PETRONILLA

THIS HAD TO BE A JOKE, PETRONILLA THOUGHT, TURNING from side to side, itching all over. The 'room' Acelina had given her was no room at all. It was a storage closet that hadn't been used in ages and was infested with every kind of blood-sucking and disease-spreading creature. Rodents ran in plain sight, hoarding remnants of food supplies in the storage. Bugs she'd never seen before took every opportunity to suck blood, leaving behind a trail of itchy red marks. She tossed and turned, pulling the covers over her face, but it didn't help. When she opened her eyes at the crack of dawn, a hairy rodent stared at her, flashing its fangs.

She sat up with a jolt, sick of scratching her right arm.

Her left arm and leg itched simultaneously, but she had only two hands. Darkness lay on the other side of the single, ceiling window the room had. The streetlights weren't on since Duality wasn't in operation, which is to say, it was morning. Not that the darkness abated a bit.

Darn it.

Resting a hand on the floor, she took a moment to rest her sleepy eyes. That's when she felt something tickle her fingers.

"Aaahh," she shrieked at the sight of a cockroach sniffing her fingers. More gathered around her white linens. Petronilla could brave a war, but cockroaches were her weakness. The disgusting, slimy brown creatures made her want to throw up last night's dinner. One of them even had wings, which it was deploying to fly to her. Petronilla crushed the insect with her bare hands and stormed out.

"Acelina!" She threw the door open, bloodshot eyes scanning the corridor for a glimpse of that infuriating woman.

And there she stood, shameless and triumphant, covered in a thin nightdress, hair spilling over her shoulders, running down the length of her curvaceous hips. The transparent white dress revealed her rosy nipples, skimming over perfectly proportioned curves. Petronilla's throat went dry. Even at six in the morning, Acelina was bewitching.

Not a road Petronilla cared to go down.

"I hope you had a pleasant night, lieutenant general." She stood a few feet from the room, barely suppressing a smile.

"You know very well I didn't," she said, scratching her arm full of insect bites. A trail of red marks lined the expanse of skin, now clearly visible in the lit corridor. She didn't even want to look under her shirt, afraid the cockroaches had gotten inside.

"Aren't soldiers supposed to be hardy? Don't tell me you can't withstand a few insect bites." Acelina brushed her fingers dismissively, eyelashes fluttering with glee.

"The storage room is infested with cockroaches!" Petronilla stepped forward, charging for battle.

"You were the one that wanted to stay here," Acelina said. "If you don't like the rooms we have, you're free to return."

"Get the storage cleaned," Petronilla shot back.

"Pests aren't easy to kill," she said, lighting her pipe and blowing out smoke. "You'll have to put up with them, I'm afraid."

"Isn't it a little early to smoke?" Petronilla hated the smell of nicotine, especially coming from her.

"Awww, if I didn't know better, I'd think you were concerned about my health." Acelina blew another puff of smoke, this time, deliberately on her face.

"Don't delude yourself." Petronilla coughed, fanning the smoke away with his hands.

"Poor Rose had to wake up to make breakfast for you," she went on, turning in the direction of the kitchen. "You better polish that plate clean."

"I hope your cook's hospitality is better than yours." Petronilla stormed off, stomping along the corridor. Acelina killed the cigarette and followed her.

They stopped outside the kitchen, which smelled of toast, eggs, and strawberry jam. Rose was young for a pleasure house cook, with curly golden hair and sunken brown eyes. If Petronilla had to guess, she was twenty-something in human years. She was a demon, though, so that made her one hundred years old. The kitchen was surprisingly clean and empty so early in the morning. Several empty pots sat on the unlit stove, and one used pan was in the sink. It was a large kitchen and housed a table for sixteen.

Rose barely looked awake, but the feast she had whipped up indicated the opposite. Crisp toast and scrambled eggs were piled on a plate, and milk boiling on the stove.

"Morning, Rose." Acelina crushed the end of the pipe on the ashtray and began rummaging the shelves.

"Good morning, ma'am," Rose said. "You're up early."

She gave Petronilla a friendly smile. Petronilla nodded in acknowledgment.

"I didn't get to sleep thanks to our new guest." She stood, her back facing the cabinets with a bottle of wine in hand. "Give her highness some breakfast."

"Yes, ma'am." Rose suppressed a smile and turned to plate eggs and toast. Despite it being morning, not a ray of sunlight was to be seen in the endless night that was Inferno. Sometimes, she missed the sunshine in Terra.

Only sometimes.

Acelina sat opposite her on the sixteen-seater wooden table and uncorked the wine bottle. As Rose placed the steaming breakfast in front of her, Acelina poured two fingers of rice wine. The smell alone was enough to throw Petronilla off. It was like drinking concentrated rodent killer.

"Alcohol at six? You're trying to kill yourself," Petronilla scoffed, biting into the warm toast.

Acelina gave her a straight gaze and swallowed the entire glass in one gulp. "None of your business," she retorted, slamming the glass on the table. A flustered Rose looked from her employer to Petronilla, worried.

"Ma'am-"

"You're a raging alcoholic. That explains your erratic behavior," Petronilla countered, eating more. This toast was really good, and those scrambled eggs were fluffy, just the way she liked them. At least the courtesan had good taste in food.

"Not all of us have taken the vows of sobriety and abstinence." Acelina poured herself more wine. "Rose, get me some of the spiced peanuts you made."

"Yes, ma'am." Rose looked unsure but fled the scene to retrieve the peanuts.

"Wine and peanuts? Do you even eat proper food?" Petronilla snorted.

"This is my sleeping time," Acelina complained, rubbing her eyes. "I didn't sacrifice my beauty sleep to be lectured by you."

"No. You sacrificed your beauty sleep to torment me," Petronilla grumbled.

"Not all of us are as petty as you." Acelina brought the wine glass to her lips, then stopped, suddenly disgusted at the sight of it.

"What?" Petronilla's head jerked up, catching Acelina's reaction. Acelina merely shook her head, pushing the glass away.

By the time Rose appeared with a bowl of peanuts, Acelina had already risen. "I'm going back to sleep," she said temperamentally, leaving the cook to clean up her wine glasses.

"What's wrong with her?" Petronilla frowned as she left. "I have no idea," Rose confessed. "She's never woken up this early before. They only go to sleep at four." She stretched, yawned, and cleared the wine bottle. "If you don't mind, I'm going to sleep."

"Ummm...sure...I'll wash the dishes."

"You can leave them. Marie will take care of them when she wakes up," Rose said.

Petronilla lingered a little longer, wondering if she should do the dishes anyway. She didn't want to be a liability to the staff. But she heeded the cook's advice and she stalked back to her room. A choking sound made her pause in the hallway. Petronilla tipped her head back to see a shadow standing next to the gutter. The lights in other parts of the district had come on, and the lamp burning in the corridor illuminated the shadow's form. Petronilla's shoes hovered on the edge of a single wooden step. She approached stealthily, recognizing the transparent white gown that molded around Acelina's peach-shaped butt. She was hunched over, the guttural sounds growing louder.

Acelina was throwing up into the gutter. Petronilla recoiled immediately, disgusted. Acelina's hands grabbed the edge of the wall and slipped, her knees weakened thanks to the utter lack of nutrition she consumed. She retched once more, her back straightening after that final onslaught.

She was done.

Petronilla backed off, feeling the wall for a place to hide, but as soon as she stepped back, Acelina doubled over, sinking to the ground on her knees, and began puking again. She was struggling to keep her strength up and summon the energy to get rid of all the alcohol that irritated her stomach.

Served her right, Petronilla thought.

Petronilla's feet slid, and only then did she recognize that she was falling. Her leg skidded down the wooden step, her butt landing with a thud on the damp garden soil. Her foot was caught on the edge of a step, from which she extricated it. Flower petals fell around her in a storm, caressed by the warm breeze, gathering in the black gutter waters.

Acelina's head snapped back, startled by the sound. Their eyes met across the gutter, and mutual disdain cracked in the air. Acelina wiped her mouth. Her eyes had sunk into their sockets, her face paler than usual.

"What—" She clutched her stomach and doubled over again, vomiting.

Petronilla reached her side and ran a hand down her back. Before she knew it, her left palm was stroking Acelina's back while the right held her arm steady. She remembered one of the women from the place she'd worked at doing it for her when she had been forced to drink too much and couldn't hold it in. It had always soothed her, even if it hadn't helped her vomit more.

Her touch shocked Acelina, whose skin pricked, but she was too busy puking to comment. Petronilla pulled her long black hair back, getting it out of her way. The smell was disgusting, and even the fragrant flowers didn't make the ordeal any better.

"This is why you shouldn't drink at six." Petronilla wasn't going to lose the chance to drive her point home.

"If you're going to lecture me, go away."

Acelina vomited her entrails into the gutter, all the while Petronilla held her hair up, stroking her back. The fact that she got to touch Acelina's body was a nice bonus. It felt so right in her hands that she regretted not holding her when she had the opportunity that night.

She didn't know how much time passed in that state. It

soothed her to know that she was helping someone. Petronilla's protective instincts had always been strong, which is why she loved being in the army. She wanted to protect others who were as helpless as her.

None of that explained why she was helping her archenemy throw up, of all things. There was nobody except them in this part of the garden, and Petronilla suspected that's why Acelina had chosen it. She hated showing her employees any sign of weakness.

A few seconds later, Acelina looked up, covering her mouth with a hand. Petronilla released her luscious black hair. It cascaded down her ass. Hurriedly, she walked to the pond and gargled clean water, drinking some of it in the process. She splashed some more on her face, rubbing it into her sleepy eyes. With water dripping down her face and collecting on her already transparent gown, Acelina stood.

"Are you okay?" Petronilla asked, stepping forward.

"I told you so," Acelina said, wiping her mouth. Her eyes were fixed on Petronilla, dark as midnight. "That's what you wanted to say, right?"

"What?" She was taken aback.

"I guess I should say thank you." Acelina splashed some water on her face.

"You're welcome," Petronilla replied before she could argue.

"For the record, I'm not usually like this," Acelina went on. "I hold my drink very well. You have to when you're in this profession." She squinted. "Another reason for you to hate what I do."

Petronilla swallowed, not knowing how to reply.

"Don't you have to go to work or something?" Acelina went on, positioning herself on the wooden step, trying to regain composure.

Immediately, Petronilla took her arm. "Rose said she was going to sleep, but we might be able to catch her to make something."

"I thought you hated me," Acelina cut in, her gaze penetrating.

'I do' she wanted to say, but her breath was sucked by the gravity of that gaze, boring into the depths of her soul. The air stood still, darkness smothering any thoughts. Her gaze trailed to Acelina's perfect rosebud lips, a swollen pink even in this state. It should disgust her to look at them after she puked all over, but Petronilla felt desire stirring in her belly. Their skin connected and her warmth flowed into Acelina. She'd never realized a touch could be so profound, making her forget where Acelina ended and she began. She wanted to take that swollen lower lip in her mouth and do wicked things to it. As if realizing what she was thinking, Acelina's fingers brushed her lower lip defensively.

She let go of her arm immediately. "I'm sorry."

She raked a hand through her hair and did the stupidest thing she'd done in her entire life.

She fled.

***

Petronilla searched the red-light district several minutes later, her mind flooding with erotic images of Acelina's mouth. Her body thrummed with the need to possess that mouth and run her fingers along those lush hips. Only a thin layer stood between her skin and Acelina's. She had been so close to giving in to that desire, which was ridiculous considering the itches on her arms were all thanks to the manipulative proprietress. She thought she'd left that part of herself in the past, but desire couldn't be locked away, no matter how many painful memories it was connected with.

A string of red lanterns lit the district, leaving no doubt where its name came from. There were all kinds of establishments here, from classy to cheap. The classier ones had closed doors with two men positioned at the doors to check patrons. They were usually clustered around Duality, in the third branch of the main street. The road in the classier part was solid stone, with a few broken stones creating troughs. As Petronilla moved towards the city, the number of establishments grew, and their quality declined. A canal ran along with the cluster of pleasure houses. Despite the moving water, it exuded a foul smell. Nevertheless, it added to the scenery, reflecting the lanterns and the moonlight.

Someone brushed past, almost tripping her over. "Hey—"

She stilled on seeing a familiar figure hooded in grey, and her senses were on alert. The stranger continued to walk, without looking back, and Petronilla was on his heels. In that salt-and-pepper hair, now quickly covered by the grey hood, she saw a semblance of her father.

It had been twenty-three years since she last saw her father, and in that time his face must've changed. She vaguely remembered a slimy-looking man leaving her twelve-year-old self at the door of the brothel saying a kind lady would come to fetch her in a few minutes, and she must listen to her. Then, he was gone.

Forever.

The lady who had fetched her was the madame, and she had been everything but kind. From the first day, she put her to work, first cleaning dishes, then helping with chores. Petronilla hated the smell of alcohol, opium, and sex that clogged the air, making her want to throw up. She'd sit by the window, crying every night, waiting for her father, but he never came. The years piled on, and then, when she began growing breasts, she was promoted to the upper floor to entertain men. And when she was fourteen...

The cloaked stranger was getting away, so she hastened her footsteps, busy itching, rubbing her eyes, and running all at the same time. It was all Acelina's fault she was in this state. She couldn't focus at all.

Cursing her thoughts into submission, she slid through the thin crowds, running down alleys and narrow passageways until she stood before a door. The door was made of wood, and a few people standing around. The cloaked figure disappeared inside, and the door bolted shut behind him. Petronilla followed him in, her heart beating in her ears.

"Hold on a second." A hand grabbed her, causing her to swivel around and stare into a rough-faced man with a broken front tooth. His bulging muscles and intimidating gaze were designed to cower her. Instead, her body itched for a fight. She shook her arm free and glowered back. He came to stand in front of the door as if shielding it from her.

"I need to get in," she continued, but he was firmly lodged.

"No." His answer was final. "What do you mean, no?"

"Entry for ladies only," he said, his words broken. Here was another one like Acelina who reeked of alcohol at eight in the morning. He gave her a once over. "You don't look like a... um...lady of the night...to me." He sized her up and down, taking her body in. Petronilla felt revulsion prickle her skin.

Dressed in a loose white shirt, and brown pants, Petronilla was the farthest thing from a 'lady of the night'. "So? I want to purchase the services of an escort," she made up on the spot. "Don't tell me the man that just went in was an escort."

His eyes narrowed. "He's a customer." "So am I."

"You're here to pick a fight," he announced. "I recognize trouble when I see it. That's what they pay me for."

"I just want to have a look," she reasoned. "Sorry," he shrugged.

"Does your employer know you're turning out customers?"

"Ask her. She'll say the same thing." He wiped the sweat from under his nose, crowding her out. "That way." He stabbed a finger in the direction of the road. Petronilla gritted her teeth, itching to kick the bastard who stood in her way. Her eyes strained to look beyond the opaque, papered windows, and the frustration in her multiplied. Causing a scene would do her no good. She was on an undercover mission and couldn't risk exposure.

Taking a breath to calm the thudding of her heart, she turned on her heel and left. Thoughts crowded her mind, but she had to keep her emotions from getting the better of her. Emerging at the street, she looped around the main road and ended back at the pleasure house's front door which was locked.

Petronilla sighed.

"You here for a job?" a plump woman with beady brown eyes asked. She wore a pink gown that struggled to contain her pudgy figure.

"Is the owner in?" Petronilla's stabbed her finger in the air angrily. "Why doesn't this place have a single, unguarded entrance?"

"Because we want our customers to feel safe." The woman stood up tall, scrutinizing her with glassy brown eyes. "What business do you have with me?"

"I just wanted to talk-" Petronilla stepped back, exhaling in frustration. That gave the woman a minute to look her over.

"I guess you'll do," she said, finishing her once-over. "They told me someone new would be coming in today-"

"What?" Petronilla took another step back.

"We're in high demand thanks to a ship that just landed. One more girl is what I need, though you're a little old to be a girl." She waved her hand dismissively as if appraising an underweight chicken. "But some men have a taste for that."

"What? No. I'm not looking for work." Her hands clamped around Petronilla's, dragging her to the door.

"If you're not looking for work..." she trailed off, showing her the way out. "Never mind, you'll get used to it."

"No!" She paused. Petronilla pulled her hand back, leaving the woman off balance and skittering to the wall. She caught her before she fell. This situation was getting more and more complicated by the moment. "I already have work. I'm here because-"

Because my rat of a father might be here. And I'm on a secret mission to find him.

No.

Telling the woman she was a spy wouldn't earn her any extra points.

"I'll come back later," she said, stepping onto the street with a quickening pulse. Just the thought of going back to one of those places made her skin break out into gooseflesh. They'd have to come up with another strategy then.

Sighing, she walked back, deciding to visit Felix.

EIGHT

PETRONILLA

IT WAS A LONG WALK FROM THE RED-LIGHT DISTRICT TO the secret service, but she enjoyed the walk despite the oppressive weather. She liked that Inferno was always dark. In a way, it hid her flaws and made her feel at home. The smell of opium and alcohol cleared and became smoke as she approached the palace area. A canal ran through the city, and she crossed a small stone bridge to get to the other side of town. Walking alone gave her time to compose herself.

The palace occupied the largest parcel of land, and the familiar shops came into view. She walked to the end of the street where the secret service building stood. It didn't have anything engraved outside, unlike the other official buildings that had plaques.

"Good morning," she was greeted by one of the secretaries of the office. With his red eyes, smooth pale skin, and friendly grin, he didn't look a day over twenty, but Petronilla knew he had already lived a century. "Felix was just looking for you."

"Is he in his office?" She didn't wait for an answer, taking the stairs two at a time.

"General Darius is here-" The secretary's voice was cut off when she turned the corner. Finding Felix's office, Petronilla knocked and barged in.

"Petronilla, we were just talking about you." Darius sat on a chair that had been cleared with a sullen expression. "Felix's men gathered some information."

"I saw him," Petronilla declared unceremoniously. On examining her reflection in the mirror, she realized she was breathless, her chest rising and falling unevenly.

At that, Darius stood up. "Where?"

"The red-light district. I couldn't see his face, but it looked like him." She paced restlessly. "I haven't seen him in so long, but something tells me it's him."

"Where is he?" Felix stalked towards her, his eyes focused on her face.

"He disappeared into a pleasure house-" She paused. Petronilla didn't like making excuses for her incompetence. "The Rose."

"You didn't get him?" Felix asked, his forehead creasing. "They wouldn't allow me in," Petronilla said. "Only courtesans

can enter, and well....I'm not one." "How did he get in, then?" Darius asked. "He's a customer. I think he's living there."

"The Rose, you said?" Felix asked, scrawling the name on a page. "We should check out the place."

"Can you send some of your men to investigate?" Petronilla asked.

"I can, but I'm worried it'll arouse suspicion. It's better if we can get in without anyone knowing and take him down in one blow."

"What do you have in mind?" Darius asked.

"There's only one way," Felix said, his eyes meeting Petronilla's. "Dress up as a courtesan and gain entry."

"What!? No!" She stepped back, her back colliding with the closed door. The thought of clammy hands on her skin made her shudder. Petronilla was never going to that dark place again.

"Felix..." Darius looked from Felix to Petronilla, hesitant.

He didn't know how to explain the situation.

"It's the easiest way in. Didn't you say they only allow courtesans inside?" Felix said. "Once you're in, you'll have access to all the rooms. We don't know which room this man uses."

"If she goes in dressed like a courtesan, they'll put her to work, and she'll have no time to follow anyone," Darius reasoned. He was standing now, holding the edge of Felix's table for support.

"She's a lieutenant general. She can defend herself." Felix shrugged. "Can't you?"

Petronilla should've said yes, but the dread pooling in her belly narrated a different story.

"It's not a question of whether she can defend herself or not," Darius went on. "For all we know, the man she saw today might not be her father."

"We'll never find out if she can't get in," Felix said. "It's just a pleasure house. You're temporarily living in one, aren't you? You know how it works. And my men will be outside to back you up." Petronilla blinked. She'd never thought of Duality as similar to other pleasure houses. Acelina maintained class and took on limited customers. She had to admit Duality was nothing like the place she'd worked in. The employees were like a large family, and the premises were clean and free of disease. Except for the storage, of course. She smiled. "What's so funny?" Felix asked.

"Nothing." Petronilla cleared her throat. "So, is it a yes or no?"

"Yes." Her sense of duty made the decision. Darius' eyebrows perked up, his head tilting in disbelief.

Only after the words had left her mouth did she realize she'd committed to dressing up as a courtesan and infiltrating The Rose.

A ballooning sense of dread had followed her back. One of the reasons she'd been chosen for this mission was because she was a female. But Felix didn't know anything about the traumas of her youth. As she flitted past the string of lanterns, she wondered if she'd ever been free of her past. It was over now, and nothing could take away the strength she'd gained through years of hard work.

Facepalming for the hundredth time since she left the meeting, Petronilla stepped through Duality's back door. She had agreed to use the back entrance so she wouldn't interrupt business, which had a goldfish pond and garden similar to the front entrance. The humidity levels were down today, but a dry heat pervaded the garden. It was a miracle the pond hadn't dried up in this weather. A relatively cool breeze blew past her, a result of so many bodies of water and trees, on the narrow sandy path to her room. After this morning's lack of progress, she didn't look forward to sleeping in that rodent-infested room. Nor did she particularly fancy the idea of seeing Acelina again.

But wishes rarely came true. When Petronilla reached the storage room, she saw Acelina standing outside, the door open. A cloud of dust wafted out, and Acelina moved away to dodge it. In doing so, she bumped into Petronilla who stood behind her silently.

"Excuse me."

Their eyes met and Acelina stilled. Petronilla felt the brush of satiny silk on her skin. Panicked, she pushed the proprietress away, narrowing her eyes at two maids cleaning the storage room. Dust flew all around, but the several boxes she'd seen last night were gone. They were stacked to her right, outside the room.

"I see you took my advice and decided to clean out the storage," Petronilla said, a wicked grin tugging at her lips.

"Make sure you leave no trace of dust," Acelina instructed the maids, straightening the black kimono she wore tonight. Then, turning to her, she said, "I didn't do it for you."

Petronilla noticed she still looked a little pale from today's morning sickness episode, the condition highlighted by the black silk kimono she wore. The sight of her exposed shoulders sent a wave of something forbidden pulsing in her belly. She coughed.

"I'm looking forward to sleeping without cockroaches sniffing at my fingers," she said.

Acelina's sharp eyes examined her arms. Petronilla had

taken her coat off during the stroll home and pulled back her shirtsleeves to reveal a column of insect bites. Acelina moved in closer, her smooth fingers brushing over the bug bites, making Petronilla's body flood with awareness.

"What are you doing?" she asked, pulling her hand away like she'd touched fire.

"You got all those from just one night of sleeping in the storage?" Acelina examined her, then sighed. Petronilla rolled down her sleeves to cover her arms.

"Follow me," Acelina instructed. Then, to the maids, she said, "Go to dinner once you're done."

"Yes, ma'am," they echoed in unison.

"Cleaning out the storage room was a lot of work," Acelina admitted, ruefully, crossing her arms over her chest, as they walked. "I had no idea that it had become such a mess."

"Of course, you did. That's why you gave it to me." Petronilla didn't realize she had spoken the words until Acelina stared at her. Then, turning away, she smiled. Petronilla connected to that smile, feeling an odd glint of bonding. As soon as that thought entered her mind, she caught herself.

Petronilla wanted to strangle whatever tender feelings were taking hold in her heart. This morning had been a mistake. She should've left Acelina alone to puke her guts out. If it hadn't been for her natural protective instinct, that's what she'd have done. Even now the words, 'Are you feeling better?', lingered at the edge of her tongue, but she cut them off with a frown. Nothing good would come out of befriending this heartless woman who sold other people's bodies for a living. The friendly exterior was merely a facade.

"Where are you taking me?" She pulled her hand away, coming to a standstill mid-way. Acelina sighed as if tolerating a petulant child. They stopped outside the proprietress' bedroom door. She slid it open, laying an arm on Petronilla's hand.

"Come in. I have something that'll help with the insect bites," she said, pulling her in.

"What? Poison?" Her natural defensive instinct came into play before her mind could formulate a rational response. "It'll put me out of my misery permanently."

"Seriously?" Acelina's placed her hands on her hips, sighing. "If I wanted to poison you, two drops in your breakfast would've been more efficient."

"There's still dinner," she suggested.

"Forget it." Acelina suppressed a smile. "There's no point talking to you."

Unlike the cramped storage, Acelina's room was large, with a four-poster bed plumped with feather mattresses. Unlike the gaudy red room, this one had neutral beige walls and a vase of dried flowers placed in one corner. A low sitting table and cushion overlooked the window, lit by a candle lamp. Thanks to the scented candle and flowers, the room smelled of lilies and roses. It reflected Acelina perfectly.

"I see you kept the best room for yourself," Petronilla remarked, as Acelina opened her cupboards looking for an insect bite remedy.

"It's your fault for being an uninvited guest." Acelina moved with a swish of her skirts, brushing past Petronilla to the other side. "Considering the circumstances, it's generous of me to house you."

She lit a lamp, casting light on the long, straight smoking pipe, scattered papers, and account books on the table. So, the woman worked on something other than her appearance. What a surprise.

"You read?" Petronilla examined the paper, which Acelina slipped away from her.

"When I have the time. I'm literate, in case you're wondering," Acelina countered. "And before you ask, they're account books."

After making sure Petronilla was far away from her precious ledgers, Acelina went rummaging through another wooden cupboard until she came up with a small tin container of something.

"Here it is." She opened the container to reveal a colorless gel that looked like petroleum jelly and smelled like aloe vera. Before Petronilla could ask what it was, Acelina nudged her to sit on the bed, and Petronilla reluctantly obeyed. The mattress felt heavenly compared to the storage's hard wooden floor. Her shoulders ached from last night.

Acelina took her arm and began rubbing the jelly on the insect bites. Petronilla pulled her arm away, distrustful. "What're you doing?"

"With this, I've paid you back for this morning," Acelina said, stubbornly taking her hand again.

'You don't have to.'

If only she could say that and pull away. Acelina's supple fingers were the balm she needed to soothe her fatigue.

"What is this thing?" she asked, instead, sniffing the balm.

"Helps with bug bites," Acelina replied. Petronilla felt

sparks of electricity wherever Acelina's fingers touched her skin. "I got it from a healer."

"For me?" Petronilla was surprised.

"No. For Turstin, if you must know," she said, skin on skin. How was this not affecting her? Petronilla's entire body was tense as a bowstring. Acelina's breath caressed her skin and up close Petronilla smelled lavender on her.

"How're you feeling?" she asked, in a desperate attempt to diffuse the tension. Her brain was losing its ability to reason. Acelina looked up, confused. "You were sick this morning."

"Oh, better. Rose made me a tonic for indigestion. She's good at things like that." She took her other arm and rubbed the balm in circles. Petronilla closed her eyes tightly to steel herself against that touch, but that only made her more aware of every caress.

"What? Does it sting?" She pulled her fingers back, blinking. "It's only aloe vera."

"No." Petronilla opened her eyes. Watching and feeling Acelina at the same time was too much.

"Why're you cringing, then?"

"I was closing my eyes." She frowned.

"Looked like cringing to me." Acelina continued rubbing balm on her hands. "Do you have bites somewhere else?"

Yes.

Petronilla had a few bites on her legs and on her back, but she wasn't going to tell her about them.

"Oh, there's one." Acelina's balm-covered fingers reached for Petronilla's neck, leaning over. Her breasts hung in a direct line to Petronilla's face, and she swallowed. Acelina nonchalantly rubbed the balm in circles on her neck, then reached lower to her shoulder, fingers sliding under her shirt. She breathed down Petronilla's neck, reviving all the little hairs on her spine.

Every cell in her body was tense, aching for more of her skin. If she strained her head up, her lips would meet Acelina's graceful neck. She wondered how it would feel to taste that porcelain perfection on her lips and lick her tongue down the smooth slope—

"I see you have some insect bites on your back. Do you mind if—" Acelina's fingers reached the opening of her shirt. Petronilla slapped her hand back.

"We spent a night together. There's no point being modest now."

"Nothing happened that night."

"Nothing's going to happen today either," Acelina assured her, undoing the first button of her shirt. "Believe me, I just want to apply medicine and be done with you."

"I can do it myself."

"I wish you could," Acelina said. "But I doubt even the invincible lieutenant general can turn a hundred and eighty degrees to reach her back."

Unwillingly, Petronilla gave in. "I'll get my shirt off." She hurriedly undid her buttons to reveal her arms, her shoulders, and her back. She had wrapped her breasts for support with a white cloth.

Acelina took one quick look at her and smiled.

"What?" Petronilla was grumpy.

"Nothing." She whistled as she applied the gel to the insect bites on her back. When she reached the bottom of her spine, she circled a little too long. Suddenly, Petronilla remembered the tattoo that was at the bottom of her spine. Fear, sharp and cutting, pierced the cloud of sexual tension blinding Petronilla. She stood up as if struck by fire.

"I—" Acelina looked up and met Petronilla's eyes. She was hurriedly pulling her shirt from the side of the bed. "Is that what I think it is?"

"No." Petronilla slipped her right arm into the shirt.

"I've been a courtesan too long to believe you," Acelina said. "You were...." She paused, her eyes fixed on Petronilla. "One of us."

"You'll forget you ever saw this."

"How can I? Oh, this is too exciting not to—" Acelina's smile was exuberant as if she'd discovered her enemy's greatest secret. She probably had.

"This stays between you and me." Petronilla's threats fell on deaf ears.

"Or what?" Acelina's right eyebrow arched. "What I just saw was a pleasure house's branding."

Her shirt sat on her shoulders but the buttons in the middle were open. "What's it going to take to keep you quiet?"

"Nothing can shut me up," Acelina said, circling Petronilla's exposed form like an eagle circling its prey. "Now, I understand why you hate me...hate this place. And to think I was lectured by you about honor." Petronilla grabbed Acelina's arm and tried to twist it. The courtesan didn't even flinch. "Violence isn't going to solve your problems."

Reluctantly, Petronilla let her go, raking her hand through her hair. She felt embarrassment wash over her.

"You have a nice figure," Acelina conceded. "Unlike me, you're not flat at all...far from it."

Petronilla clamped the edges of her shirt shut. "If you're done—"

"We could always use another girl. I pay my girls well."

"Don't even think about it," Petronilla warned.

"You can't stop me. All this time...Ha, I can't believe the great lieutenant general has such a sordid history."

Petronilla would never know if it was insanity, anger, or attraction that took over her senses, but she knew knowing couldn't have prevented what followed. She seized Acelina's arm and brought her forward. Her eyes found Acelina's lips, her finger tracing the lower lip. She laid a finger on it, cutting off Acelina's voice. The remnants of her resonant voice melted into Petronilla's fingers. Acelina's large onyx eyes surveyed her, silence taking over the room. She raised her palm toward her face as if to cup her cheek, and Petronilla closed her eyes, anticipating the touch.

"No." Acelina backed off immediately, leaving Petronilla in this half-aroused state. Putting the lid back on, she turned to Petronilla. "With this, we're even. Don't expect me to be nice to you again."

There was no acknowledgment of what had happened, which was fine with Petronilla. She couldn't quite explain it herself.

"Same here. This...." Petronilla felt the soothing coolness of the salve on her arms and still felt her breath on her skin. "It's not gonna happen again so don't get any ideas."

"I wouldn't dream of it." Acelina rolled her eyes and

threw the tin box at her, which she caught, rising. "Keep it in case you get bitten by any more bugs."

"Didn't you get the storage cleaned or something?" Petronilla ran her thumb over the aluminum tin. Acelina's fingers had warmed its rim.

"Bugs always find a way to get in." She shrugged. "Besides, your blood must be sweeter than your tongue which is why the insects love sucking it."

Petronilla came up with a lot of retorts to that but since all of them were X-rated, she judiciously kept her mouth shut. "I'll see you at dinner."

NINE

PETRONILLA

Dinner was a lavish affair at Duality. All the escorts and employees ate at seven, two hours before the pleasure house opened for business. Petronilla was now part of their small family and had spent some time learning names. Rose, the cook, was the person she saw the most, followed by Turstin, who was a voracious gossip.

The dinner table was set with an opulent display of meat, vegetable dishes, soups, and even a cake. Five bottles of wine and several glasses were laid on another table. Rose cooked a feast every night to make sure the girls stayed plump and nourished. Turstin grabbed a plate and began piling it with meat. For his wiry frame, he ate a lot. Lily followed. Petronilla was beginning to recognize their names.

"How was your day?" Lily asked. She was on the plumper side, and had a lot of fat on her, just the way Petronilla liked. Not that she needed to know.

"All right." Petronilla was shaken after what had

happened in Acelina's room. She kept glancing at the door, but there was no sign of Acelina. There was no reason to worry. Acelina was a sophisticated woman.

"I heard there were rats in the storage." Lily's blonde hair glinted under the chandelier lights, as she bent to eat her food.

"It was a nightmare," she admitted. When Lily's weary light eyes met hers, she asked, "How was your day?"

"My day hasn't started yet." Lily laughed. "I have two appointments today, and other people might come in."

Petronilla nodded mutely, sensing something was wrong with Lily. "You look tired. If you want to leave here-"

"Are you promising to take me away?"

"No." Petronilla turned away, not knowing how to answer that. "Do you like...working here?"

"It's not bad," Lily said. "I've been working here for a long time and it's way better than the last place I was at." Reading the hesitation on Petronilla's face, she added, "Acelina is kind."

"Kind?" That was the last word Petronilla associated with her.

"Most people in this field aren't as forgiving as her." Lily picked at the peas on her plate. "I'm not a big fan of peas," she paused, "But I appreciate the meat."

Acelina strode in, as graceful as ever, carrying her smoking pipe, and for a minute she felt everything go still. Their eyes met across the table, and Petronilla hurriedly turned away.

"We have a guest tonight," she announced, no trace of their interlude in the room on her face now touched up with makeup. "He's here for Lieutenant General Petronilla."

Petronilla stood up, confused. "Me? Who is it?" "General Darius," she said. "Do you mind stepping out—"

She was at the door before Acelina could finish, running through the corridor.

So, Darius had taken matters into his hands, knowing Petronilla wouldn't have the courage to ask Acelina for a dress.

"Where is he?" Petronilla asked Acelina, who trailed her down the corridor like a shadow. She paused before Acelina's open door and found Darius lingering outside. He wore a casual shirt made of cotton and loose pants, not his uniform.

"Petronilla," he said, his face lighting up. Behind him, she saw Acelina's open wardrobe with a few dresses laid out on the bed. "Acelina and I were talking about possible outfits for your undercover mission."

"You're discussing our undercover mission with her!?" Petronilla was surprised. "But nobody is supposed to know-"

"I didn't give her any details." Darius brushed off her concerns. "Just told her we need some clothes to dress you up as a courtesan."

"What—"

"Did you find anything you liked?" Acelina's entered, sly gaze sliding from Darius to Petronilla, mocking with a semi-smile. "Lieutenant General Petronilla could've asked me directly," she said, knowing fully well the woman never would.

"Our lieutenant general's a little shy," Darius said, rather cheerful for someone who was interfering.

"Shy?" Acelina was not buying it.

Petronilla shook her head, coming to stand next to Darius. "Don't you have other things to do? I'll take care of this-"

He ignored her, turning to Acelina. "Where's the dress you told me about?"

"Let me fish it out." Acelina busied herself with searching her wardrobe. Darius peered into the courtesan's room, noticing slight details like how she placed her pipe on the edge of the table, and the fresh lilies that always filled her vase. Her account book was open, showing she'd been working on it before Darius arrived. "Do you have a preferred color?"

"No," Darius said.

"I can do this without you," Petronilla hissed, annoyed. "I am capable of procuring a dress."

She shot daggers at Acelina, who sorted through garments in her wardrobe, oblivious to the tense exchange.

"I know you are," Darius said, ever the diplomat. "I just wanted to make sure you were fine. You don't like courtesans, so I decided to help you out. I can't understand why you agreed—"

"Duty comes first." Coughing, she turned the other way, and said to Darius in a low voice, "I appreciate the concern, but I can do this on my own."

"I just wanted to help," he said. "If you don't want to go-" There was a concern in his eyes, just like the one he'd had on the day the king had asked her to live at Duality.

"It's in the past," she said, turning away. "I've been living in a pleasure house for an entire week. I can manage a visit to another one without any trouble."

Darius inhaled sharply. "I should return, then. To be honest, I don't know much about women's dresses." Then, louder, "Acelina here's the expert. She's agreed to help you."

Acelina beamed at him, piling a few select dresses on the floor.

"What did you bribe her with?" Petronilla whispered.

At that moment, Acelina, who had fished out a royal blue kimono, held it up. It would look very beautiful on Acelina, she thought, as she saw the fabric held against her flawless face. Everything looked good on her.

"Oh, she agreed to help me out of goodwill," Darius said, brushing his fingers in the air. "You're lucky she's your hostess. Acelina's a gem."

He made sure the last words were loud enough for Acelina to hear. She turned back and beamed. "You're too kind."

"And the best courtesan in the Red Light District is too modest." Leave it to Darius to attract bees with honey. She couldn't imagine him being rude to anyone. It was with that easy manner that he'd made her trust him and brought her to Inferno. And that had turned out well, so she just had to trust him once again.

"It's been a while since I had to make a good first impression," Acelina returned. "But I think this should work." She handed the blue silk dress to Petronilla. "Why don't you try it on?"

Petronilla held up the royal blue silk kimono for inspection, and the first thing she saw was the low neckline followed by the long cut that stretched from the bottom of the skirt to the waist.

"I can't wear this!" She turned away, cringing.

"Why not?" "It's...indecent."

Acelina rolled her eyes. "A pleasure house isn't the place to be decent."

"Come on, Petronilla, give it a chance," Darius begged, seeing the mission evaporate right before his eyes.

"I can look for another color-" Acelina offered.

"It's not the color-" Petronilla looked at the dress like it was a specter. She couldn't imagine herself in something like that ever again.

"Let's try it on." Darius clapped.

"No," Acelina and Petronilla said together, then stared each other down.

"Why not?"

"Because I don't want to." Petronilla coughed. She stepped forward and snatched the garment from Acelina. "Thanks. I'll return it tomorrow."

"You can keep it," Acelina offered. "I don't want to."

"Get it washed before you return it, then," Acelina said, closing the wardrobe door. Petronilla scoffed, knowing this was her plan for revenge. "I'll help you put on some makeup tomorrow if you want."

"That's so generous of you." Darius smiled. "No, thank you."

"Petronilla."

"If you want to be found out and ruin your mission, that's your choice." Acelina shrugged. "Just so you know, courtesans wear makeup these days. And a lot of it."

Of course, she knew that from her long, illustrious career

as one. But she'd never liked the feel of paint on her face and the way it clogged her pores.

"I'm not trying to promote myself."

"Good for you," Acelina said. "Because I'm not sure anybody's going to buy your ruse."

Darius' eyes swung like a pendulum, the curling of his mouth revealing he perceived more than what he saw.

"And a smidge of makeup's going to change that?" She quirked an eyebrow up, disbelieving. The dress crumpled under her strong hold.

"It's nice to see you both getting along," Darius cut in, only to be subjected to two glaring pairs of eyes. "I think I should be getting home now...." He backed off, still subject to dual scrutinizing gazes, and said, "I'll see you tomorrow, Lieutenant General." Then, with a bow, "Thanks, Acelina, for all the help. I don't know how I'll ever repay you."

"There's no need for any repayment," she said. "It's always a pleasure." She paused. "If you'd like a room tonight—"

"Not tonight." He shook his head. "I'll visit soon." General Darius muttered his goodbyes and left first, leaving Acelina and Petronilla to glare at each other.

"So what's it going to be?" the proprietress asked, crossing her arms over her chest. "You want the makeup or not? I'm doing you this favor only because Darius asked me. There's nothing I'd like more than to wash my hands of you."

Petronilla frowned, weighing her choices. "I have to leave in the morning. Will you be able to wake up that early?"

"Even if I wake up that early, the pleasure house you're

planning to visit will be closed. We don't operate regular hours."

Infuriating as it was, Acelina was right. With her words heating Petronilla's blood, there was no way she could think straight.

"Tomorrow, evening, then? Seven?" Petronilla cleared her throat, shifting the silk garment in her palms.

"Even I should manage to be awake by then," Acelina said, dripping sarcasm. She adjusted the wide neck of her black dress.

"I'll be ready by seven," Petronilla finished, wrapping the silk dress around her arm. "Don't drink too much."

"Be gentle." Acelina snatched away the dress, smoothing out imaginary wrinkles. "Creases..."

"You can smooth out the creases. I'll get it tomorrow," Petronilla said, shoving the dress at her.

"Try it on to see if it fits," Acelina ordered, extending it.

"You don't trust your superior judgment?" Petronilla didn't like the sight of the dress, and the thought of wearing it before Acelina made her skin heat to an uncomfortable temperature.

"Are you blushing?" Acelina was too perceptive for her peace of mind.

"No."

"I don't know your size," Acelina said, giving her a once-over. "Though I can guess." Petronilla didn't know if that was an innuendo or an honest confession. "Tilly will make any alterations you need."

To try out the dress was the rational thing to do. Petronilla knew that, yet her heart pounded at the thought of being seen half-naked by Acelina.

"I'LL TRY NOT TO LAUGH," Acelina assured, extending the dress.

"How reassuring." Petronilla took it and glared down at the silk monstrosity.

"Do you have matching undergarments to go with it?" Acelina asked. From Petronilla's blank gawking, she must've gleamed at the answer, because she said, "Of course not. Hmmm...undergarments...you should be around Angel's size...." She turned, surveying Petronilla from top to bottom. "It might be better if you don't wear any undergarments."

"What!?" Petronilla's face heated again, the double meaning of that sentence blooming into possibilities in her mind.

"It's all the rage these days. Try it on. We'll see what needs to be fixed," Acelina sighed, putting her mind at ease a little. "I'll wait outside. Call if you need me."

"You can't be serious—"

"You might not know this Lieutenant General, but selling sex is a profession." Acelina went on in a businesslike tone, "So, you can save your blushes and modesty for later. We're working."

With that, she was gone, skirts swishing. The door slid closed, abandoning Petronilla to the silence and the provocative dress. For the first minute, she couldn't move. Only when she heard an impatient, "Are you done?" did she start stripping.

Standing naked in front of Acelina's mirror, Petronilla studied the scars that covered her body. Thanks to the balm, her insect bites had calmed down, but the scent of eucalyptus

REMAINED ON HER SKIN— not the most attractive thing for a courtesan.

As she held the dress against her body, she wanted to gag. It was a reminder of the life she'd had, one in which she'd been helpless and desperate.

"Do you need help?" Acelina called out.

"Let me dress in peace!" she snapped. The voice on the other side went silent.

Inhaling sharply, Petronilla slipped on the dress. Since there wasn't much fabric to work with, it wasn't very hard. She'd learned to dress as a courtesan, and even though it had been a long time, she found her fingers still remembered how to secure the garment.

With all the ties and buttons fastened, she looked at herself in the mirror and forgot to catch her breath. The royal blue silk cupped her shoulders, revealing a tantalizing expanse of bronze skin. The neckline dipped low, exposing her cleavage. To her dismay, she had a lot of it. She usually preferred to forget it existed, but out on display like this, it was hard to ignore. The slit on her thigh revealed her toned legs, every muscled inch of dark skin gleaming in the lamplight. Reluctantly, Petronilla admitted to herself that she looked more beautiful than she had at sixteen. It had been a while since she saw herself as a woman, but she was aware of it every moment.

Petronilla took in her flushed face, her eyes that had gone wide, and remembered what the madame had told her all those years ago,

"You have a plain face," she had described, holding Petronilla's chin between her fingers, and turning it. "Forgetable." She let go of the face and examined Petronilla in the blue dress, her breasts spilling over. "But that body will haunt a man's dreams."

That was why Petronilla had continued to get customers, despite her acidic temperament. They wanted a piece of her exquisite flesh. Back then, she'd hated her curves, the lushness of her breasts, and her long legs, knowing they were the reason she was tied to this dishonorable profession. She had made peace with them now, but seeing them once again, she wondered what it would be like to give in to her body and do what it was made for doing.

"Did you fall asleep?" Acelina burst in without a preamble.

And came to a sudden halt.

Their eyes met, locked in a gravitational pull, and Petronilla hurried to place her hands over her breasts. Acelina's jaw dropped involuntarily, and Petronilla felt a stab of satisfaction.

"Stunned?" she asked, slowly letting her hands go.

Pulling herself together, the proprietress stepped up, "I can understand why your madame kept you around," She gave her body an appreciative glance. "This could work. Blue suits you."

"Was that a compliment?"

"Why? You want me to take it back?" Acelina crossed her arms over her chest and did a deliberate once-over.

"I guess now you expect me to say it's all thanks to your excellent taste?" Petronilla's defenses rose.

"I don't expect anything from you." Acelina frowned, examining the fall of the skirts. "Does everything fit fine? Do you want anything altered?"

"Yes. This neck is too low, and this slit," She pointed to the thigh-high slit. "Sew it back together."

Acelina laughed. "Only you could say something like that," she said. "Look at yourself. You're every man's dream." She paused and added in a husky voice, "And every woman's too."

"When did you start resorting to flattery?" Petronilla glanced at the mirror again and felt a little better. Maybe being liked by other people wasn't so bad after all.

"I'm not flattering you," she said. "Just so you know, I would keep you around as an escort just for that body of yours. Men pay big bucks for—"

Petronilla cringed.

"Ah, so you know. Then, we can move on to packaging your wares better."

"Wares?" she said, clearing her throat, and remembered their previous conversation, "About those undergarments..."

"I think the dress works without them." Acelina surveyed her from the back and nodded briskly. "They're supposed to come off, anyway," she said in a matter-of-fact voice. Then, putting a hand on her shoulder to test the fit, she said, "I guessed your size right."

Acelina was taking in every bit of her, just like her

customers had. Only, this time, it felt different. She didn't feel degraded; she felt desired. Acelina brushed a finger over a cut on the back of her shoulder. Electricity sparked through Petronilla. "We'll have to do something about the scars. Some people like them, but it'd be better to-"

"Conceal them." For some reason, that suggestion dampened Petronilla's spirits. "Of course."

"You don't like my idea." Acelina crept up in front of her, sly eyes gleaming with perceptiveness.

"You're the expert." Petronilla fisted fabric in her clenched fists.

"Stop doing that. You're going to wrinkle the skirt." Acelina frowned. Moving closer, she brushed a finger over another scar on her cheek. "And, for the record, I like scars. They show character."

Petronilla felt something stir in her heart. So far, she'd only criticized Acelina, but Acelina was trying to soothe her insecurities. She didn't like this kinder version of Acelina because it made her feel like less of a human being

"But you don't have any," Petronilla said, trying to stop her heart from pounding. She remembered Acelina's smooth skin, polished to perfection. They were so close now, she felt the heat from Acelina's body near hers. Could Acelina see her elevated heartbeat pulse in her cheek?

Her eyes darted straight to that perfect rosebud mouth, full and luscious. If she bent a little, their lips would touch. How would it feel to taste her? Heat curled down her spine, a match to their volatile attraction.

"You mean I have no character?" Acelina laughed, lifting her finger. Cool air brushed the spot where her finger had been a second earlier. Petronilla wanted to argue but realized the question was Acelina's way of diffusing the tension.

"No."

"Darius seemed to be worried about you. Might that have something to do with your past?" Sometimes Petronilla hated how perceptive Acelina was.

"I don't think about it anymore." She looked away.

"But it's a part of you."

"I chose to abandon that part of myself a long time ago."

"Doesn't make it any less real."

"Are you determined to irritate me?" "Maybe."

"If we're done with the fitting, I need to get some sleep. It's been a long day."

"Yes." Acelina began arranging her wardrobe all of a sudden. "Can you put the dress back on if you take it off?"

"I can't sleep in it just because it's hard to put on!" Petronilla argued.

"Fine. Change." Acelina shook her head. "Are you going to leave or not?"

"I need to check everything before we open," she declared, leaving Petronilla inside her room. "Try not to break anything."

"Thanks for helping us," Petronilla bit out between clenched teeth. That took Acelina by surprise.

"You didn't need much help." Acelina's voice was placid, which meant she wasn't being sarcastic. "Good luck on your mission."

She opened and closed the door, but Petronilla didn't hear any footsteps.

"Will you be okay?" Acelina asked from the other side,

silhouetted by the lanterns. Petronilla closed her eyes. They stood at the end of the corridor, outside Petronilla's room, unable to tear their gazes away. The uncomfortable attraction was back again, making Petronilla's body throb. "I can ask one of the girls-"

"I'm fine," she bit out, a hand on the door. She didn't dare open it. "I can take care of myself."

They stayed on either side of the door a little longer, not knowing how to proceed.

"Petronilla?" Acelina's voice called out from outside. "Good night." She steeled her voice to murmur the polite greeting.

"Do you—"

"I'll see you tomorrow evening," Petronilla bit out, proceeding to change her clothing.

"Right...good night."

Slowly, Acelina's footsteps receded. Petronilla sank to the floor, clutching her clothes, glad she'd averted a disaster tonight.

TEN

PETRONILLA

THE MINUTE PETRONILLA STEPPED INTO THE ROSE, clad in that royal blue kimono, revealing half her breasts, she knew it was a bad idea. The smell of opium smoke, cigarettes, and alcohol descended on her like fog, throwing her senses into disarray. She coughed, climbing up the creaking stairs. Every inch of The Rose, from the artificial velvet tapestry to the ornate wallpaper, reminded her of the past she had escaped.

She'd snuck in through the backdoor, and the guard, half-drunk, had let her in, falling for her disguise. She had to admit, grudgingly, that Acelina was an expert at this. A low-necked dress, three layers of powder, rouge, and lipstick later, she looked like a veteran courtesan. Now, if only she walked like one.

The staircase curved sharply, killing her legs. Wearing heeled shoes unbalanced her, and if she hadn't hung on to the railing for dear life, she'd have slid down like a bead on a string. The Rose must've been a classy establishment before it got old, Petronilla thought. The brocade brown wallpapers lent a regal air to the place, bolstered by large glass chandeliers that hung from the ceiling. The lamps were shaped like Venus flytraps intricately carved in glass and reflected candlelight, making it seem like it bounced off diamonds.

"Who are you?" a voice asked. Petronilla spotted an escort with red lips balancing a long, lit pipe. Instantly, she was reminded of Acelina. Acelina had sent Lily to help her put on makeup. She should be thrilled about it, but Petronilla felt her absence like a physical thing. There was a part of her awareness that only came into being when Acelina was around.

"Uh...ummm...I'm the new escort," she tried, cringing on the inside. The escort surveyed her with grey eyes. Her nose was large compared to the rest of her face, and her eyes were small.

"New escort, huh?" The courtesan blew a puff of smoke straight into her face, reminding her of another rude woman in the same profession, and brought her grey eyes closer for inspection. "You're tall."

"Is that a good thing...?" she blurted, heart pounding. In the clear blue-violet eyes, she saw her trepidation reflected and hated herself for the momentary self-doubt. If she didn't project confidence, she'd be found out in no time at all.

"No," the escort placed the pipe between her lips again and sighed. "Men don't like women who are taller than them."

She didn't know the first thing about men or pleasing them. It didn't hurt her pride anymore that she wasn't made for pleasure. Back then, she'd been a helpless girl, eager to please and be accepted. But now, she'd found her place in the world, and anybody who dared look down on her could go to hell.

"Too bad for them," Petronilla said, tilting her nose upward haughtily, just like Acelina. "They're missing out."

The escort burst into laughter, a deep-throated, cacophonous sound, sending ash scattering over the floor. Petronilla crinkled her nose to block out the strong smell of nicotine.

"I like you," she said, clutching her belly, aching with laughter. "Haven't had one as confident as you in some time." Then, straightening up, she added, "How old are you? You don't look like the pure-faced virgins she usually takes in."

She'd been a pure-faced virgin too when the madame had taken her in at twelve.

"Pure-faced virgins are useless in this business," Petronilla echoed.

"I agree." The woman raised her pipe, as if in a toast. She tilted her head and approached. "What's your name?"

"Pet-Petunia."

"Petunia?" she asked, deadbeat. "Yes, Petunia."

A sillier name she'd never heard. But it was the best she could come up with at such short notice.

"Is that your real name?" Her lips shuddered with a barely suppressed smile.

"Go ahead, laugh." Petronilla shook her head.

She didn't hold back. "You don't look like a Petunia."

"My mother didn't know I'd turn out like this when she named me," she reasoned.

"You mean a six-foot giant?" she asked, pointing her pipe from top to bottom.

"I'm five-eleven." The courtesan brushed her off with the wave of a hand. "What's your name?"

"Giselle."

Giselle was considerably shorter than Petronilla with her five-three build, and dark brown hair. Her skin was smooth, but not as flawless as Acelina's. However, her grey eyes stood out in a face of angular features. Her body, on the other hand, was all fat and curves. Petronilla blinked and looked up. Why was she comparing her to Acelina, anyway?

"Don't you have clients to be entertaining?"

"Not for the next fifteen minutes," she said. Lamps cast shadows on the brocade wallpapers decorating the hallway. "And you? Do you lean towards men or women?"

Women. Definitely, women.

"Men," Petronilla lied smoothly. The person she was looking for was a man so men it would have to be. Though, the very thought of 'entertaining' one again was revolting.

"You got any booked for you?"

"The owner said The Rose was in high demand so I'm sure someone will come along." Petronilla shrugged. "I saw a handsome man enter last night. Salt and pepper hair, my height, grey cloak. Have you seen him?"

Giselle's eyebrows knitted thoughtfully. "Hmmm...I wouldn't have guessed mature men were your type. Then again, you seem like an old soul."

Petronilla coughed, not knowing how to answer that.

Giselle laughed. "I saw him last night, though I don't know which girl he spent the night with."

"He was here all night?"

"Gambling, mostly." She shrugged. "I saw him thrice between my rounds. Lost a lot. If you ask me, he'll be looking for another pleasure house by now."

"Why?"

"So that he can start his gambling tab afresh," she said. "Too many debts here. If I were you, I wouldn't pin my hopes on him being here tonight."

It was just like her father to rack up gambling debts and run away. Isn't that how she'd landed up in a brothel in the first place?

"Here you are," a familiar, stern voice echoed, making the hair on her neck stand. A shadow blanketed hers. "Giselle, stop talking and go attend to your client."

"Yes, ma'am." Giselle slipped away quickly, after throwing her a wink. The woman from yesterday surveyed Petronilla, apparently not recognizing her in these clothes and makeup. Petronilla squirmed in her dress, averting her gaze.

"And you." She came to stand before Petronilla, surveying her from top to bottom. Her heartbeat doubled, mind pounding with the realization that she could be found out anytime. "Who the hell are you?"

"I...I was looking for work," she said, watching Giselle's receding profile. "My friend Giselle recommended this place to me."

"Hmmm...you're tall," she said, surveying Petronilla from head to toe, pausing at her spilling breasts. She instinctively brought a hand to cover it, then pulled it away. How did people do this every day? Being looked at like she was a horse for purchase made her skin crawl. Taking deep breaths to dispel her goosebumps, Petronilla stood with a straight back. This was all part of her duty. She had to track down her father, no matter what the means. "But some men like 'em tall."

"Madame." A maid, dressed in tattered garments and a white apron, paused before the proprietress. "We have more customers downstairs."

"Coming," she said, grabbing Petronilla's arm. "Come with me, girl. We're short on escorts tonight."

Before Petronilla could respond, she was dragged down the flight of stairs, losing her shoes somewhere in the process. At the reception stood a tall man, reeking of liquor with a sleazy face and lust-hazed eyes. His bald head reflected the chandeliers, large fingers rising in the air to point at her.

"What's her price?" he asked, drunkenly stumbling to Petronilla. His clammy hand grasped her exposed ones in a vice-like grip, his reddened face lighting up with glee. "I like this one."

"Three hundred coins for a night," the proprietress put in, smoothly. From her expression, it was obvious she'd seen the customer before.

"That's a bit high." He doubled back, pulling Petronilla along with him.

"She's good. Experienced," the proprietress said, though why she thought that was beyond Petronilla's comprehension. Their eyes met, a hardness in the owner's calculating ones.

"Fine, fine," the man said, eyeing her breasts apprecia-tively. His thumb flicked over the exposed top of one, a broken-toothed smile parting his thick lips. "She's got big apples."

Apples?

Petronilla didn't know what she wanted to do first- gag or tackle him to the ground. Both seemed to be bad choices, so she ignored the tears stinging her eyes as his thumb traced her cleavage. It was a reflexive reaction. She'd closed her eyes on the worst days and taken it like a warrior. Perhaps, that's what had strengthened her spirit.

Or broken it.

"Good, we have a deal," the owner said. Then, in a lower voice, whispered to her, "I keep fifty percent." The woman instructed a maid to clear a room and got on with guiding the patron.

Dread stirred in her belly, alarms pounding inside her skull. Every touch of those disgusting hands reminded her of the first man who had ever taken her at the madame's brothel.

She had been only fourteen back then and didn't know what was happening to her. One of the maids, Maddie, was with her in an escort's room, instructing her to clean. Petronilla, being an innocent fourteen-year-old, had cleaned the room diligently, never wondering why the madame had given her a new dress to wear tonight. Now that she thought about it, something had been different about that day.

For one, Maddie was helping her clean, which as a kitchen maid, she never did. Then, there was the incredibly attractive gown the madame had gifted her. The madame had never been nice to her. She didn't know why she had bought a brand-new gown. It wasn't even her birthday.

The low bodice pushed up her newly emerging breasts,

just like this one did. She'd started her period last year, and ever since a flood of changes had descended on her body, leaving her confused. During nights, she felt a strange ache between her legs, especially when her monthly courses were drawing closer. And Maddie was the flame that stimulated those aches. They'd become friends soon after Petronilla started working at the brothel and were now roommates.

When she'd told Maddie about her bleeding, Maddie had said it was a part of becoming a woman and had taken her in her arms, overjoyed. She still remembered Maddie, with her pale blonde hair, friendly countenance, and clear blue eyes. She was plump and plain-looking so Madame had put her to work in the kitchens. She was six years older than Petronilla and had been her friend through the dark times.

At fourteen, Petronilla realized for the first time that she was attracted to Maddie. She began noticing all kinds of things like how Maddie's face flushed red every time the weather grew colder, and how her curves molded her tightening gown. Then, she'd noticed those lush, pink lips that made her want to kiss them. They hung over her today, those curves brushing her back as they tried to get the room clean. Petronilla's heart thundered in her throat.

"I'll do it," Maddie said, taking the feather duster from her hand. The contact sent a shock through Petronilla.

"I don't know why the madame wanted us to clean this room," she said, turning the other way, flushed. "It's already clean."

A bell chimed outside- a call for Maddie. "I'll go see what's needed," she said, speeding to the door.

"I'll go-"

"No. You stay." There was an undisguised terror in her eyes that receded to agony. "If someone comes in, be nice to them, okay?"

"Who is coming?"

"It's easier if you don't resist." "Resist what?"

The bell rang again. "I'll be back."

She hadn't come back, of course. Instead, a pudgy man reeking of alcohol had come in and locked the door, raking an appreciative glance over her newly emerged womanhood. "The madame did say you were special," he said, taking heavy steps towards her. Panic ricocheted in her head.

"You've got it wrong." She clutched the bed poster, afraid for her life. "I'm the maid—"

His hands closed over her breasts, tugging down the neck of her gown. "No!" Her protests were silenced by his damp lips. She wanted to puke right into his mouth, but he was pushing her skirts up, running a hand over her thighs.

It's easier if you don't resist....

Maddie's words flashed in her mind, and anger rose through her veins. She kicked and clawed, but the man's grasp was too strong. Ultimately, he won the battle, pushing her down on the bed and ripping off her gown. Pearls and buttons rained on the floor, rolling to the door from which Maddie had left. As the man took her virginity, she felt betrayal choke her. The pain of his invasion was swift, and tears spilled from her eyes, unbidden. He was hurting her, but she didn't care. This was her life, full of disappointments. Why had she ever believed that someone could love her?

She hated being raked by those lust-filled eyes, clammy fingers degrading her body, while he spouted rubbish from his mouth that reeked of alcohol. How many of these blurry faces had she seen in her two-year-long career?

"The second room on the right," the owner put in, pointing up the stairs. She led the way up, trying to keep a distance, but the man's hands held hers and she held his skin through the short climb. She longed to elbow his flabby gut, but she needed to be out of the owner's sight if she had any hope of getting away unnoticed. The sharp, sloping stairs hurt her legs but without the shoes, it was an easier climb. The corridor she was led to had purple brocade wallpaper, a very different aesthetic from Duality. They followed the purple carpet down to the last room.

Hastily, she opened the bedroom door and let them both in. Glancing at the darkness outside the window, she decided to be done in five minutes. The wallpaper in the room was peeling at the edges, a grey and silver brocade design. Similar glass lamps were lit, but set against the fading scenery, they appeared outdated.

"Eager for a tumble, aren't you?" The customer approached the bed while she pretended to lock up behind him. "What's your name-"

"Petunia," she said, standing behind him. Before he could blink, she hit his head, making him pass out over the billowing mattress. He lay there, unconscious, but alive. The day she'd learned how to make people pass out with one blow to the head had been the best day of her life. Looking down at him lying on the bed, she felt a surge of power, like she'd scored a small triumph over her past.

Her eyes scanned the room for possible escape routes. There was no way she was using the door. The owner watched her girls like a hawk watching its prey, and she couldn't risk being found out. So she kicked the window open, grinding her teeth when she saw how far up the room was. The flimsy dress made climbing down roofs almost impossible, but she'd have to take a chance.

Outside the room, she heard echoes of footsteps, the owner's voice cooing, "Is everything all right?"

"Yes." She hoped her voice didn't sound too hollow. Her hands simultaneously checked the window lock. "We're just getting started."

"Come see me after you're done," the owner said. Petronilla waited for her footsteps to fade before unlatching the window.

Once the footsteps receded, she pushed herself out through the window, which was thankfully large enough to accommodate her body. Her leg slipped and sent her flying down the tiled roof. The tiles brushed against her exposed legs and hands, scratching them. Grabbing onto a sewage pipe, Petronilla steadied herself and climbed down.

Well, more like fell.

Thankfully, there were no broken bones. The east of the pleasure house opened into an alley, fogged with smoke and heat. Petronilla looked around, seeing a hazy outline of streetlamps in the dark. She was just about to dash it when she heard two men whispering.

"That man who came from Terra?" The words stopped Petronilla in her tracks. She leaned against a broken wall, straining to hear the conversation between two shadows. An ember shone amidst the smoke, indicating one of them was smoking. She edged closer to the wall, making sure she remained hidden while being able to hear everything.

"I think he's planning something," another voice, slurred with drunkenness, said.

"What? A revolution?" His harsh laughter was grating.

Then, after a pause, "You can't be serious."

More silence, followed by a low whisper, "They say he's got some letters from the king."

"And he's alive?" The man dropped the cigarette and pressed it under his shoe. "I'd think King Delton would have his hide displayed in the palace by now."

"Not our king, the King of Terra." "Oh." Realization dawned. "Yeah."

"Those letters must be worth a fortune," he said. "In the right hands, those letters would be worth tens of thousands."

"Exactly. The problem is, nobody seems to know where those letters are."

"He doesn't have them?" the first voice asked. "A royal guard frisked him three days ago, and-"

The man paused abruptly at the sight of her shadow. Petronilla tried to pull back, but it was too late.

"Who do we have here?" The man's eyes lit up at the sight of her, dressed in that blue silk kimono, offering a tantalizing display of her breasts. Petronilla's skin prickled. Her head searched for any sign of Felix's men or Darius, but nobody was to be seen. She'd told Darius not to worry and had no clue what Felix's spies looked like.

"Not tonight. I'm tired." With an unsuccessful batting of her eyelashes, she tried to escape, only to be seized by one of the men- a rabbit-toothed one that smelled of ginger ale. His brown eyes examined her with undisguised lust, making her skin prickle.

"But I'm interested in the letters you're talking about," she said. "Does this man have grey hair and..." She held her hand up to her shoulder. "He's this tall?"

"How do you know?" Losing interest in her flesh, the men turned to her for information.

"I saw him yesterday," Petronilla volunteered information of her own, unusually chatty. "He's been living at The Rose. He owes me money."

The two men laughed. "If I were you, I wouldn't count on getting my money."

"Darn, it." She batted her eyelashes. "But I don't know anything about the letters. If a revolution breaks out in Terra, what do you think will happen to us?"

"The king will join whichever side wins," one of them said. "But it'd be years before the fighting stopped. I wonder what's in those letters."

"Me too," Petronilla said. "Couldn't you get your hand on the letters?"

"I'd love to, but the only person who knows anything about those letters is nowhere to be found but-" the first man paused, looking doubtful. "If you want to collect your money, you should go to Ifer."

"No way!" the other man echoed. "She won't ever get her money back if she doesn't live to see tomorrow."

"He's not that bad," the first one argued. "And he's a friend of the thief...that's what I heard."

"A friend?"

"A mutual acquaintance..."

"And where can I find Ifer?" Petronilla asked.

The first man scoffed. "You should think twice before treading anywhere near his den," he said. "He's the most dangerous boss in the red-light district. Last week alone, his men murdered-"

"I'll take my chances," Petronilla said. "Where do I find him?"

"Nobody knows." They looked at each other. "Follow the trail of crime in the district, and it should lead you to him."

Petronilla frowned, walking away from the stunned men. "She's asking for trouble," one of them said once she was

out of earshot. Petronilla walked barefoot down the street and felt an arm shoot out. She dodged immediately, pulling a shadow out of the side of the building.

"It's me," Darius hissed.

"General." Petronilla stood under a streetlamp that hit her eyes. Darius stood under it, wearing a nondescript grey coat and worn-out pants and shoes. Despite his distinct eyes, he seemed a part of the background.

"I heard your conversation," he said. "I've been following you ever since you jumped out the window."

"I think this Ifer guy might know something about the letters," Petronilla said.

"He knows of every crime that takes place in this area," another voice joined them. A brown-haired man emerged from behind them, his amber eyes scanning the area for any other known faces. "I'm from the secret service. Felix told me to meet you two. I'm Tranagard."

"What do you know about Ifer?" Petronilla got straight to the point.

"He's the lord of crime," Tranagard said. "No criminal goes in and out of the red-light district without him knowing. If a thief came here from Terra, he knows about it."

"But?" Darius prompted.

"He's dangerous," the agent said. "And we've not been able to track him down to date. He lets his minions handle the work. They're involved in everything from bootlegging to smuggling state secrets."

"That's a problem," Petronilla confessed. "Is there any way we could find out if he has the letters?"

"I'll try to find his whereabouts," the spy said. "But I doubt we'll be able to get a hold of him. This line of inquiry might be futile. But I'll try, just in case."

"How about we meet at the secret service headquarters tomorrow?" Darius suggested.

"See you." The agent left first, flowing with the rest of the crowd like he was part of a river.

"Good job, Petronilla," Darius said. "You should go back to Duality and catch some rest. I have a feeling this is going to be a long chase."

After bidding goodbye, Petronilla walked back to Duality, inviting the gaze of several curious strangers. She felt embarrassment wash over her but didn't give in to it until her feet touched Duality's gardens. Only then did she realize she didn't have any shoes on.

ELEVEN

PETRONILLA

CURSING, SHE TRACED HER WAY THROUGH THE SANDY path amidst the back garden. Her bruised feet felt every grain of sand and pebble under them. The humid air condensed on her exposed skin, helping all those open wounds clot.

"Ouch!" Something sharp lodged itself in her sole. Limping, she sat on the edge of the wooden steps, overlooking the gutter. The stench was covered by falling flowers, but disgusting nevertheless.

Clotted blood and scratches lined the soles of her feet, matching those cuts and bruises in her arms and legs. A pebble was stuck under her left foot, which she dislodged promptly. That's when she noticed the leg was exposed top to bottom, thanks to the garment piece she'd cut loose in her attempt to escape. Her hair was in a disarray, flowing down her shoulders. With sagging shoulders, she fell back on the wooden floor, seeing a face crystallize over her.

"You look like something fished out of the canal." Acelina's musical voice brought her senses back to life. Her feet shot to the ground, pulling her up to face the proprietress who was examining her disheveled state.

"Good evening to you too," she said, walking past her, scrambling for her door.

"I take it the mission didn't go well." Acelina wore yellow silk, and it made her look radiant like the sun. Petronilla didn't know anyone who could carry off that color. Her hair was pinned up in a bun, revealing the smooth slope of her neck. Red stones hung on her ears, matching her lips.

"It went very well, actually—" She paused, realizing Acelina had come to stand before her. Her sooty lashes cast a shadow on her pale cheek, and Petronilla felt her gut tightening. Her muscles, joints, and cuts ached, yet all she could feel was this awareness, consuming her like a fire.

"A courtesan's job wasn't too hard for you?" she asked, intending to provoke. She deliberately crept closer, unbalancing Petronilla, who held the door for support.

"Don't you have customers to entertain or something?"

"They can manage without me," she said, a finger brushing over the scratches on Petronilla's arms. Blood clotted under her bruises. "Does that hurt?"

With one touch, she made her forget all the unpleasantness of the evening.

"No." She swallowed, and swallowed, and swallowed, but the desire pooling in her belly refused to dissipate.

"Come on, I'll patch you up," Acelina said, holding Petronilla's arm.

"No, thank you. I can patch myself up," she said, pulling her arm away.

"You're being stubborn." Her eyes narrowed, and the onyx depths became a black hole, pulling her in.

"It's not your job to take care of me," she bit out. "I can look after myself."

"You're my responsibility as long as you're under my roof," Acelina said with finality.

"I'm not one of your employees. You've got no obligation to mother me."

"I'm not mothering you. I don't want you to catch anything and pass it on to my employees."

"I'm not catching anything."

"Ugh. It's my fault for trying to be nice." She stomped her foot, uncharacteristically ruffled.

Their argument was cut short by Turstin, who approached them shakily.

"Ma'am..." a terrified Turstin lingered at her door, knees quaking.

"What is it?" both of them spat together. Turstin took another step back, fearful. His dark eyes were large, the edges of his curly hair sticking to the beads of sweat lining his forehead.

"Turstin? What's the matter?" Acelina walked to him, placing a hand on his shoulder. The fight went out of Petronilla as she realized something was wrong.

"Lily...she...." Turstin's words faded. "Please come." He tugged at Acelina's arms, and the next second, she was on her feet, rushing to the main rooms. Petronilla followed her with Turstin, wondering what had happened to frighten the boy.

"Lead the way." Acelina nudged Trustin, who hurried.

Footsteps pounded on the wooden floors, passing several doors before coming to a stop in front of a closed door.

"I heard Lily screaming—" Turstin's voice was unsteady. "You know she screams sometimes-"

Turstin shook his head. "You should have a look."

A muffled scream decided for her. Without thinking twice, Petronilla threw the door open. What they saw behind those doors horrified her. A sharp crack resounded. A hand flashed across the dull scene, and Lily's pained voice echoed. Petronilla froze, watching a scene from her past replay before her eyes. The man- a bulky, middle-aged monster who smelled of a mixture of alcohol and perfume hit Lily, whose face turned the other way because of the force. Her face was stained with tears, as she muffled sobs with blankets. Her shoulders were exposed, but she held a blanket around the rest of herself when she heard the door open.

"You're old," he said, his voice raspy and slurring. "Can't even do your job properly."

The dullness of the lamps, the artfully arranged flowers, the neutral wallpaper, and the silk sheets didn't make the scene any more palpable. The white bed covers were ruffled, a drop of something— blood— staining it. Since Lily was no virgin, it didn't take a genius to figure out where that came from. One side of Lily's lips, where the light fell, was bruised.

"I'm sorry..." Her voice broke as he gripped her hair.

Petronilla's first reaction was to freeze, as her skin tingled with emotional memory. The past washed over her, thoughts swirling into a toxic cocktail. How many times had she been that woman? Nausea weakened her stomach.

She saw a rustle of yellow flash in the periphery of her

memory. A petite hand grabbed the man in a strong grip. The man who was hurting Lily snapped his face up, irritated at the sight of Acelina.

"What are you doing here?" he asked, still not relenting. "Sir, please get off." Acelina's voice cut like glass.

"Get off?" His irritation intensified. "I paid for this."

"If you like it rough, I'll assign you to another escort. Lily isn't-" Acelina went on, unblinking. Turstin hadn't moved an inch from the door. "You can't hurt her."

"No. I want this cow...er...woman." His breath reeked even from this distance.

"That wasn't a suggestion." Acelina's voice sharpened to a dangerous warning. Throwing away his hand, she lingered over Lily. When she touched her finger to Lily's face, she flinched. That was enough impetus to thaw Petronilla.

"Or what?" he asked, raising his hand again. He stood facing Acelina's nose but a few inches away.

She recognized the sort. He didn't want sex; he wanted to make them suffer, to establish his power and dominance. She'd seen many sadists like that in Terra. They wouldn't stop until she cried with pain. It was sick, but as an escort, she'd not been in a position to question it. But she wasn't an escort anymore, and she wasn't helpless. Snapping out of her daze, she stepped forward. She balled her fists to hit him, but Acelina's hand stopped her. Their eyes met and came to a silent understanding.

"I kindly ask you to leave," she said, showing him the door, after wrapping Lily in the blanket.

"Leave? Are you kidding? Is this the service you offer to your clients?"

"I'll refund your money-"

"I don't want a refund, damn you!" He was bellowing, throwing vases on the floor in a full-blown tantrum. "I want her."

Lily didn't move from the bed, burying her head in the mattresses. She was too shaken to say anything.

"You can't have her," Acelina said. "My girls aren't vases you can break."

"She can hardly be called a girl!" he scoffed. "You are supposed to respect her."

"What respect? She's a whore!"

Petronilla flinched, her body reacting on instinct. Her punch went straight through his jaw, sending him reeling back. Acelina shot her a cold stare. "Don't sink to his level," her voice was a gentle whisper. She shook her head and Turstin left the room, nodding with comprehension.

The patron approached Acelina, surveying her icy facade. Fingers brushed her cheek, and she drew back reflexively. It was just like Acelina to believe she could solve all the world's problems with words. Some bastards needed a taste of violence.

"So are you," his rant went on, and Petronilla's patience snapped. "I'll have you kneeling—"

Petronilla seized his arm before he could touch Acelina. Acelina's eyes flew open, her hands stilling mid-air. She'd been prepared to do the same.

"Time to leave," Petronilla gritted out.

"Or what?" he tried to snap out of her grip, but she was too strong for him. Petronilla twisted his hand behind his back until he was writhing in pain.

"This is how others feel when you hurt them," Petronilla said, squeezing his hands tighter. She ground them together harder, longing to hear those bones snap. Maybe then she would feel better.

"Petronilla." Acelina's hand made contact with her again, and her grip loosened. She cast her a worried look but Petronilla didn't let go.

"Let's go," she told the patron, hauling the man off. He struggled and tried to kick her, but she kicked first, rendering him weak. He was no match for a trained soldier like her.

When she emerged in the corridor, she saw someone she hadn't seen before- a large, well-built man with shaven hair.

"Elias," Acelina's voice echoed from behind her. "We're having some trouble. Please take care of our customer."

"Yes, ma'am." He took the errant customer from Petronilla's hands and hauled him out. She heard his screams all the way.

"I won't let this go," he yelled. "I'll kill you...have this place shut down..."

His voice faded, but Petronilla's heartbeat didn't. "Are you okay?" she asked Acelina.

"Better than you," Acelina replied, recognizing how shaken she was.

"Good job getting Elias here." She turned to Turstin who had come out of hiding. "And thanks for coming to me."

"No problem," he said. "I heard her screams and had a feeling something was wrong."

"Thank you," she said, placing a palm on his hand. "Lily's my friend too," he said. "I knew something was
wrong when I heard her scream."

Acelina nodded. "Thanks to your quick thinking, we were able to avoid disaster."

"Will she be all right?" he pressed on, his eyes indicating he didn't think she would.

"I'll take care of her. Get back to work."

"Yes, ma'am." Reluctantly, he left, peeking back several times.

"Sorry, but I can't keep you company tonight," Acelina said, heading in past Petronilla. The door closed behind her, but not before Petronilla followed.

Petronilla continued staring at Lily, who was still naked and crying in bed, unable to lift her head. Acelina sat beside her, covered her with a bedsheet, and stroked her quivering back soothingly.

"It's okay, Lily," she said, holding Lily like a mother. Petronilla's gut clenched, affected by kindness more than sensuality. "He's gone."

Lily looked up, her eyes red with tears, and pressed her face against Acelina's bosom. Acelina's hands came around her, and she continued to stroke gently. "It was...I'm sorry...I... I should've done better."

"It's not your fault." Acelina's voice was icy, despite her warm manner. "You can't think you did anything wrong."

"What... if he... comes back?" Lily's eyes glistened with tears. Petronilla turned away, not knowing how to console her.

"Don't worry. I'll take care of him," Acelina said. "Are you okay?"

Lily cried in response to that question. "I'm...I tried..." Her tears spilled down Acelina's kimono, but she didn't care, moving to stroke her hair gently. Petronilla noticed it was disheveled too.

"Did he pull your hair?" she asked, caressing her light hair.

"Yes..."

Petronilla closed her eyes, anger rising again. Maybe she shouldn't have let him off so easily. But it hadn't been her decision to make.

"Lily..."

"I'm sorry..." she kept saying, unable to stop crying.

"It's not your fault," Acelina said. "He didn't know how to treat you well."

"I'm a nobody..." Lily sobbed. "And he's right... I'm getting old..."

"You're the most beautiful courtesan in Duality." That invited a broken laugh from Lily.

"You're too nice to me." Lily brushed away her tears and looked up. "I wouldn't have stayed this long if it weren't for you."

Acelina's smile was wan. "You don't have to stay," she said. "You're allowed to give up fighting when you're tired."

Petronilla blinked. The words went right to her heart, making her remember the terrible nights when she wanted to stop being strong. But she'd had no choice but to keep fighting. If only someone had said that to her and held her like this. Emotion choked her.

"I can't. You know that," Lily said, sniffing. No fresh tears spilled as she wrapped her dress around her body.

Acelina hugged her tighter and said in a low voice, "Take the rest of the day off."

"No, I—"

"Shhhh, listen to me," Acelina said. "I'll have someone else take care of your customers."

"Thank you." Lily sniffed burying herself in Acelina's shoulders, and Petronilla exited quietly.

"You don't have to thank me," Acelina said, rising. "But do better next time. You're nobody's fool. You have a voice, you have a body, the same as him. Don't think he holds any power over you."

Petronilla's heart beat loudly, wishing someone had told her that a long time ago. Their eyes met again when Acelina exited the room, and Petronilla followed.

"Rest here for as long as you want," she said, before closing the door. Without acknowledging Petronilla, she went the other way.

Petronilla traced the slow steps to her room, wondering if she would ever be able to forget tonight. The creaky storage door opened, abandoning her to a sliver of pale moonlight. Once inside her room, she sat in the darkness for hours, not bothering to light a candle. Her bruises and tattered clothing were forgotten.

You're nobody's fool.

Acelina was made of steel, and it was only now that Petronilla saw it. She cringed at the recollection of all the things she'd said to Acelina. What if she had been prejudiced?

The uncomfortable consequences of that couldn't be pondered on in her hungry state. As the minutes passed, lights dimming outside, she got down to treating her wounds and changing clothes.

TWELVE

ACELINA

Acelina sat in her room after Duality wound down, working on the account books. The candle had almost burned out, signaling it was time to sleep, but sleep was the farthest thing from her mind. Thanks to the events of that evening, her brain was a mess. The sight of Lily being forced was vivid in her mind, making her blood boil. If Elias hadn't broken all of his bones, he was being too kind. She remembered Petronilla's reassuring presence that made her heart flip. Not that she'd needed her there.

The candle went off, abandoning her to darkness. Thoughts converged, each more disillusioning than the other. She'd have to let Lily go soon. After tonight, she couldn't let her continue in good conscience. But the future was a patchwork of uncertainties, and uncertainties were never favorable to the powerless.

Lighting another candle, she pulled out the envelope of notes she'd prepared for Lily's farewell and counted them.

The crisp notes crackled against the bright flame, their scent invading her nostrils. This bundle would have to do. Lily had no family, just like her. Acelina hoped her little gift would help her start over and find something or someone she loved in life. It also reminded her how old she was. Lily and Acelina were the same age, and if it was time for Lily to retire, maybe her time was coming too. She shoved the notes back into the drawer, shoulders slumping.

Duality was her life. Without it, she was lonely— a shell without a soul. But even with it, she was becoming the same. As she looked at her empty queen bedspread over with fresh linens, she longed for someone's reassuring touch. No matter who she entertained, she always spent the night alone in her bed after looking over account books. She was there for her employees, but she'd never let anyone into her life, always believing she was too strong for comfort.

She was strong, and she liked being alone but on days like today, she wished someone warmed that bed, held her in their arms, and kissed her good night. How would it feel like to fall asleep with a companion who shared her sorrows, burdens, and joys? Someone who loved her even when her beauty faded and time claimed her vitality? She'd never thought of being in a relationship before, preferring the freedom her work offered. She didn't need a protector, and she didn't need anyone's name, but she needed support.

"Stop thinking!" her mind commanded. Thinking about the future was a destructive path. Her future was a shroud of darkness, made of uncertainty and decorated with disappointment. Which was why she took it one day at a time.

Acelina closed the book and lay down on her spacious

bed, feeling the fine linen against her exposed skin. Her thin silk nightgown left her arms and most of her back exposed. She liked it because it was perfect for the warm weather, but tonight, even the fine fabric couldn't calm her mind buzzing with thoughts. She hugged a pillow to calm the anxiety she felt. The dissatisfied customer's threats rang in her ears, sending shudders down her spine.

Closing her eyes, Acelina remembered the feel of Petronilla's arms on her back. She wanted to melt into those strong arms, knowing they'd always be there for her. How many times had she thrown up last night's excesses alone at the crack of dawn, while her employees were sleeping? Before that day, she didn't even know she needed someone to soothe her.

She shook her head violently. Petronilla was the last person she needed. Her tongue was barbed wire, and her past was nothing less than a ticking time bomb. Her temper was flammable, and she was a fortress that couldn't be breached Acelina had no desire to walk on eggshells for the rest of her life.

Her eyes met the dark ceiling. Acelina swallowed, her body heating. No, this wasn't the way to go. Petronilla hated her, and she didn't like the lieutenant general much either. There had to be some other way to make herself feel better. Hugging the pillow closer, she closed her eyes, letting the air cool the goosebumps on her skin. What could she do to make these destructive thoughts go away?

An idea lit up her brain.

Alcohol.

That's what she needed. Some strong liquor was the best way to drown her thoughts in oblivion.

Lighting a candle, she slid off the bed and made her way outside, sure to keep her movements quiet. The entire corridor was dark, echoing with light snores. Thank goodness everybody was asleep. This was a side she wasn't proud to show her employees.

The path to the kitchen was quiet and dark, with everyone off to sleep. The candle she carried lit the way. The kitchen door had been left ajar, something for which she'd scold Rose tomorrow morning. For now, she stealthily stepped in.

And found a candle burning. A face looked up, and she knew she was caught in those brown eyes like a spider's web.

Petronilla lounged on a chair with her legs on the table, watching the flames flicker. She had changed out of her tattered kimono and was wearing her usual full-sleeved grey linen shirt. A few scratches persisted on her arms, but most of them were covered.

"Good morning," Acelina said, taking a deep breath.

Petronilla's eyes carefully watched her cross the kitchen. "Good morning." Petronilla's legs dropped, and she straightened. "You're up early."

"Technically, I didn't go to sleep." She crossed the threshold, resigning herself to fate. "What're you doing here at this time, Lieutenant General?" Acelina came to pause before Petronilla, whose back rested against the spirits cabinet, the bottles lining the shelves over her head. It was five in the morning, and everyone was asleep but them. In front of Petronilla lay an unopened bottle of strong liquor.

"Do you even know what this is?" Acelina picked up the porcelain jar.

"Alcohol?"

"Of the highest concentration," she finished, plucking it off the table. "I don't think you should drink this. What if you get sick and die? I won't be responsible for our country's army losing its prized lieutenant general."

Petronilla didn't acknowledge her words, instead standing up, "Which one do you recommend?" She pointed to the bottles on the top shelf.

"That one's my favorite." Acelina pointed to a white ceramic bottle that held a weaker rice wine. Petronilla plucked it from the shelf and placed it on the table, rummaging through the lower cabinets for matching glasses. Acelina sat on the chair next to hers, watching her place a glass on the table.

"I only need one," she said, reaching for the bottle.

"The other one's for me." The candle painted a flawless picture of Petronilla's face, the sharp edges smoothed by light. She had the right balance of shadow and light, Acelina decided. Her chin was sharp, her eyes the color of hot chocolate. Her skin was olive, a rich and deep color, and the dark hair that framed her face completed the haunting portrait. Hers was a face you'd remember in your sleep.

Her eyes widened. "You're drinking? At four in the morning?"

"Just tonight." Petronilla's gaze was averted.

"I would be the last person to judge you." The bottle shook in her hands, she realized. Petronilla clamped her hand over Acelina's to steady it. Instinctively, Acelina pulled her hand away. Thankfully, Petronilla caught the bottle before it spilled, and placed it on the table. "You go first."

Acelina cautiously took the bottle, while Petronilla sat back down and retrieved her glass. She poured herself some rice wine which had a strong smell, thanks to its high alcohol content. "I'll pour," she said, reaching for Petronilla's glass, but Petronilla clamped a hand over hers.

"I'll do it myself." She snatched the bottle from Acelina. "Why—"

"Because I can," she said, carefully pouring. "I'm not one of your customers."

Acelina's heart lurched a little. Her eyes a little blurry, she brought the tiny cup to her lips and swallowed the drink in one gulp. Petronilla didn't touch hers, focusing her attention on Acelina's empty glass instead. Quietly, she poured.

"I can do it myself too." Acelina was just being stubborn.

But Petronilla already held the bottle. Their fingers brushed again, and Acelina was ready to argue to drown out the electric sparks alighting in her belly, when Petronilla said, "You've had a hard day."

Her head snapped up, eyes widening. She was shivering again, and she didn't know why. "If I didn't know better, I'd think you cared about me."

Petronilla inhaled sharply, drinking some more. They were both trying to ignore that inevitable attraction that was the third person in the room. "I can't help but care after what happened this night." Acelina merely sipped, letting the words disappear. "I wouldn't have handled the situation as well as you did."

"How are your bruises?" she asked, attempting to change

the topic. The liquor slid down her throat, burning her esophagus.

"Better," Petronilla said. "Getting hurt is part of fighting." Her eyes rested on the liquor. Acelina reached for the bottle, but Petronilla placed a hand over hers and poured her some more.

"Thank you."

Awareness prickled her skin. Acelina didn't know how long she could keep up this charade. It felt nice to be served by someone else for a change. But this was rapidly headed for disaster. She could handle Petronilla's hate, but her concern was stripping away at her defenses.

"I can leave if you want to be alone."

"No." The word had come out before she could think. Though her mind wanted Petronilla to leave, the weaker part of her wanted her here. "Stay."

Wordlessly, Petronilla drank another sip. "How's Lily?"

"Sleeping."

"Lily told me you're the kindest employer she's ever had." The introduction didn't prepare her for what was coming. "What're you going to do about her?"

"You know what happens to women who are too old to work," Acelina said, smiling. It was at moments like this that she remembered Petronilla had once been a courtesan.

"They are tossed out into the street," Petronilla said, without any emotion.

"I can't toss her into the street," Acelina sighed. Petronilla filled her glass quietly, noticing it was empty. "I won't. She was my first employee, you know." The alcohol was blurring her thoughts. She slapped the glass on the table, and it was refilled without question. "She's family to me. They all are. I don't know who my parents are. We courtesans are like that... no past...no future...no promises..." She swayed unsteadily in the chair. Petronilla's palm clamped over hers.

"Are you drunk already?"

"Far from it." She rubbed her eyes, seeing Petronilla's face. "I'm going to give her a gift. I saved up for this day...I saw it coming. It's not much but it should tide her through a few years."

"Do you think she'll be happy with that?"

"I hope so. The sum will help her start over in life," she reasoned. "I don't know what she'll do, but it's all I can do."

Petronilla inhaled. "Why not give her another job here? Something like a cook or a maid?"

"Once you've been a courtesan, you can't be a maid," Acelina countered. "She's lived in luxury all these years. I can't expect her to scrub the kitchen floors."

"There are other things she can do."

"Why, Petronilla, are you giving me business advice?"

"No." Her hand backed away. "I'm sorry, it's none of my business. I was...just thinking about what you said..." She swallowed the tortured expression back on her face. Acelina wanted to run her thumb over the creases on her forehead. "If she's your family, will you be able to let her go?"

Acelina blinked, having never thought of that before. Giving her money was one thing, but never being able to see Lily again was another. Was she ready to let her go forever?

"What if something happens to her?" Petronilla continued, reading her thoughts. "What'll she do once the money

you give her runs out? The only profession she knows is...
being an escort. Reality can be cruel to women like us."

Women like us.

She'd heard that.

"I...I never thought about that before," Acelina said,
ruffling her hair. "I guess I didn't think I'd have to let her go so
soon."

"It might be better to keep her around," Petronilla said,
holding the glass up. "Want some more?"

Acelina nodded, and she poured.

"You're good at this." Acelina giggled, halfway drunk. "At
what?"

"At being there," she said. "You're a good listener."
"You're complimenting me?" Petronilla was incredulous.

"I am." Acelina drank, turning the idea over in her head.
"You've drunk too much, then."

"Not nearly enough," she said, her tone bleak. "I saw you
freeze at the door tonight." At that, Petronilla put the bottle
on the table with a clank. "Did...Since I'm drunk, I might as
well ask you this...." Acelina paused, the tension in the air
pressing down on her collarbone. "Did something like that
happen to you?"

Petronilla closed her eyes. "I'm sorry."

"Worse," she said in a small voice. When she opened her
lids, their eyes met and the barrier that had always existed
between them was incinerated. "Maybe you were right...
maybe I judged you based on my past," Petronilla admitted in
a low voice, after a long pause. "I wish someone had shown
me the kindness you did. I wish someone had held me when I

was abused..." She rubbed her eyes which were red. "You're a better person than I gave you credit for."

Acelina stopped drinking and blinked. "Please tell me you're drunk."

"I haven't touched my glass," Petronilla confessed, rubbing her eyes.

"I must've died, then. The almighty Lieutenant General Petronilla is admitting defeat?" Acelina's lips curved in a cat-like grin.

"I'm not admitting defeat. It's just...it's honorable to admit you've made a mistake."

"You think you made a mistake?" Acelina forgot to drink and surveyed Petronilla under a microscope. Her clammy hands kneaded together under the table.

"Yes."

"I won't hold it against you," Acelina said. "Mistrust is all you know. Some girls are like that when they come to me."

"What do you do to them?"

"Nobody can fight their demons for them," she said, looking into Petronilla's eyes. "I can hold your hand when you scream at night, but you must slay your own demons." Petronilla's breath was caught in her throat as if containing a flood of emotion. "But you already know that."

Acelina reached for her cup, but she'd lost the will to drink. Her eyes were transfixed on Petronilla's lush lashes, covering the conflicting concern in her mahogany eyes.

"I'm good at taking care of myself," Acelina assured her.

Petronilla finished her drink and set the glass down, cringing. "How do you drink this stuff every day?"

"Alcohol is a courtesan's most loyal companion," she said,

looking dazed at the cabinet over Petronilla's head. "It's there for you on days nobody else is."

Petronila blinked. "You mean on days like today?" Acelina took the bottle from her without answering, but

Petronilla clamped a hand over hers.

"I think you should stop. You've been throwing up for the past two days. I don't want you to wake up puking into the gutter tomorrow."

"My indigestion is better now. And you're the one that's been pouring me all these drinks," Acelina said, wresting the bottle. Petronilla didn't look so sure.

Then, she did something unexpected.

She relinquished her hold on the bottle. The animosity in those brown depths had been replaced with something else, something that looked like respect. A lump formed in Acelina's throat. In her centuries of being a courtesan, people had loved her, hated her, lusted for her, and been afraid of her, but nobody ever respected her as an equal. She didn't know how to react.

"You're not going to argue?" she said, standing. Arguing, she could deal with it, but she had nothing to defend herself against whatever this was.

"No," she said. "You said you can take care of yourself."

Acelina squinted her eyes. "Who are you and what did you do to Lieutenant General Petronilla?"

Petronilla didn't smile, her eyes pulsing with deep pain.

She stood up. "I should go to sleep."

But she didn't leave. Instead, she inched closer, hovering over Acelina. Unable to meet her gaze, Acelina shrugged.

The air had grown warm and thick with unresolved attraction.

"Good night." Though the words left Petronilla's mouth, she still didn't move, watching her carefully, as if asking for permission to give in to her impulse.

"You're not leaving," Acelina noted, her eyes gazing up to meet Petronilla's. Her bones were liquid, eyes threatened to water.

"No." Petronilla's fingers brushed over Acelina's arm now, thumbs rubbing the hem of her sleeves. Every slide of skin against skin was exquisite torture, fanning her lust.

"You don't want to leave..." Her voice was a husky whisper. Petronilla shook her head.

She couldn't think straight. She'd walked from the frying pan to the fire. The whole reason she was drinking was to forget Petronilla's existence. But here she was, pouring out her insecurities to the prickly lieutenant general.

It felt an awful lot like companionship. Like respect. Like understanding. And like all the things she longed for but never had. Never could.

What would it feel like to make love to someone who was her equal? To someone who hadn't paid for her? To receive as much as she gave?

Desire flickered to life, spreading tentacles around her brain. Petronilla's eyes were blank, and she didn't know if it was a good idea to give in to what she felt.

So, Acelina took a chance. Grabbing her collar, she pulled Petronilla down.

"What—"

And claimed her lips in a hard kiss.

Sensation exploded, heat enveloping Acelina's entire body. Petronilla's hand gripped her waist, trailing lower to squeeze the bulge of her perfect ass, while the other wrapped behind her back. Delirious with lust, Acelina sucked on Petronilla's lips that tasted rice wine. Her brain was swimming, unable to distinguish between fantasy and reality.

Petronilla sucked her lower lip, making her body tremble with need. This was unlike any kiss she'd experienced before. The pleasure was mutual. Their lips needed each other like oxygen. She didn't have to put on a show to please. She let herself go, kissing as she'd never kissed before, and in return being kissed as she'd never been kissed before.

Petronilla's kisses, like her personality, were honest and straightforward. One of her hands trailed over Acelina's shoulders, steadying her, while the other wrapped around her waist, pulling her closer, deepening the kiss. All their breath was consumed in keeping that fire alive, in breathing in every part of one another.

As if remembering where they were, Petronilla backed away. Their mouths separated and she felt the loss of sensation. Acelina's heart plummeted, watching hesitation flicker over her face.

"What?" she asked, impatient.

"Are you sure?" Petronilla was worried. "Do you want to do this? You might end up regretting it tomorrow."

"Yes, I want to do this." Acelina's palms enveloped her face, looking her straight in the eye. She knew this had been coming for a long time. "Kiss me."

Petronilla seized her mouth in a possessive kiss, branding her with passion. Acelina reciprocated with equal intensity, thrusting her hot tongue into Petronilla's mouth, making the stubborn lieutenant general part her lips. When their tongues melted into each other, devouring, she lost all track of time.

Hot and quivering with suppressed lust, their second kiss was like a nuclear explosion. Ecstasy came in waves, drowning her. She'd never been kissed with such fierce passion before like nothing in the world mattered. Acelina moaned, angling her face to deepen the kiss. Their faces brushed soft skin on soft skin.

Frenzied, Petronilla tore her mouth away and began trailing hot kisses down her jaw and neck. Acelina clung to her, while she gently bit down on a sensitive spot on her neck.

"Oh god..." she gasped. This was torment. But she wanted it. Her body had throbbed with a need while she was alone in her room, not for a random stranger, but for the incomprehensible lieutenant general.

Petronilla's hands tugged at the opening of her nightgown. Carefully, she parted the front folds, a hand reaching inside to cup her breast. She kneaded the breast roughly, the pad of her thumb rasping over Acelina's sensitive nipple. Acelina gasped, feeling her entire body shudder with pleasure. How was it that Petronilla had such a strong effect on her? The ache between her legs got sharper.

Minutes ago, they'd been enemies, and now all animosity had melted into a mass of smoldering passion that razed every rational thought in its path.

"Please..."

Petronilla cut off her begging moans with another hot kiss. She fondled her other breast, kneading and lightly pinching. Her skin was warm and Acelina felt the roughness of her skin against her nipple.

"Mmmmmm...." Tingly, warm sensations washed over Acelina.

The world ceased to exist, time a mere illusion. Only the two of them were real, consumed by an inferno of passion. She'd always pleasured but never been made love to. Never been kissed with such sincerity and devotion.

Petronilla's other hand ran up Acelina's exposed thigh, feeling every inch of her skin. Acelina's fingers dug into her hair, rumpling them, then trailed down Petronilla's jaw, reveling in each inch of beautiful bronze skin. Unable to hold on any longer, she wrapped her legs around Petronilla, who picked her up and placed her firmly on the table.

"It's like a dream..." she said, seeing Petronilla's flushed face in the candlelight. Her thumb ran over her perfect nose, feeling her lips calloused with kisses. Leaning in, Acelina peppered feathery kisses up her jaw, all the way to her ear. Then, she licked the shell of Petronilla's ear. "I never thought you'd kiss me..."

"Ummmm..." Petronilla moaned, her arms tugging up her nightdress.

"You like it," Acelina noted, kissing down the slope of her neck. Every inch of that perfect, golden skin inflamed her. When she reached the base that met her shoulder, she kissed harder.

"Go easy on me," Petronilla said, closing her eyes to feel the sensation. Acelina wondered what it would be like to see a love bite on Petronilla's neck tomorrow, knowing she was the one that had put it there. Smiling, she backed off.

"What?" Petronilla asked, confused at her sudden amusement.

She shook her head, still amused by the thought. "Nothing, Keep going."

Petronilla took control again, her lips trailing down, showering kisses over Acelina's shoulder, collarbone, all the way to the top of her breast, branding her, possessing her. Acelina was only too glad to surrender to the responses that Petronilla incited in her.

Something flashed in Petronilla's eyes, then she went down, claiming an aroused nipple with her mouth. Acelina gasped, the sensation ricocheting right to the tormented spot between her legs. She quivered, tortured sensation pooling between her legs, while Petronilla's tongue circled her bud with languid strokes like they had all the time in the world.

"Hurry." Her last words were stolen by a guttural moan. Petronilla stopped sucking her right nipple and trailed kisses over the other breast. "Goodness, you're going slow deliberately." Acelina rolled her eyes. Of all the times to be stubborn, she had to choose this one.

"I want to savor you," Petronilla said, then took her other bud in her mouth. This time she sucked on it until Acelina was blind with pleasure.

"You're too good at this, darling," she said, her voice trailing off, her hands in Petronilla's hair.

"You make me lose control." Her breaths broke against Acelina's sensitive, suckled peaks that became more aroused when the cool air of her breath brushed them. Petronilla's rosy lips drank her in with a hunger that left her knees weak.

She felt those calloused lips rough against her breast, and that aroused her even more.

"Just do it." She tightened her legs, arms wrapping around Petronilla.

"Bossy, aren't we?" Petronilla's right hand parted her thighs, her mouth pulling away. She shifted Acelina against the table to hold her firmer. Acelina buried her face in her shoulders.

Then, they heard voices.

At first, she closed her eyes, hoping they'd go away, feeling Petronilla's steady fingers on her inner thigh, so close to giving her pleasure, but they only grew louder. Petronilla's hands stilled, eyes meeting in panic. She'd heard them too.

"Do you hear something?" The echo of Tustin's voice startled both of them.

They instantly pulled away, breaking the kiss abruptly. Petronilla pulled down her nightdress and adjusted the collar to cover her breasts. The magic was broken in a moment, replaced by frenzy. They fixed all the buttons and folds, making sure to appear normal.

"Your hair." Acelina patted down Petronilla's hair, while the lieutenant general put her clothes back in place. A heated glance passed between the two, frustration filling Acelina's body.

"Who is it at this time?" Petronilla sounded annoyed.

They managed to get everything looking normal just in time for the door to open. Turstin and Lily stood there, their gazes flickering from a flushed Acelina to a startled Petronilla.

Petronilla's entire body vibrated, her face flaming red. She was a bad liar.

"Are we interrupting something?" Lily's eyes widened. "No!" Petronilla's voice was too high to be convincing.

Lily looked so much better now, laughing with Turstin about something. The trail of tears was gone, and her usual exuberance replaced it. They looked at each other, and a smile tugged at her lips, amused by the transparent gesture. It made Acelina's heart skip a beat.

"What're you two doing here?" Petronilla asked, raking a hand through her hair, an eyebrow crooked in annoyance. It was kind of cute, Acelina thought.

"I thought you were sleeping," Acelina put in, crossing her arms over her chest to hide the open neck of her nightgown.

"I couldn't fall asleep, so I took a walk," Turstin said. "And Lily—" he gave her a tense look.

"I was...uh... taking a walk too. I thought it'd be good to clear my mind."

"You look better," Petronilla said, her voice conveying gladness.

"What were you two doing in the kitchen?" Turstin asked, suspicious. "Together." She ran a pleasure house, for goodness sake. Of course, they'd guess.

"I was hungry." Petronilla had retrieved her ability to think.

"Me too." Acelina's voice frayed.

"We're hungry too," Turstin said, examining the table. "Should we wake Rose?"

"No, there's no need to wake her up." Acelina was already retreating to the door. "We're done."

"All you ate is alcohol?" Lily pointed to the table, eyebrows knitting with suspicion.

She had to admit the entire setup looked dubious.

"I'm not that hungry," Acelina said, contradicting herself. "Can I have the cheese you bought last week?" Turstin asked.

"Go ahead and help yourself," Acelina said, at the door. "I should go. Good night."

Then, without so much as a backward glance, she left the kitchen, head held high. She heard footsteps—Petronilla's—following woodenly behind her, but ignored them, choosing to retreat to her room.

The corridor was dark, but she knew the way. Throughout the short walk, her heart thundered. Her body still hungered for Petronilla's touch, but, if she went all the way, she wouldn't be able to face herself the next morning. Whatever existed between them didn't have a name yet, and probably never would.

"How could I be so stupid?" Acelina facepalmed, once safely inside her room. Of all the people in the world, she had to choose Petronilla. She flopped down on the bed, feeling the soft silk brush all the places where Petronilla had kissed her. Acelina turned the candles off and went to sleep but her heart was thudding violently.

Hugging the pillow between her legs, she tossed and turned. This was going to be a very long night.

THIRTEEN

ACELINA

When Acelina awoke the next afternoon, Petronilla was nowhere to be seen. The first place she went to was the storage, which was predictably empty. She asked Turstin and the others if they'd seen Petronilla, but their answers had all been negative. Ultimately, Rose told her Petronilla went out in the morning after breakfast. She hadn't returned ever since.

After wandering in the doorway for a few seconds, Acelina decided to visit Lily's room. Though there was no light inside the room, Acelina opened it, making sure not to disturb Lily. Unlike her room, Lily's was smaller and messy. The wooden floor was overlaid with clothes she needed to put away. Some garments hung on the side of her bed, squeezed under Lily's right leg that protruded from the bed covers. The small window on one side was completely barricaded with blankets, allowing very little light to seep in. In her attempt to navigate the room, Acelina accidentally hit her leg against a low table.

"Ouch!" She doubled over, falling on the blanket of clothes that littered the floor. Lily writhed like a caterpillar under the blankets, then went flat. Snoring sounds filled the room.

"Lily, wake up!" Acelina said, only to be greeted with a reluctant groan. She tried to extricate herself from the tangled clothes. "Lily!"

"What?" Lily flipped the blankets aside and sat up, her voice croaky. Stifling a yawn, she said, "What're you doing here so early?" She reached for a candle near her bedside and lit it. Her sleepy, red eyes had dark circles around them, but her face was radiant.

"I wanted to talk to you," Acelina said. "And it's almost three-thirty."

"So? I never wake up before four. You know that." Lily stretched, kicking the rest of the sheets away. Under the sheets, she wore nothing but her silk undergarments. Her arms were smooth, thanks to a generous lining of fat, and coupled with her immaculate complexion, she had a body to die for.

"Come talk to me once you're done with breakfast," Acelina said, turning to leave.

"What? You're leaving already?" Lily's eyes flashed open.

Her generous thighs emerged from the legs kicking the blanket away. "After waking me up?"

"Go back to sleep." Acelina waved her hand.

"I'm awake now," she said, climbing down. "Tell me about last night."

The words made Acelina's spine straighten. She stood still in her spot among the discarded clothes. "You need to clean your room," she said.

Grabbing a kimono-style dressing gown, Lily stood before her, tying the sash. "What's going on between you and that lieutenant general?"

"I don't know what you mean." Acelina's lips pressed together. "I came to talk about—"

"Weren't you two making out in the kitchen last night? Turstin's ears went red. Poor thing couldn't look you in the eye."

"Lily!"

"What? This is a pleasure house, you know. We aren't exactly innocent." She came to stand before Acelina, her light eyes narrowing. For the first time in many years, Acelina felt herself blush.

"I'm not here to talk about myself. I'm here to talk about you," she said, taking hold of the derailed conversation. "How are you feeling?"

Silence descended, a pained expression passing over Lily's eyes. Acelina regretted bringing up a painful memory, but it had to be done. "You know me. I bounce back pretty fast." Lily wasn't fine. She was just pretending to be.

"I did some thinking," Acelina said, clasping her fingers.

"And?"

"Listen to me with an open mind." Her voice was a little shaky, and she took a breath to steady it. Meeting Lily's gaze, she went on, "You're like a sister to me. When I started this place, you were the first one to join. Duality owes its success to you, as much as it does to me."

"What's with you?" Lily asked.

"I feel it's time for you to retire." Her heart was heavy like she'd pronounced a death sentence. The words hung in the air, weighing it down.

"What? No." Lily moved away, feeling betrayed. "You're kicking me out because of one customer-"

"I'm not kicking you out," Acelina said, holding Lily's hands. She retrieved the envelope filled with notes from the folds of her clothing and handed it over. Lily glanced at the stack of notes in shock.

"What does this mean?" Her eyes went wide.

"I've been preparing for this day. I've known I would have to let you go someday," she said.

"Why? Am I not beautiful anymore?" Heartbreak was stamped in her voice. When Acelina met her eyes, they were filled with tears. She moved in closer, opening her arms for an embrace, but Lily shrank back, sobbing into her hands. "Is it because I'm old?" Another broken sob echoed. "Of course... that's it, isn't it? You think I'm too old."

"No..."

"It was considerate of you to think about me." She flashed the envelope. "I guess I should find another place to live now that I'm being kicked out."

Acelina's face flushed red. So far, this conversation was going nothing as she imagined. She'd never thought Lily would be hurt by her pronouncement. But Lily wasn't mature for her age. Acelina had always made decisions for her and protected her, and that had left the courtesan with the personality of a child. "You're welcome to live here as long as you like."

"And, how long... is that?" Lily handed the envelope back to her. "I don't want money...I want...to...continue...this..." Brushing tears clumsily with the back of her palm, she went on, "This is...my only home...my only family...the only thing I know... Where will I go?"

With a sinking feeling, Acelina knew that Petronilla had been right. Severance pay wasn't good enough. Duality was the only home Lily knew and taking it away from her would be cruel. She'd been a courtesan all her life and didn't know any other way to survive.

"You're right. I can't let you go into the world with just money," she said, swallowing the lump in her throat. "I didn't think it'd come to this, but if you're okay, I want you to stay here and help me."

"What?" Lily brushed tears away, tilting her head.

"I need someone to help me with the administration. If you don't mind learning about numbers, I'll teach you how to keep track of expenses," she said. "I know, it's not what you'd like to do, but we could ease into it slowly. You know everyone and everybody knows you, so they'll be more comfortable having you around as a manager."

"What're you talking about?"

"Lily, you and I both know you're growing too old to remain a courtesan," she said, knowing those harsh words had to be spoken aloud. "But turning you out isn't the answer. If you want to stay here, you can help me with running Duality. That should keep you away from rude customers like the one yesterday."

"Acelina?" "Yes?"

"Are you feeling all right?" she asked. "Just a minute ago, you were asking me to leave."

"I'm giving you another choice." Her lips were pressed, tense. "Someone told me I should."

Lily eyed her suspiciously. "I know nothing about accounts or managing a pleasure house," she said, placing a thoughtful finger on her chin.

"I didn't know those things when I started either. You could learn," Acelina said. "I have people to help, but the question is, would you like to learn?"

"I like being the center of attention," Lily said, walking around the bed, the cogs of her brain turning. "But I guess we all grow old. Learning to manage a place like this would be...a new adventure." She looked up at Acelina, "So, when are you retiring?"

"Soon," The question was always at the back of Acelina's mind. Ever since she opened this place, she was semi-retired. Yet, if she stopped seeing clients altogether, she didn't know how she'd fill the emptiness. She was a people-pleaser, and some part of her wanted to be admired, even if by strangers.

"You're older than me," Lily reminded.

"I'll think about it." Acelina shrugged. "We're here to talk about you. I won't take any bookings for you starting today. That should give you enough time to learn about numbers and how Duality works. You used to help me when we started. It'll be like the old days."

"The old days, huh? Well, I'm glad I won't have to leave," she said. "Still, it feels horrible to know I'm not number one."

"You'll always be number one to me, Lily," Acelina said. She still remembered her from two hundred years ago, a young, confident girl standing at her doorstep and telling her she'd become the most requested girl in Duality. She would never forget the first employee she hired.

"Awww...is that how you got to the lieutenant general?"

"We're not talking about her." Acelina turned her face away.

"Now that my future is sorted out, I'd like to know what happened last night." Lily's bout of sentimentality was replaced with a wicked gleam. Aside from being the most-requested escort, she was the biggest gossip around town.

"Nothing." Acelina turned away, closing the door behind her.

"You can't hide forever," Lily's voice echoed behind her. When were her employees so interested in her personal life?

FOURTEEN

PETRONILLA

PETRONILLA WASN'T HAVING THE BEST DAY. SHE'D FOUND an excuse to get out of Duality before Acelina awoke, making her way to the secret service. The streets were damp, thanks to a rare spell of rain. As she crossed the famed pleasure houses, the smell of cheap perfume mingling with gutter residue made her nauseous. The humidity had shot up during the day, leaving Petronilla sweating. As she passed another escort batting eyelashes at her, she felt sexual frustration rise in her bloodstream.

Last night's kiss had been a drunken mistake, but she wasn't stupid enough to think her lingering attraction to Acelina could be brushed over with an apology. She'd tossed and turned all of last night, the memory of Acelina's wicked tongue brushing over the shell of her ear washed her anew, sending waves of pleasure. Yes, she hated her profession, and everything the courtesan stood for, but yesterday, she'd seen a side to her that she'd never seen in any other person. It was much easier to think of Acelina as a courtesan than as a person. If she was a human being just like Petronilla with honor and flaws...Petronilla didn't know what to make of her.

If not enemies, then what were they?

The cream-colored building came into view, and she realized she'd been thinking about Acelina all this time. Exhausted, and with a heavy head, she turned to the street-lamps that stung her eyes. She was beginning to understand the appeal of living in a place where the sun never shone. In the darkness, she felt comfortable with her tangled thoughts.

"Petronilla?" General Darius's voice met her ears. She saw him walking holding a stick. He wasn't dressed in uniform, and she noticed that the buttons of his dark blue shirt were inserted in the wrong holes. That gave her pause.

"Good afternoon, general," she said, moving closer to him. He swayed unsteadily, making Petronilla wonder if he was drunk, but she smelled no alcohol on him, and he was known for being professional. "Are you feeling okay?"

He looked up at Petronilla, as if looking right through her, and sighed. "For some reason, my vision is blurry today," he began. "I wonder why."

"Did you drink last night?"

"No," he replied. "I don't think drinking caused this. Do you mind guiding me inside? I don't want to miss a step and hit my head."

"Of course." She held his hand, the one without the stick, and guided him in. They were surrounded by the chaos of the secret service as soon as the door opened. The staff was busy decoding a message they'd received from Elysium.

"I'm hoping to be better by tomorrow, but you'll have to

work alone today. I'm sorry." He climbed the stairs, his hand firmly in hers. Though he was taller than her, she guided him in, watching for potential sources of collision.

"Don't worry." She paused. "I mean, it's my job to find my father, and I'll find him."

"I'm lucky to have someone as reliable as you," he said, smiling at her.

"Watch your step." Petronilla held his hand as he felt his way to the railing. Slowly, they ascended the steps, one at a time. He missed a step, but she caught and steadied him.

"I feel like a two-year-old learning to walk." Though he laughed, there was no humor in his voice.

"Have you had vision problems before?" she spoke in a soft voice, not wanting to startle him.

"Once," he admitted. "The day we went to Duality for the year-end party."

"You spilled wine," she remembered. Then, connecting the dots, "Because you didn't see it."

"I'm sure it'll be gone by evening," he said. "I sometimes get headaches that make it impossible to see."

She nodded. "I hope you feel better soon."

With that, they were on the final stair. Felix's door opened before either of them could knock. His eyes were a startling color of red today, as demon eyes sometimes got when they were angry or under stress. He came to a stop upon seeing them.

"Is everything all right?" He looked at Petronilla, a grey eyebrow raised.

"I'm not feeling well today," Darius volunteered. "Petronilla is helping me out. I think I'll return home after today's meeting. There isn't much I can do in this state."

"Should I have something made for you?" Felix asked, unsure how to handle Darius' extremely rare bout of illness.

"Nothing."

Petronilla led them both inside and helped Darius sit on the sofa. From the corner of her eye, she spotted Tranagard nestled in the shadows between the curtains.

"This affair is messier than I thought," Felix said. "If your father, the thief from Terra, is planning to start a revolution, Ifer is probably involved. We haven't been able to catch hold of him for over a century. I don't even want to think what'll happen if he has the letters."

"I tried tracking down an illegal shipment his cronies were bringing from Elysium," Tranagard spoke. "But so far, I haven't met with any success."

"One of the men I posted at the red-light district thinks the thief might still have the letters," he said. "There have been no signs of him meeting Ifer. Regardless of Ifer's intentions, I think we still have a chance to find him with the letters before they're gone for good. We must all tread carefully and make no mistakes." The last three words were heavily emphasized.

"We should find him before we decide about the letters," Tranagard said. "He's still at the red-light district and has already been banned from six pleasure houses. Information travels fast there."

"I suspect he's going to try and get into one he hasn't been to before," Felix said. "Keeping you at Duality was a good move. He might go there next."

Petronilla stopped breathing.

"I'll send more agents to watch Duality," Felix said. "You need to be on your guard, Lieutenant General. We're counting on you."

Petronilla gave a terse nod.

"I'll look into other pleasure houses tonight," Tranagard said. "You should return and watch Duality. If I find him, I'll send a message. The sooner we take care of this issue, the better."

"I agree," Felix said. Then, to General Darius, "Should I see you home?"

"No need." He stood up. "One of the royal guards will do."

Petronilla and Tranagard left first, parting ways at the red light district. On her way back, she passed The Rose, taking a moment to watch at the back door. Patrons went in and out, but he was nowhere to be seen. By now, the madame would've found out she'd hit her client unconscious last night and escaped through the window. After that debacle, she hadn't dared to ask Acelina for another dress so here she stood, wearing a nondescript grey shirt and pants.

"He's not here tonight," a sharp voice told her. Swirling abruptly, she saw Giselle standing behind her, rumpled purple skirts sweeping dust.

"Giselle."

"You look different today." She eyed Petronilla's clothes. "You're not a courtesan, are you?"

Before Petronilla could invent an excuse, she continued. "I know you escaped through the window last night after hitting your client in the head." She laughed, surveying

Petronilla head to toe. "I liked you much better in yesterday's dress, though."

She blinked, throat burning. Her lie had been caught and she didn't know what to say. Petronilla was forthright and no good at trickery and deception. Damn Felix and his plan. "I'm sorry."

"You're sorry?" Giselle burst out into musical laughter. "I was so amused I laughed all night...nobody's ever left after making a patron pass out within five minutes...you're something else..."

"Huh?"

"Are you looking for the grey-haired guy from Terra again?" she asked, sly eyes flitting over an opened fan.

"You know where he is?"

"Who's he to you?" Giselle asked, fanning herself furiously.

"Nobody." Her voice was a tad strained to be believable.

"Then, why are you looking for him?"

"We have a score to settle."

"A score, huh? Isn't he too old for you?" Giselle's mind was headed in a completely different direction.

Bile rose in her throat. "Not that kind of score-"

"Uh-huh, keep talking." Giselle motioned her fan forward.

"He...owes me money," Petronilla said.

"Owes you money?" Giselle's eyes narrowed, and Petronilla wasn't sure if she was buying it or not.

"Have you seen him?" Petronilla pressed, stepping forward.

"No. He hasn't come around since two days ago," Giselle said.

Petronilla deflated.

"But I heard some men talking about him visiting other pleasure houses. I think they mentioned Duality."

"Duality?" All of a sudden, her pulse pounded in her ears.

"Yeah, I think that's what they said. Though I don't know how he managed to—"

"Today?"

"Nobody else is going to let him in. But I don't think they know of his record at Duality yet—"

Blood pounded in her ears, her body taking flight. "Thanks."

Before Giselle could complete her explanation, Petronilla was running, passing people and lights in a blur. Thoughts popped into her mind, changing and dissipating like a kaleidoscope. She was so close to getting her hands on her father. She needed to finish this mission and return to her old life as soon as possible.

FIFTEEN

ACELINA

IT WAS ALMOST EIGHT IN THE EVENING WHEN ACELINA sat in her room, applying makeup. She thought back to last night. She'd woken up aroused and dizzy this morning, her mind buzzing with thoughts. Her skin ached for those hot, drugging kisses, her nipples tightening at the thought of Petronilla's mouth on them. An ache built between her legs, requesting the completion of what they started last night.

The powder brush slid down, clanking on the floor. Acelina couldn't summon the strength or clarity of thought to pick it up. Her eyes burned holes in the mirror that reflected her painted face. In them, she saw her past, present, and future, until those images were interrupted by last night. Sitting alone in the kitchen drinking and listening to each other had felt oddly like...companionship. Though she hungered for more of those intoxicating kisses, what she hungered for even more was that feeling of knowing someone would catch her if she fell. Petronilla, of all people, gave her that feeling. She was sturdy and dependable. But was that enough?

Acelina had learned to cultivate inner strength early in life, knowing if she fell, nobody would pick her back up. Nobody was strong enough to outdo her will, to be her rock. She'd been abandoned by her parents before she took her first breath and had been raised in this world. This world was all she knew, and she liked it, with fleeting relationships and bloodless bonds. But, when she looked at families, she always wondered what it would feel like to have somewhere to come back to, to know you were loved by someone even on the worst days of your life. Now that she was getting older, she was beginning to think of who would care for her once she couldn't go on. The people at Duality were her family, but as their employer, she was supposed to be someone they could look up to. They derived their strength and comfort from her, but could she turn to them?

Long ago, she'd decided that if she was going to make this work, she needed to be her own strength. What she'd never imagined was meeting someone whose strength matched hers. Petronilla hated her, and she made her living sleeping with random strangers. Petronilla's strong sense of honor would never let her be with a person like Acelina. Maybe last night had just been a moment of drunken passion, and she was attaching too much meaning to it. That had to be it. Because if not, she didn't know what she'd do.

"Are you ready?" Lily asked, knocking at her door. "Your client arrived early."

She sighed, for the first time not looking forward to sex. Thoughts ate her mind, leaving her unable to derive pleasure from anything. She wondered if this lack of interest was a sign that she needed to retire. Or, maybe, it was someone else she wanted to have in her bed tonight.

"Coming." Acelina turned around, carrying herself with the grace of a seasoned courtesan. Decisions could wait until tomorrow.

"He looks weird to me," Lily suggested as they made their way to the main building. "He ordered the finest wine and food, but..." she paused. "He reminds me of someone."

"Who?" Acelina asked, her heart feeling heavier by the second. She didn't want anyone else tonight.

"I don't know," Lily said. "But be careful. I get a strange feeling about him."

"Have Elias on standby," she said. "Is Lieutenant General Petronilla back yet?"

"Not yet." Lily stopped outside the VIP room door. "Have you been thinking about her all day?"

"Nothing is going on between us, just so you know," Acelina said, throwing the doors open. Lily slipped away quietly.

SIXTEEN

PETRONILLA

THE ROW OF RED LANTERNS ENDED BEFORE A QUIET stone wall beyond which lay the most famed pleasure house in the red-light district. Duality was composed of two wooden buildings with a pagoda. A constant stream of water flowed down the broken bamboo pipes in the manicured garden. Petronilla's feet pounded over the wooden bridge, startling goldfish, as she rushed into Duality's main building. The smell of expensive liquor and sweat hit her nose instantly, coupled with the sight of several men. Lily was in the waiting area tonight, trying to sort out appointments.

"Where's Acelina?" Petronilla asked, panting. Her eyes searched the vicinity for Felix's men, but she had no time to try and find them now. God only knew how long her father was going to stay here. Since there was no provision for gambling, she guessed not very long.

"You okay?" Lily asked, turning from the line of patrons to her. "Acelina has been looking for you."

"Why? What happened?" Her heartbeat grew to a crescendo. She couldn't start thinking about Acelina now when duty was breathing down her neck.

"Nothing. She has a customer tonight," Lily said, returning to welcome patrons. "You should pay her a visit later."

"Customer? What customer?" The hammering of Petronilla's heart began anew, mingling with a deep-rooted disgust. After what happened last night, the thought of Acelina with anyone except her made her uneasy.

"She's a courtesan," Lily said as if reading her thoughts. "That's what she does."

She was right, of course. "Which room?"

Lily narrowed her eyes. "You're not going to barge in there, are you-"

"Which room?" The words came out a command, her mind flooding with thoughts. Her father was in one of the rooms, and for all she knew, it could be Acelina's.

"The green one."

Petronilla blinked away the tears of frustration that lined her eyes. That's where they'd had their year-end party. That's where they'd dared her to spend the night with Acelina. That's where they'd met—

She had more important things to do, like figuring out where her father was hiding.

"Thanks."

She hurried up a flight of stairs, listening for any familiar sound. The rooms were all closed, making it hard to see who was in there. She wondered if she should alert Tranagard, but she didn't want to call him here if he wasn't here. Storming down the corridor, she arrived at the green room. Acelina's musical laughter resonated on the other side. She closed her eyes, willing herself to act rationally. Anger only made everything worse, but it was all she knew. She threw the door open with a kick, bracing herself for whatever was on the other side.

What she saw on the other side, made her blood freeze. Her weasel-faced, slimy father sat half-naked in a robe exposing the mass of grey hair covering his chest. Acelina poured her father drinks, dressed in her most alluring kimono, her hand sliding into her father's robe. The old man's face was flushed with joy, each touch of her smooth hand, titillating him.

Petronilla saw red.

Upon hearing the door open, Acelina pulled her hand away, onyx eyes meeting hers with a question. She glanced from Acelina to her father, both half-naked and disheveled, and rage rose like mercury in her veins.

Bursting in, she flipped the table, sending alcohol splashing and china breaking. Her father and Acelina backed away immediately before the broken shards hit them.

"There you are." All trace of calm gone, she grabbed her father by the throat.

"What're you doing?" Acelina stood behind her, pulling her hand away.

"You." Petronilla stabbed a finger in the air, in the throes of emotion. Even in her sleep-deprived state, his face was vivid. Her memory stood in human form. She remembered his unrepentant eyes that left her at the brothel's doorstep without a coin. If it weren't for Acelina's hand restraining her, she'd have pushed her father to the ground and killed him on the spot.

"Where are the letters?" she asked, her eyes still on his throat.

"Get off my customer right now!" Acelina ordered to no avail.

"Welcome back, daughter dear," he said, choking. "Daughter?" Acelina's fingers stilled on hers, and Petronilla could hear her heartbeat ricocheting through her skull. "Where have you hidden the letters?" She shoved him

back, checking his clothing for them.

"I wouldn't bring them to a place like this," he said. "They're in safe hands."

Petronilla tightened her grip on his throat. "Whose safe hands?"

"I...do not have to...tell you that..." He was choking.

"You can't escape. The King of Terra is looking for you," she said. "You better tell me where you've hidden those." When he said nothing, "Is Ifer involved?"

"Ifer?" He raised an eyebrow as if he hadn't heard that name. That at least eliminated one possibility. Her hold on his neck tightened for a second. In her fit of rage, Petronilla hadn't seen him pick up a flower vase from the table. He hit her with it, smashing the porcelain.

Acelina shrieked.

She let go of him, and he ran to the window. She looked up, holding the right side of her head that was wet with blood. There was a venomous glint in his brown eyes as if challenging her. Then, he dove out of the window. He'd always been fast— something Petronilla had inherited.

"You're bleeding." Acelina touched her forehead. Watching him get away, she broke out of Acelina's grasp, knocking her to the floor in the process.

"Acelina—" Her head snapped back, just as she heard her father's footsteps on the roof outside.

Acelina was on the ground, her back against the floor. She'd shoved her too roughly, leading her to fall. Their eyes met, making time stop for a second. Guilt seeped through her brain, drowning out the realization that her father was running away. All she saw was Acelina on the floor because she'd roughly pushed her away in the heat of the moment.

"Are you okay?" She extended a hand to Acelina, helping her get to her feet.

"Go after him!" she said, signaling to the window.

"Are you hurt?" Petronilla asked, jogging to the window.

"I'm fine." Acelina's eyes were fixed on her. Then, abruptly, she turned to the window and said, "That side leads to Blu, the pleasure house next door. He could've gone there." Still, Petronilla didn't move, making sure Acelina was all right. Their eyes remained locked, a silent conversation taking place in those stolen moments. "Go."

Petronilla scanned the scenery outside the window, looking for any secret agents. When she didn't see any, she muttered a curse and burst out of the front door. She bumped into a customer on her way out and startled Lily with her speed. Once the air hit her face, she ran down the street, to Blu's entrance.

Like the name suggested, Blu was a blue building decorated with red lanterns. In her rush, she ignored their lawns and emerged straight at the reception teeming with patrons. The red lanterns made her see light spots.

"Excuse me." She flew past the proprietress, into the main hall. It was decorated with cheap-looking velvet draperies, porcelain vases, sofas, and rosewood tables.

"Where is he?" she asked the proprietress who was following on her heels.

"Who?"

"The man who jumped from Duality's roof. I saw him come in."

"I don't know who you're talking about." Her face was blank. Had her father not come here, then?

Petronilla raked a hand through her hair, panic eating at her brain. She had to get him tonight or things would become more complicated.

"Who are you?"

She rushed out, breathing in the humid air, scanning the garden for any trace of her father. She checked the trees, the shadows, the lakes, the fences, hunting like a madwoman. Despair filled her when she came up empty. He was gone, leaving behind nothing but flashing red lights.

If only she hadn't bothered to help Acelina, she'd have made it in time. But seeing the object of her affection with her father made bile rise in her throat. The ugly scene replayed in her mind, as she turned to go back home.

Home.

When had she come to think of Duality as her home? "Lieutenant General." Tranagard materialized along with two other agents outside the gate. "The thief was here."

"Yes," Petronilla uttered, breathless. "He jumped out of

the window. I tried looking everywhere but..." She swallowed her voice, not having the courage to admit failure.

"We've been trailing him," the other secret agent said. "I saw him come out of Duality and we followed him in but-"

"He's not here," she finished. All the promises she'd made to Darius and Felix played through her mind. She couldn't believe she'd let them down. It was her fault for not being able to catch him when he was at Duality. She shook her head.

"I can see he hit you and ran away," Tranagard said, eyeing the trail of blood running down her forehead.

"It's nothing. We should wait and get him when he comes out."

"If he comes out." The other secret agent gestured to the pleasure house that looked benign. Petronilla's head fell back. "If none of us could find him in there, he's gone."

"Felix won't be happy about this." Tranagard sighed.

"It's my fault," she said, guilt closing in on her. "I shouldn't have let him get away. I should've informed you when I found out he was in Duality."

"Why didn't you?" Tranagard asked. She had no answer to his question.

"We spotted him right away," the other agent said. "But he's like a shadow."

"We'll watch the place, and get him when he comes out," his colleague said as if to make her feel better. But nothing made her feel better. The bitter taste of failure was on her tongue.

"I'll stay with you," she volunteered

"Don't you need to get that wound treated?" Tranagard asked her.

"Catching a thief is more important," Petronilla said.

Tranagard handed her his handkerchief which she used to blot the wound.

It was going to be a long night together, but when they were done, she was determined to have the letters.

SEVENTEEN

PETRONILLA

THE LIGHTS WERE STILL ON WHEN PETRONILLA STEPPED into Duality, a burden weighing on her chest. Four hours of waiting and investigation had led nowhere. They were back to square one.

Tonight, she'd finally been lucky to find him, but her emotions had taken over at the cost of her mission. How was she going to explain the debacle to Felix? How could she face Darius? Never before had she failed to capture a thief, especially one as amateurish as her father. No matter how fast he was, she was a professional. But her mind had been distracted all night.

The sight of his lips lingering near Acelina's skin sent venom spiraling down her bloodstream. He had no business putting her filthy hands on her. But then again, that's what she did for a living. Midnight kisses couldn't change that.

With drooping shoulders, she crossed the corridor,

noticing the light in Acelina's room was on. As if sensing her presence, the door slid open, and Acelina stood there, eyeing her with sympathy.

"How's your wound?"

But she didn't want sympathy. She wanted an argument that would numb her to pain, that would end their fragile relationship forever. She didn't want to like Acelina despite her profession. She didn't want to give in to this attraction that was at the breaking point. She'd always known nothing could come out of it. If she didn't play this well, she'd never walk out with her pride intact.

"Petronilla, are you—" Acelina reached for her. She slapped her hand away, shrinking back.

"Have you no standards?" she roared. Her suppressed feelings poured out in an angry outburst.

"What?"

"You're going to sleep with anyone who gives you money?" Her voice was thunderous.

The words irritated Acelina, just like they'd been intended to.

"Who I choose to sleep with is nobody's business," she snapped. "Especially not yours." Her eyes turned to daggers, her magnificent porcelain shoulders cast over with a blush. Petronilla wanted to kiss that expanse of creamy skin down to her flawless rounded breasts—

"He's a wanted criminal." She checked herself, tearing her gaze away from her shoulders. But no matter where she looked, Acelina's presence filled her like air from which she couldn't escape. "I expected you to know that. He's the reason Darius sent me here."

"How was I supposed to know when I've never seen him?" Acelina pulled out a long pipe and lit it, exhaling a puff of smoke. She only smoked when she was annoyed. Petronilla's nose scrunched, sensitive to the smell of nicotine. Sometimes she thought Acelina deliberately smoked to annoy her.

"Stop smoking. I hate the smell," she snapped.

"I don't exist for your convenience." Acelina's voice turned cold, rings of smoke coming in rapid succession. So, they were back to arguing. Petronilla felt an odd sort of comfort at that. The only feeling stronger than attraction was anger. It was the only thing that could douse whatever was between them. So, she held on to it.

"You agreed to cooperate with us." Her voice rose. "You should've made it your business to check."

"I agreed to house you, not become a part of your mission."

Petronilla huffed, too far gone to end the episode harmoniously. "You have no taste in customers, just like draperies."

She'd offered the same criticism on their first night together. For some reason, it stung. It stung to hurt Acelina.

"I'm under no obligation to take criticism from you." She exhaled another cloud of smoke. "Or do you think you have some special claim over me because of last night?"

So, she hadn't forgotten.

Petronilla's breath got stuck in her throat. 'Yes, I do,' she wanted to shout. Possessiveness came as naturally as breathing to her. But she knew she was out of line.

Why did she have to be stupid enough to go and develop an attraction for someone as unattainable as Acelina? Sleeping with people was her profession, and she wasn't going to change just because of one kiss. One act of kindness wouldn't erase her past.

"I have no such illusions," she said instead.

"Good, because you're mistaken if you think you can tell me what to do." Another ring of smoke dissipated before her eyes.

They were arguing again, just like they always did. Just like Petronilla feared they always would. Beyond the fuel of their united animosity was a feeling neither of them wanted to face. Acelina was the oxygen to the flame of Petronilla's volatile temper. Every time they were in a room, sparks flew and ignited. Nothing good could come out of this aggravating association.

"You didn't get him? What's wrong with our capable lieutenant general?" Acelina was downright baiting her now, annoyed.

"It was because..."

Because of you.

I couldn't think of anything except you.

Heaving a sigh, she lowered her head, and said in a low voice, "He got away. I failed. Are you happy?"

"Failed?" she goaded on.

"Failed to perform my duty," Petronilla ground out. "Drowning in self-pity, are we?"

"I'm doing no such thing," she snapped.

"Self-righteousness, then?" Acelina fanned herself. "You think it's my fault you failed."

"No." She paused, their eyes meeting again. Her temper had cooled a notch. "I'll catch him next time."

"I'm sure he'll be back," she said, moving away with a

swish of her silk skirt. "You're his dearest daughter, after all."
"I'm not." Petronilla's voice was tight, her eyes darting back to
Acelina's receding silhouette. She stood at the threshold of
Acelina's room, candlelight falling on her face,

unsure of her welcome. "He hates me."

"You don't get along with your father either?" Acelina
exhaled an angry puff of smoke, straight in her face, knowing
fully well she didn't like the smell of nicotine. "What a
surprise."

Before Petronilla realized, she had grabbed Acelina's arm,
jerking her forward violently. The pipe dropped on the floor,
the orange embers on the cigarette extinguishing under
Petronilla's shoes. "Listen to me. He might've given me life,
but he isn't my father."

"Why? What crime did he commit except participating
in your creation?"

"Sold me to a brothel? How's that for—" The words were
out before Petronilla could think. This woman drove her
insane with her verbal barbs and constant challenges. Acelina
flinched, just as Petronilla let go of her arm. Acelina stared at
her, her face devoid of any expression. A heavy silence
descended upon the room. "Scared?"

She was still for a few more moments, which was time
enough for Petronilla to regret revealing something so
personal. She'd never made this mistake with anyone before.
All these years, she'd made sure never to get drunk so she
wouldn't start spilling unsavory bits of her past. She hated
who she had been until Darius found her and brought her
here.

Something akin to sympathy came over Acelina's usually

hard eyes. "No, something like that doesn't scare me. I've seen worse." However, Acelina moved closer, dropping her voice to a whisper, "But you didn't tell me your father sold you."

"I don't need your sympathy," she spat, heart, thundering. "Good, because I'm not giving you any," Acelina said,

stepping forward until only an inch separated them. Petronil- la's ragged breathing echoed between their bodies. "What I'm giving you is comfort." Then, she wrapped her arms around Petronilla's shaking body. She hadn't even real- ized she had been quivering until those frail arms held her, suffusing her with warmth. "You need it."

She'd never been held before. Since her birth, she'd been thrown on the streets to fend for herself, never receiving kind- ness or comfort from any human being. Not that she wanted it. But this...there were no words to describe this. All she wanted to do was break down and cry, spilling centuries' worth of unshed tears.

Her body tingled, and the fight went out of her. She didn't know how to respond to a gesture such as this, so she let her body take over and hugged Acelina back, burying her face in the smaller woman's shoulder. Her knees were wobbly, threatening to give out.

'This is wrong. Get away now,' her mind screamed, but her body held on for dear life.

"I don't need comfort..." Her voice was shaky, her fingers shakier but she didn't move.

"This is where you shut up and let go," Acelina advised. "You know, we have more in common than I thought."

"Did your father abandon you too?"

"I don't even know who my father is," Acelina said, her laugh cracking. There was a moment of silence in which Petronilla pushed her mind to think. She couldn't let things head down this road, where she had no control. There had to be a way to stop whatever was igniting between them.

"How much do you charge for comforting?" she asked in a last desperate attempt to stop the inevitable from happening.

"It's free." Her voice was husky and low, filled with emotion.

"Nothing is free," Petronilla's shaky voice retorted. But that wasn't right.

Everything Acelina had given her— friendship, generosity, and a place to live—was free. And, in return, she'd been argumentative and ungrateful.

"Was that supposed to put me off?" Acelina asked, running her palm soothingly up and down her back. "Try harder, darling."

Darling.

She liked hearing that.

"You should get away from me," she said, even as she clung to Acelina, her fingers exploring the smooth silk she wore today.

"You always do this when you feel your self-control slipping away," Acelina said. "You shrink back and become defensive."

"I want you to leave me alone." There was no conviction in her voice.

"Do you know you say the exact opposite of what you

feel?" Acelina's cheek rested on her shoulder, tugging at her heartstrings. "You should've told me about your father before. I would've understood."

"I didn't think you'd understand." Petronilla hunched, her head resting on Acelina's shoulder. Acelina's hand caressed her back.

"I've been thinking of you since this morning," she confessed.

Desire warred with sadness, the former coming out stronger. She wanted to forget tonight and take this hand that was being offered. So, she bent down, and pressed a kiss on Acelina's bare shoulders, tasting salty, smooth skin. Acelina's skin pricked, but she stood, unmoving.

"Sorry. I couldn't stop myself." Petronilla tore her lips away.

"I didn't ask you to stop," Acelina said, ceasing the stroking. Their eyes met, hazy with desire, and the grief was forgotten. Where her defense was broken, the light now entered.

Acelina's fingers reached her cheek, brushing away the tears. She felt their smoothness soothe her dark memories.

"Me...too..." The anger was gone now, replaced by something more powerful— lust.

"What do you want?" Acelina asked.

Ugly scenes from the past flooded through her mind, the incident this morning and the sight of her father mixing into a toxic cocktail. But even those unpleasant memories couldn't stop the words that came out of her mouth.

"I want to go back to being a lieutenant general...never having to face a past that I hate."

"I meant what do you want right now?" Acelina smiled, holding her in place. Her eyes twinkled.

It was a question that had only one answer.

"I want you." Petronilla's low voice reverberated in her body.

"Good, because I want you too."

Desperate for oblivion, their mouths met, squeezing hands that hung between them. Acelina's soft pink lips parted, tasting nicotine, liquor, and something fruity. Petronilla hated all three, but on her they were intoxicating. She deepened the kiss, breathing her in.

Acelina groaned, holding Petronilla closer, swinging them both into the closest room. Her leg reached out and pushed the door shut. Just as Petronilla was about to tear away, the courtesan's tongue darted out and licked her, making her moan with pleasure. She joined, their mouths exploding with passion. Petronilla threw her against the closed door and trailed kisses down her mouth, jaw, and cheek, nibbling at the sensitive flesh of her neck.

"Slow down." Acelina's giggle vibrated against her lips.

She pulled apart the side seams of Petronilla's kimono to reveal even more of her shoulder, kissing her smooth porcelain shoulders.

"I've always wanted to do that," she whispered against her creamy skin. "It drives me crazy to watch your bare shoulders."

"It's a day of revelations." Acelina's hands raked her hair, her voice chiming with musical laughter.

Her fingers undid the sash, loosening the kimono to reveal her breasts. Petronilla admired them for a moment— flawless globes with pale pink nipples — better than her wildest fantasies. Better than she deserved. The paling candlelight didn't do them justice. She kissed her way down Acelina's breasts, capturing a pink nipple in her mouth. When she licked, a moan escaped the escort's lips.

"You're so beautiful." Petronilla's breaths echoed. "I want to taste all of you."

Petronilla resumed sucking again, teeth joining tongue. She bit down lightly on the taut pearl. Pleasure exploded in Acelina's belly. She grabbed Petronilla's hair, fingers quaking. "You're driving me crazy."

"We're even, then." Petronilla bit down lightly on the nipple.

Acelina was grinding her hips, begging for release. She kissed her other breast, suckling another nipple. The sweetness intoxicated her senses. Her teeth came in, biting lightly, and sucking ardently. Acelina's body exploded with sensation, grinding harder and harder, arousing Petronilla even more. She stopped suckling and let her sash fall. With it went the rest of the robe, pooling at her feet.

Petronilla forgot to breathe. There were no words to describe the beauty who stood before her. Her body was so flawless it appeared to be carved with marble. Creamy shoulders melted into pert, small breasts, and shapely curves. Acelina was blessed with abundant hips, embodying a goddess of fertility. Candlelight flickered over her naked form, turning Petronilla's brain to mush.

"You're magnificent," she said, breathless.

"High praise indeed, coming from you," Acelina said with a coy smile.

She was looking at that perfection anew, this time no chains on her desire.

"Come to bed with me," Petronilla said, feeling like a third person watching herself from the distance. When had she become this wanton? No, she had to stop thinking. Her mind couldn't focus on anything beyond the beauty in front of her.

"My pleasure, darling."

Acelina crossed over to the bed on the other side of the room. The memories of her father were erased, and only the two of them remained. Petronilla pulled off her coat, unbuttoning her shirt.

"Let me." Acelina sat up, snapping the buttons one by one, each brush of her fingers sending desire pooling in Petronilla's stomach. When her fingers roamed her shoulders, pushing her shirt and undershirt away, she couldn't hold on any longer. Pushing Acelina onto the bed she began kissing her toes.

"What're you doing?" Acelina asked, looking up. "What do you think?"

"You don't have to—" She was silenced by the kiss Petronilla placed on her inner thigh. "God. Are you sure you don't want to join this business?"

Petronilla stilled, just for a second.

"Petronilla?" Acelina sensed her stillness. "I was kidding."

"I know."

"I'm sorry."

"Don't be."

Petronilla captured her mouth, silencing her protests. Her

hands felt every inch of that delectable skin. Acelina had the right amount of fat and muscle. Her body was a work of art. Acelina's fingers joined hers in exploration, touching her arms, and her back, tracing the dents in her spine. When she felt a hand brush under her breasts, she broke contact.

"What—"

Petronilla kissed her way down her neck, making Acelina moan. She licked a clavicle, moving to kiss down her body, her breasts, her stomach, and further down, kissing the inside of her thigh.

"Hmmm..." Acelina's guttural moan was music to her ears.

Then, she kissed her between her legs. It was pure instinct— something she'd wanted to do during all those years but never got to. Acelina's hips buckled, arching upward.

She groaned, letting Petronilla's tongue trace the outline of her intimate lips, plunging deeper, drinking in her taste. She tasted like honey and woman, swirled into a heady mix. The taste of her drove her crazy. She eased her tongue deeper, plundering the liquid essence of her.

"You're so wet," she said, pressing a kiss to her core.

"Oh my..." Acelina's breath came in jagged puffs, her body ready and primed. When Petronilla took her bud in her mouth, Acelina gasped.

Her hips bucked, driving to a climax. She teased her bundle of nerves with a warm tongue, making her wetter, hotter, and needier. She'd wanted to do this on the night they kissed. She wanted to give Acelina all of herself, to take or leave. It had always been all or nothing for them.

"Ummmm..." Even the vibration of her voice made Acelina writhe. Petronilla suckled her little pearl, licking and tantalizing it with strokes of tongue, while her hands squeezed her ass.

"Do it," Acelina begged, her body covered in a feverish flush. Petronilla pulled away.

"Gladly." Two fingers slid inside her moist folds. A guttural moan escaped as Acelina buckled, unable to hold on any longer.

Then, she came, body spasming. Sweet, sticky wetness drenched Petronilla's fingers. Her muscles convulsed, a wave of pleasure sweeping through her sweaty body. Every nerve ending short-circuited. Acelina fell flat on the heap of mattresses, eyes open, and a smile on her lips.

And they both knew nothing would ever be the same again.

They lay side by side, sated and quiet, staring at the ceiling. Acelina couldn't remember the last time she'd felt this good. Her life had always been about pleasuring others. But today had been different.

"Are you going to say something?" Acelina asked, turning her face to meet Petronilla's vulnerable eyes.

"You know I'm no good with words." Petronilla inched closer, their bodies brushing under the sheets.

"Remind me of that when we argue the next time," Acelina said.

"Even in this state, your tongue is sharp as a blade," Petronilla remarked.

"I'll stay quiet, then."

"No!" She panicked. "That's one of the things I like about you. You speak your mind."

"I was kidding. I'm not that easy to change."

Petronilla turned, weight resting on her right arm. "What happened between us..." She didn't know where to start and where to finish. Inhaling several times wasn't helping.

"Look at you, all nervous," Acelina took Petronilla's face between her palms, brushing a soft kiss on her lips. "I like you. I think I've liked you since the moment you pointed your finger at me and said you wanted me."

"Really? I was so rude to you the first time."

"You were." Acelina stared into her eyes. "But even so, I dreamt of you lying in this bed next to me on nights I was lonely." She turned and met Petronilla's gaze, expecting a reply. "There's something dependable about you..."

"I don't know where this is going," Petronilla admitted, setting her gaze steadily. Butterflies danced in her stomach, but she knew she had to do the right thing. "But I want to know. I want to give this," she signaled to the space between them, "a chance."

"You are hesitant."

"I can't help it. I've had an uncertain life," Petronilla said. "It's taught me to prepare for the worst. I wish I could always have the security of knowing what comes next."

Acelina moved closer, holding her. "You're not alone anymore."

Petronilla's heart warmed, stirring with feelings that had been dormant for centuries. "Has anyone told you how wonderful you are?"

"What's with all the praise today? Stop or I'll have to call a healer to get your head checked." Acelina's laugh was high-pitched and musical. She always kept it down before her customers, but here, she was free.

Petronilla laughed, too. "We've always been at odds. But I think underlying that animosity was this explosive passion."

"I'll have to add philosophy to your list of virtues." Acelina laughed again. Then, turning serious, "About what I said earlier...you being an escort again. Did I hurt your feelings?"

Petronilla pulled her fingers apart and kissed them, one by one. "No. I can't win against my past. General Darius tells me that all the time," she said. "I can only hope to move on one step at a time."

Acelina's embrace tightened. "Those experiences are a part of you, darling, and I like you all the more because of them."

Petronilla smiled sheepishly. "What?"

"I could get used to you calling me darling." Her thumb brushed Acelina's cheeks.

"You like it?" She nodded.

"Then, I'll use it more often," she said, so close their breaths mingled. "What else do you like?"

You.

Every inch of you.

"You don't need to remember the things I like. I'm not your customer," Petronilla said, indignant.

"Occupational hazard," Acelina confessed. "I'm a natural people-pleaser."

"I don't know how I resisted you for so long." Her face

turned to Acelina and looking at her face radiant with the afterglow of pleasure filled her heart.

"I attribute it to your stubbornness," Acelina said. She crawled over Petronilla.

When their lips met again, all the uncertainty was forgotten, and only ecstasy reigned.

EIGHTEEN

ACELINA

WHEN ACELINA AWOKE THE NEXT MORNING, SHE FELT much lighter. They had moved to her room and made love again before falling asleep. Petronilla was already awake, a candle burning next to the bed. She looked down at her, observing without a word. Being here in her arms was the closest thing to happiness that she'd experienced in a long time. Last night had changed something fundamental in her. The animosity between them was gone, replaced by something wonderful.

"Good morning," Acelina croaked, her eyes opening. The candle Petronilla lit illuminated her arms and shoulders that peaked out of the duvet. "Is it morning yet?"

"It's afternoon."

She turned, their naked bodies brushing, sending another wave of desire coursing through Acelina. Upon seeing her stir, Petronilla nibbled at Acelina's ears, all the way down to her neck, awakening her completely.

"You're insatiable," Acelina complained, turning. "Let me sleep for a few more minutes."

She was intoxicating like a drug, and no matter how much Acelina tasted of her, she would always want more.

So, this was what happiness felt like.

She could get used to it.

"Do your clients know you snore?" Petronilla asked, breaking contact.

"No, I never stay the night," Acelina said, eyes opening wider.

"Except when I asked."

"You're special," she said, her hand cupping Petronilla's face, her thumb brushing her cheek. "Besides, you kicked me out for snoring. I couldn't sleep after that, you know."

Petronilla cringed. "I'm sorry."

"I wasn't criticizing you." Acelina rose from the bed, sheets slipping from her body. Petronilla's throat went dry. Self-consciously, Acelina pulled up the bedsheet to cover her breasts.

"Let me look at you," Petronilla said, standing. She had already slipped on her shirt and dressed before Acelina awoke. Acelina turned away. "What's the matter?"

"You know, the last time you said my breasts were small for a courtesan," Acelina said. Petronilla would've thought she was kidding if it wasn't for the emotion in her voice. "I'm sorry. I seem to be picking bones this morning."

In a flash of movement, Petronilla covered the distance between them in two strides and enveloped Acelina in a back hug. The naked skin of their thighs pressed together, and the bedsheet she held fell to the floor. Petronilla's hands traced their way up, caressing her hips, and drawing patterns on her stomach that quivered with every touch. Acelina shifted, rubbing her hips against Petronilla's.

"The first time I saw you, I thought you were magnificent," Petornilla's voice was husky but serious. She weighed her breasts in her hand. "I thought your breasts were glorious and they'd fit right in my palms..." she went on, brushing a sensitive nipple that pebbled under her touch. "And I was right."

With a swift movement, she swirled her around, bent down, and kissed the valley between her breasts. Acelina gasped, digging her fingers into her hair. Her lieutenant general was full of surprises.

"You're blinded by lust." Acelina's voice was breathy. "I'm sorry for what I said," she said. "I wanted to hurt you

because I thought you were like the people who abused me."

Acelina looked at her hesitantly, trying to gauge the sincerity of her words.

"I believe you," she said, pressing a kiss on Petronilla's cheek.

"Your body is perfection," she went on, turning her attention to the other breast when they parted.

"I get it. You don't have to do this." Acelina's voice was foggy with need.

"Do what?" Petronilla broke away. "Make me feel better," she said.

"That's not what I'm doing," Petronilla said. "You've consumed my every waking thought since that first night. I hate myself for saying those things to you."

"It doesn't matter," Acelina said, her naked body wrapping around Petronilla with equal fervor. Petronilla was as moldable as clay in her arms. "It's all in the past. But hearing you admit your mistakes makes me feel better," she added with an impish smile.

Petronilla's lips trailed down, pressing kisses on her belly. "Let's do it again."

"Time to go to work," Acelina said, patting her shoulder. "If we start this, you'll be late."

"You want me," Petronilla said, taking in her flushed face.

"I also want to salvage my dignity," she said, pointing to shadows lingering outside the doors. The employees had woken up early to witness their employer's blooming love affair. They were stacked one on top of another, almost bursting through the door. Petronilla laughed.

"You're right," she straightened, slipping on all her clothes and striding to the door. "See you tonight," then, after a pause, "Darling."

The employees scrambled away just as the door opened. Several sly gazes were aimed at Petronilla who sailed out without a word.

Acelina dressed, smiling to herself throughout. How long had it been since she'd taken a lover?

Maybe forever. It felt good to have someone to sleep and wake up with. And in her room, of all places, which had always been her private sanctuary.

When she stepped out, she saw six of her employees, all wearing knowing looks. She wasn't going to give them any fodder for gossip, however.

"Time to get to work." Acelina's voice cracked like a whip.

They cleared away, casting each other sly smiles. Turstin, the novice, was left behind. "The last time I checked, your job didn't include keeping an eye on me."

"I'm sorry." Turstin was flustered but the maids cleaning the corridor couldn't smother their obvious grins fast enough. Why was everyone up so early today?

"Where's Rose?" she asked, referring to their cook.

"Sleeping, I think," Turstin said.

"I need to eat." She was ravenous, but all she could feel was joy lighting her body like sunshine.

Acelina checked on Rose's quarters before entering the kitchen for breakfast. The cook, who was supposed to be asleep, was awake now, busy fixing her apron strings. She turned her perceptive eyes to Acelina, laying dishes on the table. There were eggs, toast, and bacon.

"Good morning," Acelina said.

"Good morning." Rose smiled at her, a knowing grin.

News traveled fast here.

"What's for breakfast?" she asked, even though a spread was laid out before her.

"You're not usually up this early." There was a hidden message in the cook's not-so-subtle gaze. "What's the occasion?"

Tact was clearly not her strong point.

"You know what," Acelina said, suppressing a smile.

Rose got on with making oatmeal, whistling a bright tune.

"It is official, then?" She was trying hard to contain a smile.

"I don't know," Acelina said, pressing a cold palm onto her heated face. "I don't know where this is going."

"Life's like that. You don't know what's going on until you do," Rose said, slapping a bowl of oatmeal onto the table. She'd also fried some bacon and eggs to go with it. "You've gotta take whatever comes your way or the opportunity will pass you by. And for the record, I always knew you liked her."

"What gave it away?"

"You argue too much. I've never seen you argue with anyone else."

"Doesn't that mean I hate her?"

"No, it means you're fighting your attraction. There can be no love without hate."

"Who knew you were so perceptive? Maybe I should put you to work in the front," she said, smelling the bacon. All of a sudden, her stomach was queasy, nausea rushing past her throat. Her face took on a pallid coloring, eyes searching for the nearest place to throw up.

"Are you okay?"

Acelina rushed out, humid air hitting her face. Two escorts— Emmeline and Sakura watched her rush past the storage into the garden. Holding onto the wooden pillar for support, she threw up into the gutter, away from the gazes of the curious escorts. Her stomach churned, from hunger and pain. She couldn't remember what she'd eaten last night, but it'd felt alright until this morning when she saw those pieces of bacon.

Her stomach muscles clenched in pain, struggling to throw up the nothing she'd eaten. From the corner of her eye, she saw her staff gather in the corridor, watching curiously as she puked into the gutter. Closing her eyes, she remembered the time Petronilla had run her hands over her back, holding her hair up while she threw up. The thought did her no good because now, her heart began aching with her stomach.

If this kept on, she'd have to see a healer about it.

NINETEEN

PETRONILLA

THE SECRET SERVICE WAS BUSIER THAN USUAL THAT DAY. As Petronilla stepped into the reception area, she saw no sign of Tranagard. Despite the happiness warming her heart, a thread of trepidation coiled in her belly. Felix wasn't going to be happy about last night. She didn't know how to face General Darius yet.

"Petronilla!" His chirpy voice cut through the noise.

Speak of the devil.

"Good morning, General." He appeared alert in a beige shirt today. "How are you feeling?"

"Fit as a fiddle," he said. "Looks like the blurry vision was a temporary thing."

"I'm so glad," she said, a little too honestly. General Darius was known for his quick reflexes and sharp mind. Seeing him so lost due to bad vision was heartbreaking.

"You look...different today," he ventured. The downside

to the return of his sharp senses was being a victim of his perceptiveness. "Did something good happen?"

"N-nothing."

"How is Acelina doing?" The benign question set her on edge.

"Fine," was her monosyllabic reply. "Do you see a lot of her?" Petronilla nodded.

Thankfully, Tranagard's appearance cut their conversation short. His amber eyes examined them. "It's good to see you looking well, General," he ventured cautiously. "Has Petronilla briefed you about last night?"

"Not yet." Darius turned to her.

She closed her eyes, not looking forward to writing a report on last night. "He got away," was all she said.

"Got away? You mean you found him?"

"He was in Duality when I came in," Petronilla said. "I tried to contain him but—" She shook her head. "I'm sorry. I let him get away."

"He smashed a vase on Lieutenant General Petronilla's face." Tranagard made her excuses, but Darius' gaze was fixed on her.

"He doesn't know who Ifer is," Petronilla divulged. "I asked him, but his face was blank."

"At least there's a silver lining," Darius said, but he appeared tense. Petronilla hated to be the one that put him in this mood. She should've caught her father last night. He'd been right in front of her. "Let's go upstairs and tell Felix what we know."

Tranagard went first with Darius and Petronilla following

him. Darius touched her upper arm in a quick gesture. "Don't be too hard on yourself."

"I'm sorry. I'll take responsibility. I was distracted."

"Acelina can be distracting." He smiled. Petronilla stilled on the last stair as Tranagard opened Felix's office door and went in. She would be a fool to underestimate Darius. The question was, how did he know?

"Coming?" he asked.

"Y-yes." She shook the thoughts away and entered.

When Petronilla walked home that night, the red-light district, with its cheap red lights and gaudy decorations, appeared beautiful to her. Her body felt light and agile, itching to jump and touch the clouds. She had touched the clouds last night when they made love. A blush crept across her cheeks, spreading to her ears. Running a finger over her lips, she felt the remnants of their morning kiss.

After last night's debacle, Darius, Petronilla, and Felix had spent the whole day tracing her father's whereabouts. Like Acelina, Darius too believed that her father would be back to see her, hence the best way to bait him was to frequent the areas he went to. Other than The Rose, Blu, and Duality, he'd been to the market at the center of the red-light district. She had a feeling that he'd evacuated the red-light district completely. There was no trace of him.

Tomorrow, she'd visit the inns and pleasure houses Felix's guards missed that night. But for tonight, all she wanted was to see Acelina's face again. Tranagard believed there was a chance he would visit Duality again, so Petronilla needed to stay there, just in case. She, on the other hand, didn't think her father would make the same mistake twice.

Petronilla crept up the back garden, which was buzzing with activity. Several patrons stood out, excited and chatting. Passing by the crowd, she ducked her way under an errant branch and entered the living quarters.

Two solitary lanterns decorated the corridor. The light in Acelina's room was off, so Petronilla guessed she must be in the main building. Their sleep timings were the opposite. Petronilla worked all morning and slept all night while Acelina worked all night and slept all morning.

It was an especially humid day. Dust mingled with sweat on her skin and became grime during her walk between the buildings. As soon as she entered through the back, she heard the clanking of pots and pans in the kitchen and frenzied shouts. Throwing the kitchen door open, she stood to look at a battlefield. Several maids and cooks helped Rose who barked out orders without a pause. All the stoves and surfaces were occupied. Serving maids collected bottles of wine and refreshments while cooks fried food on autopilot.

"Petronilla?" Somehow Rose spotted her amidst the chaos. Her light eyes were rimmed with dark circles, and she wore an apron that disguised her grey dress. They stared for a moment as if Rose wanted to say something but was too busy to remember what.

"Uh...good evening." Petronilla squeezed herself in, wading through an army of annoyed maids and chattering serving girls. Steam rose in the air. Dishes piled up in the sink, which the maid was trying to wash at a breakneck speed.

She smelled a mixture of delicious food- fried potatoes, rich meats decorated beautifully in ceramic plates, the savory smell of garlic and ginger. As she reached the main stove, she smelled fish, looking at a whole fish being bathed in an exotic oily mixture of chilies and spices by Rose.

"Did you need something?" Rose wiped a bead of sweat on her forehead with her shoulder. "We're really busy today."

"I'll come back later." Petronilla stepped back, threading past kitchen staff running in and out.

"Acelina is at the reception." Rose's eyes were trained on the food. "We have a lot of customers tonight."

Rose's words were swallowed up by a serving maid's rushing in. Petronilla left, walking back to the storage room. She didn't want to disturb Acelina while she was working, and she needed a bath badly.

A flicker of streetlight entered in a single ray from the narrow window on her ceiling. She lit candles but decided against placing the lampshade on them at the last minute. The light revealed worn-out wooden floors, crates stacked to the ceiling, and a solitary twin bed made of iron with white bedding. On a crate, Petronilla had stacked her belongings, deciding to use them as a nightstand. Her clothes were placed in a bag on a high crate where the pests couldn't eat them.

The number of rodents and bugs had reduced since the cleaning, but the storage was still stuffy owing to a lack of windows. Petronilla went to the bathing area first, deciding to fill a bucket with water but changed her mind when she saw a wooden tub. She needed a proper bath tonight. The tub was light and made of wood, so Petronilla carried it back to her room. She had to clear some stuff to make space for it but it fit in. She then began filling it with water from the water pump outside. After carrying pails of water up and down, she looked proudly at a full bathtub. How she was going to put it back was a question she didn't want to contemplate yet.

Stripping her clothes off, she grabbed hold of a bar of soap and placed it on the crate next to her, and sank into the water. The cold water soaked up the stresses of the day, making the grime dissolve. As the rest of her stresses melted away, the questions buzzing at the back of her mind remained like rocks during low tide. She wanted to find her father, now, more than ever. But her mind kept going back to last night. One part of her wanted to get the entire thing over with and leave this place, while another wanted to hold on to whatever it was she and Acelina had going on between them. Sighing, Petronilla reached for the soap.

The door creaked open, making her turn abruptly. She hunched. A flicker of candlelight penetrated the room, followed by a pale face.

"Acelina." Her thoughts skittered to a halt. She felt the cool air brush her wet, exposed skin.

"Rose told me you were back."

The proprietress stood between the door and frame, watching the room overflowing with lit candles. Petronilla preferred solitude for thinking, but with Acelina standing before her, watching her naked in the tub, she lost all capacity for rational thought. The proprietress' tongue stuck out and licked her lips which were red as sin. She wore dark-colored silk that was either blue or black and revealed her shoulders and a perfect amount of cleavage.

"You've got a romantic streak," she said, pointing to the multitude of candles Petronilla lit around the tub. "This setting calls for something more than just a bath, don't you think?"

Acelina quickly shut the door, locked herself in, and placed the candle on a carton next to the door frame. The candlelight painted Petronilla's exposed shoulders and arms in an artistic light and shadow portrait, the clear water thinly veiling her body. Her legs which were too long to fit in the tub dangled over the edge, droplets of water sliding down her calves.

Acelina edged closer silently, as if unable to speak. Petronilla sank deeper into the bathtub, wanting what was coming next but scared at the same time.

"I thought you were working tonight."

Acelina sunk on the floor behind her, skirts billowing on the wooden floor. "I can spare a few minutes for you." Her breath caressed Petronilla's neck as she sat behind her. Their eyes met, lust for lust in the darkened room, and bathing was forgotten.

"How far along are you?" she asked, picking up the bar of soap.

"Just started." Petronilla smiled, her legs hooked on the edge of the bathtub. "How did you know where to find me?"

"This is your room, isn't it?" Acelina's fingers splayed over Petronilla's shoulder, massaging the tight muscles of her neck.

"Ummm..." a moan escaped, her muscles loosening under Acelina's touch.

"You like it." Acelina continued plying the sore muscles loose, lathering her back with soap. The soap slid down her arms. She sat forward so that Acelina could reach the rest of her back. The soap bar slid down her spine as Acelina's fingers explored every indentation.

"You can touch me anywhere and I'd like it," she said, resting her back on the wooden edge of the tub now that Acelina had splashed water over it.

Acelina continued her exploration. "Really?" She flicked her thumb at the bottom of Petronilla's neck, stroking down, flicking soap over her collarbone. Petronilla's core tightened, buzzing with anticipation. Acelina's fingers moved lower, dancing on her wet, bronze skin until they reached the swell of her breasts. From there, she inched downward, flicking a teasing touch over her nipple.

"Ummmmm...." Another moan made her throw her head back. She relaxed, resting her head on Acelina's shoulder. Acelina's firm fingers cupped her breasts, kneading them with soap-covered hands.

"How about here?" she asked. "I like it."

"Just like?" Her breath broke on Petronilla's shoulder, indicating she'd moved in. Before Petronilla had a chance to react, her lips were on her ear, licking a bead of water that traveled down to her neck, nibbling her collarbone, then sliding between her breasts. Sensations danced on her skin.

"Oh, god." Her knees wobbled, desire flickering to life. "Stand up," Acelina said. "I can't reach the rest of your body."

Petronilla looked at her for a second, then, clutching the edge of the tub, stood up. Water slid down her naked skin in a storm of droplets. Only the part below her knees remained submerged in the pool of cool liquid. Acelina's breath whooshed out of her lungs from the look of it. Her gaze raked

Petronilla's completely naked wet body, her eyes drinking in the sight.

"Have I told you you're the most beautiful person I've seen?" Acelina asked. "That body is every woman's dream."

Petronilla smiled a shy, hesitant smile. On the inside, she felt a little light come on.

"I'd like to make every fantasy come true. I want to spend all night exploring you, kissing every inch of your skin." Acelina's fully clothed body stood two inches from her, the courtesan's soft fingers brushing her lower lip. "I don't know if one night will be enough." Her legs shook. "I don't know how my legs haven't given out already." A broken laugh followed.

"Come here." Petronilla's arms snaked around Acelina's waist and pulled her in for a kiss. She felt the warm brush of silk, smooth against her damp skin. Their lips met. Acelina's hands slid to steady her back, and Petronilla's mouth hungrily ravished hers, tasting a faint whiff of lemon and mint. She nibbled at Acelina's lower lip, every cell of her becoming one with Acelina. For those few moments, the world was theirs, time and space a mere illusion. Acelina stepped back, their mouths melded, their tongues dueling, as her back hit the wall. She groaned at the slight contact but didn't let go. That kiss was a drug, making them feverish and hungry with each stroke of the tongue, plunging them deeper into an oblivion from which there was no recovery. Every wet stroke, every touch was igniting a firecracker inside her.

Acelina broke the kiss, getting hold of the bar of soap.

"Let me finish what I started." Her breathing was ragged, her eyes hazy.

"We're still going to pretend you're bathing me?"

Acelina smiled, then set the soap aside. "You'll need another bath once I'm done with you."

"I'm looking forward to it," Petronilla said, as Acelina's lips trailed down her neck. Her kiss was deep and intense, a little teeth pressure joining her lips and tongue.

"You're going to mark me." Petronilla couldn't think, lost in a fog of pleasure. Her nerve endings came to life, aching for Acelina's touch. Her other hand traveled down her back, cupping her ass, squeezing it.

"I already have," Acelina said, parting her lips. Cool air brushed over exposed skin, craving the feel of her lips again. The courtesan's fingers gently rubbed the spot she'd kissed and sucked, trying to help blood flow. She pulled her hand away. "You're mine."

The streak of possessiveness made her heart hammer. She didn't want to examine what that meant yet, urging Acelina to go on. From there, Acelina went on to lick her way down her breasts, suckling each nipple until they puckered. She lost control, feeling a heady ache building between her legs. She groaned, the guttural sound spurring her forward.

Acelina pushed Petronilla back against the wall. Then, she spotted Petronilla's bed and guided her there. Once Petronilla's back was pressed to the sheets, Acelina climbed over her. "I like you so much better when you're naked." There was only room for one in the twin bed that creaked with the pressure of them, but they'd have to make do. Laying out Petronilla like a feast, Acelina backed off, sliding off the bed.

"Where are you going?"

Acelina kissed her toes, one at a time, taking the smallest

one in her mouth. Petronilla decided to just lie and back and be eaten alive. Her nerves were filled with liquid fire, her body feverish, aching, and ecstatic like it'd never been. "I love every part of you." Acelina resumed kissing her way up Petronilla's wet calf. "I really liked it when you did this last time."

"You weren't kidding when you said you were going to kiss every inch of me." Petronilla's voice was terse but light. "You're going to shatter me."

"That was the idea." Acelina's wicked lips moved to her knee, then up and up until she felt a kiss on her inner thigh. Tension coiled inside her belly. Acelina's head shot up, and she pressed a kiss to Petronilla's stomach, her thumb rubbing circles on it. Petronilla quivered, and all escape routes closed. Pleasure was the only option open to her.

The feel of Acelina's silk garments on her wet skin was something she'd never experienced before. Longing to feel soft skin on soft skin, she tore at the low shoulder, her other hand undoing Acelina's sash. The kimono loosened, even as their contact intensified.

"Acelina..." she moaned her name when Acelina kissed her inner thigh again, turning her legs to jelly. Her body was as moldable as clay, completely surrendering to Acelina's pleasuring. "I'm... ready for you."

She felt her release building, making her body burn like a flame. Acelina's lips continued to tease the other thigh.

Though pleasure tore at her, she felt a small knot of trepidation build up at the base of her stomach.

"Acelina." Her body was tight as a string.

"Patience." Acelina's fingers reached the apex of her

thighs, and she pushed them apart. Petronilla's heart began hammering faster. The pleasure began to drain as air brushed her opening. She shut her eyes tightly, determined to block out the terror that poisoned her system. Her arms clenched, and all the pleasure Acelina had given her became dark as smoke. Acelina's fingers found her core, thumb massaging the wet opening, priming for penetration.

The minute she felt that solid weight brush against her entrance, Petronilla stilled. Memories washed over her, drowning out the ecstasy she was so close to achieving. She associated penetration with pain, remembering all the times men had pushed into her. She remembered the horror, the pain, the shame, and the guilt. Every muscle went rigid, and her thighs clamped shut, trapping Acelina's hand.

"What happened?" Acelina asked, pulling her hand back instinctively.

Her body fought the exposure, the uncomfortable sensation of having her legs wide, open, and vulnerable for someone to exploit. She hated being under someone who held power over her. Every time she had been penetrated, she'd felt violated. Now, all those feelings washed over her, as she struggled to keep her tears at bay. She was so close to giving in but couldn't let go of that last shred of resistance. Forcing her eyes closed, Petronilla felt her eyes heat with tears.

"I'm sorry...."

Her eyes blurred, dredging up unpleasant memories. The ceiling appeared fuzzy, tears clamoring like needles at the back of her eyes.

"What's wrong, darling?" Acelina's thumb brushed the

tears that stained her cheeks. Her dark eyes loomed over Petronilla, softening with concern. "You're crying."

Petronilla had never thought she'd be the one to cry while being made love to. It wasn't her first time, after all. But you live and you learn. She held her arms over her face, trying to shield herself from embarrassment

"I'm sorry...I...just can't..." she said, swallowing any coherent words in sobs. "Can we try again?" She tried to open her thighs, but they wouldn't move. They were stuck in place, heavy like iron.

"We don't have to do anything you don't want to," Acelina said, laying a hand on her elbow. She slid off her, coming to sit on the edge of the bed. Petronilla's tears silently fell as Acelina sat there and watched her, a hand holding Petronilla's. Petronilla felt strength entering her where their fingers intertwined. She still lay on the bed, unable to move.

Her body still thrummed with remnants of Acelina's touch, but fear tore pleasure to shreds, reducing it to dread. Her knees came up, clamped even tighter now. A sinking dread permeated one side of her mind, while a keen sense of loss lit up the other. Acelina let her hand go, walking across the room to bring back a towel. She laid it over Petronilla.

"Do you want me to dry you?" Petronilla grabbed the towel and wrapped it around herself. It soaked the moisture on her body, leaving her shuddering. With her back against the headrest, she numbly stared at the ray of light that filled the room. The candles had burned down, three of them going out, leaving only two lit.

"I'm sorry," she whispered, her voice sounding distant even to her ears.

"It's okay." Acelina sat beside her. "Can I hold you?"

Petronilla rested her head on Acelina's shoulder as her arms came around her body. Acelina was tinier than her, but her body seemed to contain a warmth hers didn't.

"I...I don't like being violated," she confessed. "It reminds me of... the past."

"I wouldn't hurt you, you know that." The concern in Acelina's eyes touched the depths of her soul. Her thumb grazed Petronilla's cheek, blotting the last of her tears.

"I know," she said, holding Acelina's arm. "My mind knows but my body reacts on instinct."

"Let's stop here for today," Acelina said, Petronilla's head resting on her breast. "We can try again when you're feeling better."

"I'm sorry," Petronilla began, lingering on the edge of the bed. The dread in her belly was nowhere near dissipating. Even though she should leave, she felt whatever they'd started tonight wasn't over yet.

"You don't have to apologize," Acelina said, pressing a kiss on her wet cheek. "I shouldn't have rushed...knowing your history."

"No," Petronilla shook her head. "It isn't your fault. I never told you." She moved in closer, hugging Acelina who now sat beside her. "It was dreadful...all those years, I just wanted to run away. If Darius hadn't come for me, I would've killed myself."

"Oh, dear..." Acelina held her, while she poured her heart out. The air stilled as Petronilla let silence be a prelude to her tale.

"I...I was sold to a pleasure house at twelve," she swallowed the discomfort and went on. She'd never told anyone this before, but she owed Acelina an explanation, at least. Petronilla disengaged from the embrace and rested her head on Acelina's shoulder, their backs pressed against the head-rest of the cot. Acelina's fingers raked through her hair, and she found it oddly calming.

"That night when Darius came in, hoping for a rest, I held a knife to his throat and said I'd kill him and go to prison because at least that way I would be able to get out of that place." She swallowed ugly scenes from those days passing before her eyes. Acelina's fingers tightened in her hair. "From the day my father left me there, I wanted nothing but to get away. For the first two years, the madame made me work as a maid. I didn't like the work but at least it was honest work. I pitied the escorts who had no choice in the use of their body. Who knew I'd become one of them myself?" she scoffed. "I hated those men, each one of them."

"They forced you." Acelina's voice was light and full of understanding.

"I always knew I wasn't attracted to men," Petronilla said. "The other girls would talk about how guys made their hearts flutter, but I felt none of that. The only person that made my heart flutter was...." She trailed off, closing her eyes. "I probably shouldn't tell you this."

Acelina caressed her shoulders patiently. "You probably should."

"Every night, I entertained a new man, and every night, I grew more and more disillusioned. I felt nothing for them, and the minutes spent in a man's arms were pure agony to me."

"Did you tell anyone how you felt?"

She shook her head. "Back then, relationships between people of the same sex were prohibited in Terra," she said. "I had no choice but to take in men. Sometimes what I did worked, but mostly it didn't. I had no idea how to please them, and on days more than one customer complained about me, the madame would make me starve."

"And there was Maddie..." She trailed off, her vision blurry again. "Even now, I wonder about her...Would we have ended up together if she hadn't betrayed me? She was so kind...she brought me food, and when I failed to escape, she came to get me, bringing me food in the room downstairs where I was locked."

"She was your first love." Acelina's voice was breathy, but her fingers still caressed. It was strange to be talking about her first love in front of Acelina, knowing how possessive she was. She deserved to know.

"It's all in the past. But yes, that's what I believed," Petronilla said, her throat tight. "She was eight years older than me and taught me the ropes of being a maid. When I hit puberty, I knew what I felt for her was more than friendship...." Her grip on Acelina's arm tightened.

"I'm here," she said, interlacing her fingers in Petronilla's. "I was young back then and couldn't comprehend what I was feeling." She was making excuses, worried her story would unsettle Acelina.

"I know," Acelina said. "Tell me about Maddie. I can handle the truth."

"I loved her...whatever I knew of love at that age," she said, her eyes misty. "She was the sunshine in my dreary world, and I thought someday we'd run away to Inferno and start a new life here. But..." She willed her choked throat to open. "She left me in a room one day, dressed in fine clothes, and told me when a man came in, I shouldn't resist. It'd go easier that way."

"Oh, dear..." Acelina's eyes turned misty, and she embraced Petronilla. Petronilla's head was cushioned in Acelina's clothing, but she continued talking.

"When I confronted her about it, she broke down and said the madame agreed to let her go if she inducted me into the profession. Maddie was pregnant with her lover's child, and they planned on getting married. When I heard that, I felt abandoned. For days, I told myself that it was a lie...that it'd go away. I'd always thought she loved me but carrying another man's child...was the most physical form of betrayal. It hit me hard. The madame gave her some money, and I never saw her again."

"That's not loving," Acelina said. "She was cruel to you. She sold her friend."

"I know," Petronilla confessed. "But it broke my heart, anyway." The smell of Acelina's faint jasmine perfume filled her nostrils. "Every time someone tries to...penetrate me...I remember those men," she went on. "That's why I swore off drinking and sex...it reminds me...of them..."

"Have you told anyone about this?" Acelina asked, now soothing her back.

"Only you," she said.

"Thank you," she said, squeezing her arm. "For trusting me. I know it was hard for you."

Sitting on the bed naked and depleted, Petronilla didn't

feel vulnerable. She felt safe, enveloped in Acelina's arms. Inside her heart, it was a riot, unknown feelings bubbling to its surface. She wanted to put a name to that emotion but was too afraid to.

"I should get dressed." She broke from Acelina's grasp. "And eat something."

Fishing out new clothes from one of the crates, Petronilla slipped them on, aware all the while that Acelina sat behind her, observing quietly.

"I'll get back to work," she said, reaching for the candle next to the door. "I'll send someone to get rid of the tub and some food."

"Don't bother," Petronilla said. "I'll clean up myself."

"But..."

"I need some time." Petronilla's voice was low.

"I understand." Acelina stood and picked up her lantern. Petronilla heard the door open. Their eyes met. "Sleep well."

Acelina's tiny voice was gone as soon as the door shut with a quiet thud.

TWENTY

PETRONILLA

PETRONILLA COULDN'T SLEEP THAT NIGHT. SHE TOSSED and turned, hoping the morning would come, but at seven in the morning, there was no sign of life. Boring holes in the darkness, Petronilla cuddled a pillow between her legs, trying to clamp down the thread of frustration that remained even after she had eaten dinner. Mosquitoes sucked her blood, but she didn't care. The scene from earlier that evening kept replaying in her mind, pausing over her teary confession. With the truth out in the open, her heart felt much lighter. Was this what people meant when they talked of shared burdens?

Petronilla had never imagined herself divulging these intimate details of her life to anyone before, but telling Acelina about her past felt right. Even now, she knew she'd been right to trust her. She shut her eyes, forcing her brain to sleep to no avail.

As Petronilla mulled over thoughts, the lights outside

dimmed and sounds faded. For another hour or so, she lay on the bed, watching the last of the corridor lights go out. Then, she stood up and ventured out, her next course of action clear in her mind. Hesitation was not her strong suit. She was a lieutenant general, and good at making quick decisions.

The passage outside Acelina's room was dark. Nobody roamed the corridor at this hour, and that meant all the candles were gone. Petronilla could see well in the dark, so she hadn't brought along a candle. Her feet attached them- selves outside Acelina's door, registering the darkness inside. She knew Acelina was asleep, but that didn't stop her from gathering her fingers into a fist.

A knock resounded.

She pulled her hand back and waited.

At first, there was no reply. She knocked again. This time, she heard something hard hit the floor and Acelina's sleepy moaning. A candle flame came on within seconds, its fuzzy light seeping through the edges of the door. The door opened soon after, and Acelina stood there, a candle burning behind her.

The flickering candlelight Acelina held illuminated her sleepy face, as her other hand suppressed a yawn. A translu- cent nightgown flowed over her curves, and she wore no makeup now, her unadorned pink lips and black eyes contrasting her magnolia skin.

"Petronilla?" Her head poked out and looked around the corridor. "Is something wrong?"

The sight of Acelina made her heart quicken. Her eyes trailed to the rosebud lips, bare and utterly kissable, and moved further down.

"I want to try again." Petronilla's voice was low, her eyes holding Acelina in their intense gaze.

"What?" She rubbed her eyes, angling her head to catch Petronilla's face.

"I want to finish what we started this evening."

"Now?" Acelina was taken aback, her eyes opened wide.

All traces of sleepiness left her face.

"I'm sorry. If you're tired, we can try again tomorrow—" Petronilla turned to leave, but Acelina caught her arm.

"No. Come in," she said, sliding the door open.

Petronilla was pulled inside, and once they were both in, Acelina slid the door shut, and held the candle up, examining Petronilla. "You're nervous." She swallowed and nodded. Acelina placed the candle on her desk, and asked, "Should I put it out?"

"No. I want to see you." Acelina blinked, appearing touched by those words. "And I want you to see me."

"I'll leave it burning, then." She moved to the bed, pulling the covers aside. "Do you want anything to drink?"

"No." Acelina sat on the bed, motioning Petronilla to sit next to her. "I couldn't sleep." Their eyes met, and Acelina read the redness in her eyes.

"No?"

"No."

"Was it the rats?" Acelina leaned back, slipping under the silk covers.

"No."

"Come on." She held the duvet up, signaling Petronilla to get in.

She slipped into bed, next to Acelina, who snuggled close.

"So, what brought on this sudden change of heart?" she asked, reaching for Petronilla's shirt button. Petronilla's hand covered hers, and she stopped.

"I couldn't stop thinking about you...what happened earlier." The candlelight illuminated Acelina's face, and her nervousness was mirrored in her eyes. She let her hand slide away and felt a cool brush of air on her skin where the buttons had parted to reveal her breasts.

"Let's take it slow," Acelina said, pulling her shirt out, and away. "Tell me what you want." Acelina's fingers moved to the button of her pants, and her stomach clenched. The fingers stopped.

"Keep going." Petronilla's voice was tight.

"You're not going to the gallows," Acelina said. "Relax."

"I know. I'm sorry." Petronilla felt control slipping through her fingers.

"Sorry again?" Acelina asked. "You woke me up at seven to be sorry?"

"I'm..." She exhaled roughly. "This played out differently in my head."

Acelina laughed. "What were we doing in your head?" Petronilla held her hand and guided her to the button,

breaking it open. She wriggled out of her pants, kicking them onto the floor. Her hands skimmed Acelina's shoulders, parting the thin straps. She pulled up the nightdress from the bottom, and Acelina pulled herself up, letting Petronilla pull it over her head. Their naked bodies brushed against each other, tentative and questioning.

"What else did we do in your head?" Acelina's musical laughter chimed.

"This."

Their lips met in a passionate kiss. Limbs meshed and legs intertwined, Petronilla suckled Acelina's lower lip that tasted of fruit wine. Acelina hips ground against hers, setting the flame between them alight. She lightly nibbled on her lip until Petronilla struggled to find her next breath. Their eyes met again, and the kiss intensified until they were numb with pleasure. Acelina's tongue darted into her mouth, hot and needy. The smoothness of her skin exemplified Petronilla's own.

"You've got a lot of energy for someone who spent the whole day working," Petronilla rasped, kissing them and pulling them apart in a teasing rhythm. Her hands slid down Acelina's body cupping her bare ass. She loved that ass.

"When it comes to you, I'm insatiable." Acelina trailed kisses down her jaw, stopping to gently brush one on the love bite she'd given her earlier. The candle flickered over Petronilla's skin, illuminating the mark. "You're going to have to find a way to hide that."

"Are you regretting giving me a love bite?"

"No," Acelina said, continuing the descent of her lips. "I love knowing you carry some part of me with you. That you're mine."

Her lips hovered over Petronilla's breasts, pulling the sheets down. In the candlelight, Petronilla now saw scars on her hands, stomach, under her breast, and on her legs. They were visible starkly, despite it being darker than before. She pulled away, self-conscious. Acelina's eyes followed the trail, pausing over each of them, making Petronilla's heart beat faster. Compared to Acelina's flawless skin, hers was a patchwork of unpleasant memories. She reached for the bedsheet, pulling it up, but Acelina stopped her. "I know they can be too much. Maybe we should just—"

Acelina kissed one on her upper arm, sending shudders down her spine. "I wonder how long it'll take to kiss them all."

"Oh, we'll be here all night," Petronilla said. "I've been accumulating scars for a long time."

"I like this one too," Her lips moved to a brown line on her stomach with serrated edges. "How did you get this?" She ran a finger over the damp flesh, making Petronilla's belly tighten with molten heat.

"I was stabbed," she replied, nonchalantly. Acelina quirked a charcoal eyebrow. "It was several years ago. Luckily one of my comrades found a healer, and we managed to stitch the wound."

"Your job is dangerous," Acelina remarked, proceeding to kiss the scar under her breast.

"Not so much anymore," Petronilla admitted. "We haven't had any major battles in a while."

"That's a good thing, isn't it?" Acelina was moving down, pressing a kiss on another long scar—an old burn scar— that lined her right thigh. Acelina kissed her way up, all the way to the inside of her thighs, under the nest of dark curls. Up closer, Acelina noticed it had a pattern. Her head snapped up. "The pleasure house branded you here?"

To Petronilla's ears, that sounded like a soft shriek. "Back in the day, that's how they did it."

"Not here," Acelina said. "For the record, we don't brand people at Duality. But I was branded once." She held up her hand and showed Petronilla a scar under her upper arm. "It hurt to have hot iron stamped on my skin. That's why I don't do it to others."

"I'm so glad to hear that." Petronilla pulled Acelina down, and held up her arm, kissing the branding. "I didn't notice this before."

"Neither did I." Acelina backed off, running her finger over Petronilla's inner thighs. "It looked like just another scar."

Acelina pressed another kiss to the star branded on her inner thigh. Petronilla had been uncomfortable when she discovered another star at the base of her spine. Now, she was glad it was her.

"With that, you know every last one of my secrets," Petronilla said. "I don't know how I feel about that."

"Do you trust me?" Petronilla heard a quiver of vulnerability in Acelina's voice.

"I do," she said, finding her voice. "I do."

At that, Acelina put a hand between her thighs, urging them to part. Petronilla fought the uncomfortable feeling of exposure that made her skin prickle. Petronilla's brain clamped shut, her thighs freezing mid-way.

Acelina looked up. "Having second thoughts?" "I..." her throat closed up. "I'm sorry..."

"Tell me what to do to make you feel safe," Acelina asked, kissing her thigh. Her heart warmed, letting her legs loosen.

"Let me do it," Petronilla said. Acelina backed off, letting Petronilla open her legs of her own volition. It took her a few seconds and a lot of deep breaths and sighs to manage to get her thighs far enough. "Take me."

Acelina laughed. "You look like you're laying down your life for the country," she said. "Let go, Petronilla."

"Easy for you to say."

When she nodded, Acelina's head bent down. "What happened to you wasn't sex, it was...a crude display of power." A ragged moan escaped Petronilla as Acelina's breath fanned her intimate curls. "But this," her tongue licked the sensitive spot between Petronilla's thighs, reducing her to a puddle of desperation, "this is lovemaking." Her voice came out raspy and breathless. Wicked lips pressed a kiss to Petronilla's hot core, burning with desire for Acelina. Only then did she realize she'd opened for Acelina. "Sex isn't about domination or control," she said, another hot lick penetrating her core. "It's about allowing yourself to be vulnerable." Her tongue reached into her sensitive folds, licking and teasing its way to her bundle of nerves. "Let yourself go. Surrender to this..." Acelina's tongue teased its way inside. "I'll start you off gently."

"You call that gentle?" Petronilla's fingers dug into the sheets, knuckles turning white. "I'm dying here."

"You have no patience, darling." The vibrations made her writhe. In exquisite torture, Acelina's mouth captured her clit, teasing her with wet strokes of her tongue. An intense pleasure broke through her senses, making her cry out. She was so close to coming, she could feel it.

"High-strung already?" Acelina backed off, kissing her way down her thighs. Her finger reached out into her wet, hot opening, gently prying it open. When one finger pushed inside, she came undone.

Centuries of desire burst forth. "Oh...my...god...."

Acelina inserted one more finger, stretching her, and breaking her, opening her. When a third finger joined in, rubbing against her sensitive spot, she surrendered. Her body shattered, the residue of her past leaving behind lightness. She came with a scream. Her body quaked with release, every cell, and nerve ending awash with bliss. Her body cracked open, and she experienced a force greater than herself. It consumed her entire being. For one short moment, Petronilla thought she'd never come back to the world of the living.

Acelina's head popped up, a sly smile curving on her lips. "You alive?"

"This is the best thing that's ever happened to me." Acelina nudged her, coming to lie down beside her. "You're the best thing that has ever happened to me."

They lay side-by-side, sated and spent, watching the ceiling. The sole candle had burned out, abandoning them to the dark.

"You're a lot of work," Acelina said, finding a cloth to dab between her thighs.

"I'll do it." Petronilla snatched the cloth from her and cleaned herself. Acelina rested her back on the bed, still naked with sweat condensing on her body. Throwing the cloth away, she said, "I feel..."

Transformed.

"Like the world has shifted on its axis...Like I've been born again..."

"Well, that's the best compliment I've received all month." Acelina smiled, putting away the cloth. They lay side by side, fingers interlaced in each other.

Their eyes met. "Thank you," she said. "That word doesn't even begin to describe what I feel for you."

"You're welcome, darling." She put a hand on Petronilla's sweaty face. Petronilla saw the exhaustion on her face and felt a little guilty.

"I should go. You need to sleep." She slipped off the bed, but Acelina caught her, pulling her back up.

"Where are you going?" Acelina asked.

"Back to the storage." She blinked, finding her clothes on the floor.

"You don't have to," Acelina said, tugging at her arm. "Stay."

Acelina let her hand go, but Petronilla held on. "What if the others find out?"

"They already know." Acelina shrugged. "News travels fast in Duality."

Petronilla lay on the bed, propping herself up on the arm to face Acelina. "Are you sure?"

"Yes. I can't make you sleep in the storage after this. What kind of lover would that make me?"

Lover.

They were lovers.

Petronilla smiled. "A bad one?"

"Starting today, this is your room too." Petronilla was speechless. She pressed her hand to Acelina's in silent gratitude. "It was killing me inside to make you sleep in the storage with rats," Acelina confessed, suppressing a yawn. She couldn't summon the energy to pull her clothes back on.

"The rats are not that bad," Petronilla said, spooning Acelina. "But I like you better."

Their fingers interlaced together and lay before Acelina's stomach. They stared at the candle. Silence filled the gaps in their conversation, abandoning them to peace in the end. Petronilla only thought about sleep once she heard Acelina's snoring.

Smiling, she whispered, "Good night." And, with their bodies huddled together, she slept like a baby.

TWENTY-ONE

PETRONILLA

PETRONILLA PULLED HER COLLAR HIGHER IN AN unsuccessful attempt to hide the love bite on her neck. It was blazing hot in Inferno, so turtlenecks were a lost cause. She'd slipped out of bed three hours after their lovemaking, making sure Acelina still snored soundly. Her heart was lighter than it had been in decades. Now, she had someone to share herself with. Petronilla frowned as she passed by the row of red lanterns, watching her reflection progress in the canal. She liked being marked by Acelina, she decided. It was proof that there was someone she belonged with.

As she entered the palace area, she spotted a shadow that merged with hers. Moss green eyes half-shut with exhaustion looked at her.

"At least one of us had a good night," Darius smirked, his eyes fixed on her love bite. This time, she pulled her collar up and blushed. "No need to be shy." She cleared her throat. "I spent all night trying to track down a criminal."

"I'm sorry." She lowered her head.

"No, it's better this way. I found some information." His eyes lit up. "Do you know about Skera?"

Petronilla's heart pounded, and she hoped it hadn't come to the worst. "Yes," came her breathless reply. "The King of Terra owns the country, but they want independence. So far, their attempts haven't gone anywhere."

"That's right. It looks like one of the leaders of the rebellion wants evidence to hold over the king's head should a revolution break out," he said.

"The letters..." Petronilla quickly made the connection. "Now, we just need to figure out where they are meeting."

"The docks," he declared. "You're not going to like this..." He rubbed his eyes. "They are meeting on a ship headed for Skera. Once the exchange is complete, your father will flee to Skera."

"Where neither Inferno nor Terra will be able to get hold of him," Petronilla finished, gritting her teeth in frustration. "How soon can we get him?"

Darius shook his head. "Tonight," he said. "There's a ship leaving Skera from Inferno tonight. I think he'll use the first opportunity he has to get out of here now that he knows we're on his trail."

"Then, that's where I'll be," she said. "I won't let him get away this time."

Darius watched her for a moment, a strange mixture of emotions crossing his face. "I'll tell Tranagard. Meet me there in the evening."

TWENTY-TWO

ACELINA

THE EVENING CAME, IMMERSING DUALITY IN A FLURRY of activity. Customers flowed through the door like a river, and all her escorts were occupied instantly. When the flood died down, Acelina sat in her room and counted the money she'd made. There were so many notes, as usual. Lily had counted them with her and noted the amount before going to sleep. Now, Acelina sat alone in her room, ears straining to hear any sound of the door opening.

She remembered why she'd run away from the pleasure house where she was working several years ago, determined to take charge of her destiny. She was in charge of her destiny now. She'd built her palace, her sanctuary from the ground up and now it towered over the red-light district. Her high standards were what made Duality a success. The years had passed peacefully, but they'd left a need for more. She was still as alone as she'd been the day she ran away from the pleasure house with nothing but a few coins. She was only half a person, having no existence of her own other than as the proprietress of Duality. She liked her life, but sometimes she craved to be seen for who she was— a human being with flaws and feelings.

Last night had shown her another possibility. This morning had cemented her resolve. The warmth of their embraces lingered, but the warmth was rapidly being replaced by a deep longing. She'd watched the door all evening, waiting for her stubborn lieutenant general, secretly disappointed when someone else showed up. Even after the last customer was gone, she didn't arrive.

Acelina locked up the money and stood up, going to check on the front door. A dark corridor greeted her, the lights having been put out by the escorts who had taken off to sleep. Acelina emerged outside, watching the flower petals fall into the pond. She watched them create ripples on the surface. And she watched the gate until she was sure the shadows were nothing but shrubs and trees. The night droned on, stinging her bleary eyes until nobody was left on the porch except her. All her muscles ached, but her heart wouldn't give up. A shadow emerged behind her and, filling with hope, she whirled around.

"I have been waiting." The words died when she looked into Turstin's face, instead of Petronilla's. His curly hair was messy after a long night and dark eyes that were going red looked at her.

"Aren't you going to sleep?" Turstin asked, suppressing a yawn.

"Why aren't you asleep?" she asked.

"I just finished cleaning," he said. "What about you?" His eyes darted to the back entrance. "Waiting for someone?"

"I'll stay a little longer," she said, resting her face on her palms. "You go on first."

"Okay...good night," Turstin said. He didn't move away, though. "Lieutenant General Petronilla is late tonight. She's usually back by the time we open."

"Something must've come up." Her eyelids drooped but she rubbed them constantly in an attempt to stay awake. Turstin's shadow vanished, and she was relieved when she heard his door close.

She'd missed Petronilla all evening, reminded of her every time a customer came in. Her red silk kimono had been chosen with care to seduce, but she'd taken no customers. She didn't think she could sleep with anyone else after last night. The prickly lieutenant general had left an indelible mark on her heart. And it burned every time she was away.

So, she watched the night fade, surrendering to dreams on the hard wooden floor.

TWENTY-THREE

PETRONILLA

THE DOCKS APPEARED HAUNTED AT NIGHT EVEN THOUGH there was a huge crowd. A veil of mist spread over the water, ships appearing like sea monsters with their large bodies. The blood moon looked down on them, and a row of streetlamps that looked like gigantic candles lit the harbor, going all the way to the city. General Darius and Petronilla stood several feet away at the entrance, watching for any sign of her father or someone from Skera. Tranagard was on the ship to Skera, disguised as a sailor. Several of his colleagues from the secret service were scattered over the docks, dressed as sailors, captains, customers, and even revolutionaries from Skera. They were determined to retrieve the letters tonight.

Several men in dark clothes looked very suspicious.

"Ifer's men," Darius said. "They're here to ensure the ship sails safely to Skera. This area is under his thumb."

The docks had been safe years ago before Ifer gained control of them after buying properties in the area. Now, it was a thriving hotbed of bootlegging, illegal immigration, and crime. In the last year alone more than two hundred people had been murdered by the dockside. The crown couldn't gain control of the place, thanks to Ifer. Most of the illegal immigrants visited either through the Terra border or the Elysium border. The black waters stared at Petronilla.

"They've begun to arrive," Darius said. From the corner of her eye, Petronilla spotted someone that looked human arriving with a document to board the ship to Terra. Felix's agents approached him first, but she saw shadow figures approach them from behind. She stood up, but Darius grabbed her arm and pulled her down. "Observe. Don't act." He watched the secret agent who was dressed as an officer check the documents while the men in black clothes looked on and admit him to the ship. She breathed a sigh of relief. The men backed off.

More people began appearing in the same direction.

"Do you see him?" Darius asked. Petronilla shook her head. Two other passengers, both of whom looked normal, appeared next. Ifer's men were keeping a close watch on their turf. Petronilla counted; there were six of them. Including Tranagard and all the spies, there were twelve of them. Ifer's men were outnumbered. Petronilla felt a warm tingle of satisfaction at that. They were going to get her father tonight.

But as several more passengers climbed in, she felt hope diminish. The ship was full, just fifteen minutes from setting sail but there was no sign of him yet.

"Did they discover us?" Darius wondered aloud. "He should've been here by now."

"I'm going to look." Petronilla stood up. Her legs were cramped from sitting and waiting.

"But..."

"We've got the agents covering the docks," she said, taking off in the other direction. She walked past the entrance of the docks which was a large arched gate made from stones. They'd been here for hours, and it was already past midnight.

She followed the streetlamps, mixing with the crowd. When she looked at her reflection, she wondered what Acelina would be doing at that moment. She stopped, catching the glint of something shiny on the abandoned house window. She turned sharply, her eyes latching onto a bracelet. She recognized the bracelet instantly- her father. The last time she'd spotted him at Duality, he'd been wearing the same bracelet.

Her gaze shot to the man who wore the bracelet. His grey hair was visible under his cloak which was large enough to conceal the letter. She walked nervously, glancing around at strangers as if looking for someone. Her feet moved on their own accord. Their eyes met across the crowded street. She'd recognize his face anywhere. Too bad he recognized hers as well. His legs sprang into action. He broke into a run, frantically elbowing and tearing past the crowd.

Oh no, she wasn't going to let him go this time.

Her feet sped up, cutting across an alley, pushing drunk and waddling people out of her way. The gleam disappeared into another alley, but she didn't let up. He smashed against carts and threw bottles at her- all of which missed. He was running for his life, but so was she. The roads curved and curved until it was hard to tell one from the other. She was too busy keeping her eyes trained on his slimy form to notice where she was heading. The number of people dwindled as they ran further. Finally, she came to a stop at a dead end.

She had seen him head here, but he was nowhere to be seen. She looked all around, taking in the water dripping from iron pipes over her head. Stony walls and abandoned houses surrounded her. There was very little light, most of it coming from a single streetlamp. The ground was broken, grime clinging to the edges of broken stones. Moss grew on the wall to her right, the smell of stagnant water spreading.

"Show your face," she said, her voice echoing in the clearing. There was no response. She looked to her other side, catching a shadow. As soon as she approached it, it disappeared. She rubbed her eyes to keep them open.

A light jingling sound caught her ear. She reacted instantly, just in time to see her father coming at her with what looked like a knife. Catching his arm, she turned him over, slamming him against the wall. The knife skittered to the ground, landing with a soft thud. His weasel-like features came into the light, his rotting broken teeth laughing. His eyes were the same brown as hers, though she hated to think of her having any part of him.

"Hello, daughter. We meet again." He was struggling against her grip. Twenty-three years ago he'd been bigger and stronger than her and she was dependent on him for survival.

Not anymore.

"You stole letters from the King of Terra." She got straight to the point, digging into his cloak, and checking his pockets. "Where are they?"

His eyes scrutinized her, pausing to linger on the love

bite. Immediately, her hands flew to cover it, but it was too late.

"You're sleeping with that whore, huh?" he went on. "I should've expected that from the way you reacted-"

"Shut up." She slammed him against the wall, rage, disgust, sleepiness, and jealousy all mixing to fuel her movements.

"Like attracts like, they say," he scoffed. "You became a lieutenant general but you can't wash off your past."

"Are you going to shut up?" Fury pounded on her ribs. Her mind was crowded with thoughts. She shook her head, fighting to maintain focus amidst the chaos in her mind and heart. "You have no right to speak about anyone else when you sold your daughter to a brothel!" Petronilla's throat was tight, but she kept looking for the letters in his clothing.

A gleam flashed in his eye. "That's all you were worth. You were never good for anything else."

"You're wrong," she said. "I'm worth more than you could ever imagine. Now, show me the letters."

"Is that any way to talk to your father?" he slurred. It was then that she stumbled on a stack of something wrapped around his calves. She pulled his pant leg up, exerting force to keep him pinned and saw a stack of letters wound around and attached to his leg. Tearing the ribbon that bound them, she gathered the letters. There were three of them, in total.

"Is this all?" Petronilla asked, trying to steady her emotions. She pushed him harder against the wall until he squirmed. She couldn't believe she had come from a person like him. Their brown hair, tan skin, and dark eyes were the only things they shared.

"Of course not," he said. "Ifer already has the most important one." Petronilla didn't know whether he was telling the truth or baiting her. "You're no match for him. None of you are. He'll have his revolution, I tell you."

"You've seen him?" she asked. Ifer was notorious for never having been seen by anyone. He was a phantom- part-fiction, part-reality— and the reality of him had very few facts to support it. Yet, his deeds were very real. "Why does he want a revolution in Skera?"

"Escayton, not Skera." Her father was usually chatty today but she chalked it up to her thigh pressing him against the wall. "Skera is only the beginning..."

"Tell me where the letter is!" she spat.

"You're so impatient," he said. "Your escort wouldn't tolerate you if you didn't pay her."

Petronilla couldn't control the flash of fury that pulsed through her. Before she realized it, her fist pounded on his face, bloodying his nose.

"I don't have time for you," she said. "Where's. The. Letter?"

Her father flashed a smile that made all the warnings ring out in her head. "Goodbye, daughter-"

She saw a shadow behind her— one of Ifer's men. But he was fast. Thankfully, General Darius was right behind her. He attached and she watched him crumble to the ground as the sound of flesh hitting flesh echoed.

"Petronilla!" Darius stood behind her. Her father took the opportunity to elbow her and ran away. Darius ran after him, and Petronilla followed, clearing the haze in her head. She slipped the letters into her pocket.

As soon as they turned the corner, they were attacked by two large men. Petronilla dodged instinctively. Darius was quicker, dodging and elbowing the assailant.

"Ifer's men," Petronilla bit out, her eyes fixed on the large, rough-looking man in front of her whose sole aim was to stall them. Petronilla flew at him, kicking, punching, ducking, dodging, and elbowing until he lay on the floor. Skipping over the bodies, Darius and Petronilla chased her father, skipping past strangers, dodging carts, and keeping their aim focused. Predictably, he ran towards the dock, eager to escape.

Darius and Petronilla's pace quickened. Her knees felt weak, reeling from the effects of starvation. She hadn't eaten anything all day in her relentless pursuit of her father. But she wasn't going to slow down now. Brushing the exhaustion aside, she took the final leap between the street and the docks.

The first thing she noticed was that the ship to Skera had left port, six feet of water now lying between the harbor and the vessel. Ifer's men had left, their duty complete. However, Felix's agents now stood around the port, encircling her father.

"No, don't leave me—" In a last-ditch effort, he tried to jump into the ocean. Tranagard pulled him back by the collar of his cloak. Petronilla hurried to the edge of the pier, helping the agents steady her father. He spat and kicked to no avail. The agents tied his hands and legs and stuffed his mouth until he was relatively still.

"Good job," Tranagard said.

"He's in league with Ifer," Petronilla burst out. "I retrieved three letters from him, but he's already sold the most important one to Ifer."

At that, her father wiggled in the secret agents' grip. Annoyed, they carted him away saying, "We'll hand him to the royal guards."

Tranagard nodded.

Once they left, he told her, "Come in tomorrow. Felix will want to know the details." He suppressed a yawn. "I'm going to hand him over then go to sleep. We've been awake forever."

"I agree," Darius said, his red eyes matching Tranagard's. Tranagard and his team left first, leaving Darius and Petronilla behind.

"Good job," he told her. "I know you were being hard on yourself because you let him go once. But it all worked out in the end."

"We still need to get him to talk about the letter," Petronilla said. "And before I forget." She pulled out three letters from her pocket. "These are the letters I managed to retrieve. You should take them to the king."

"The only place I'm going from here is my bed," he said. "But I'll take them in tomorrow."

Petronilla bade him goodbye and watched him leave.

Only then did she begin walking home.

Truth be told, Petronilla was tired. Her heart was pounding extraordinarily fast, and she felt dizzy. She'd spent all day searching for her father, and she didn't want to think of him for even one more second. To add to it, an embarrassing growl emanated from her stomach.

. . .

WHEN PETRONILLA RETURNED to Duality after the episode, it was six the next morning. Bone-deep exhaustion claimed her. She was looking forward to going to sleep. The night had settled into a predictable and quiet rhythm. The wind was still. As she crept up the porch area behind Acelina's quarters, she found her sleeping on the floor, right behind the door. Acelina's crumpled red dress fanned out like a blanket under her body. One side of her face met the hard floor, becoming imprinted with a pattern of lines.

She'd looked forward to seeing Acelina again, but she didn't expect her to be sleeping on the doorstep. Why would she be here? Could it be-

Petronilla smiled down at her. Acelina had been waiting for her. Feeling a tug of warmth in her chest, she scooped up the snoring Acelina. She felt the smooth, cool silk brush against her skin. In the red dress, Acelina looked like sin itself. If she had a little more energy, she'd like to explore the perfect body under that dress. But she needed to sleep and so did Acelina. Light-footed and strong, Petronilla carried her inside. Everybody was asleep, and the corridors were dark. She found Acelina's room right away, nudging the door open with her foot.

She entered to find a dying candle on the table and open account books. Quietly, she laid Acelina on the bed. She stirred a little but didn't wake up, soundly snoring.

Stripping her outer clothes, Petronilla climbed into bed next to her, watching Acelina's even breath as she slept, their legs entwined. For all the seductive charm, the courtesan slept like a baby, holding onto her like a pillow. Petronilla continued to wait for her even breathing to transform into light snores, her eyelashes casting a shadow on that flawless skin. She looked so beautiful like she was from another world, up close like this.

Her heart pounded with the realization of her impending departure. Now that she'd caught her father, it was time to go. Her heart twisted and turned in her chest, uneasy. Feelings she didn't recognize stirred in its depths. Petronilla brushed a strand of hair that had fallen on Acelina's face, but as soon as her fingers touched skin, she was overcome with desire. Leaning in, she pressed a kiss on Acelina's closed eyelids, feeling the slight movement of her eyeballs underneath. Her heart stirred.

Acelina moaned but after a little stirring resumed sleeping. Once she was sure, Acelina was snoring again, she kissed the other eyelid, embracing her tighter. This time, her eyes opened, drugged with sleep.

"I'm sorry. Did I wake you?" Petronilla's head jerked back.

Acelina smiled like a Cheshire cat with half-open eyes. "You're back."

"I found you sleeping at the front door," Petronilla said, relaxing.

Acelina leaned in closer, brushing a gentle kiss on her lips. "I must've fallen asleep while waiting for you. What took you so long?" Before she could answer, Acelina brushed another light kiss on her lips. "I missed you."

The confession made Petronilla's heart still. Scraps of Acelina's silk dress brushed the exposed skin of her arms, but she'd forgotten to breathe. Acelina held on tighter, her legs coming around her. Her hand brushed Petronilla's collarbone, pushing down her shirt. Her eyes were tired, dark circles showing under them. There was nothing Petronilla wanted more than to make love to this beautiful woman who had given her a place to return to. But she couldn't. They were both tired, and she had goodbye lingering on her lips.

"You're sleepy," she said, grabbing Acelina's arm that was tracing circles on her collarbone.

"I am but—"

Petronilla returned the hand to Acelina's side. "Sleep, then. I'm not your client. You don't have to please me when you don't feel like it."

Acelina yawned, cutting off another knowing smile, and pulled her arms around Petronilla. "This is why I love you," she said, snuggling. "Good night."

Acelina fell asleep almost immediately, a loud snore echoing in the room. But there was no way Petronilla could sleep after what she'd heard.

I love you.

She'd heard those words. Granted Acelina was sleepy and not fully aware of what she was saying, but...what if she meant it?

"Love." She tasted the word on her tongue. How that word changed the world.

Made her see hope where there was none.

Made her believe in the future when she lived from one day to the next.

"Good night." Her voice was tight, but her arms wrapped

around Acelina, strange sensations wreaking havoc in her heart.

When the morning came, she'd have to go.

And that scared her.

TWENTY-FOUR

PETRONILLA

Petronilla awoke early the next morning, her mind plagued by thoughts. She slipped out of bed quietly, finding her room among the maze of doors. The cook was up, chatting in a loud voice with one of the maids, as the smell of oatmeal filled the air. She ate breakfast quickly, stuffing her empty stomach with anything she could find.

"How's work?" Rose asked, eating breakfast with her. She woke up at three in the afternoon, keeping in line with the courtesans' timings.

Petronilla stopped eating, the toast turning to ash in her mouth. "Good." It wasn't a lie. Her voice dropped. "I think it's time for me to leave."

"Leave what?" "Leave Duality."

"Permanently?" At that, Rose's eyes went wide.

"Yes. I have a home in the city," Petronilla said, her lips pressed together. "You probably don't know this, but I came here as part of a mission. It's over now, so I must leave."

"Did Acelina ask you to leave?" Rose's eyes bore into Petronilla's, her forehead creasing with confusion.

"No. She doesn't know." Petronilla paused. "Yet."

"I think you should talk to her about it." Rose stood up with her finished plate. "The rest of them will be coming soon. Finish your breakfast in peace while it lasts."

Petronilla finished her breakfast, thanked Rose, and then went to the storage. Sneaking in, she gathered her belongings and began packing. The paltry light from the ceiling window, the crawling cockroaches, the stuffy scent, and the crate she'd converted into a nightstand. She sat on the bed, watching the large open space in the middle of the room where she'd once installed a bathtub. The memory brought back the feel of Acelina's fingers on her. Petronilla closed her eyes. Even this depressing, rat-infested storage had become important to her now. It bore happy memories.

Petronilla hadn't brought many clothes, knowing she could run back to her place anytime. But, as she stuffed her bag with five sets of clothing, she felt a sinking blackness envelop her heart. Last night, when she saw Acelina sleeping on the floor, she felt at home for the first time. Her house in the city was merely a place to sleep with four concrete walls and a comfortable setup. It wasn't home. Nobody was waiting for her there.

But she couldn't go on living here, could she?

She, who had spent her entire life avoiding pleasure houses, now wanted to live in one. The irony of her situation made her laugh. For a moment, she contemplated asking Acelina to let her stay. She hated pleasure houses but if it was with Acelina, she wouldn't mind living in a dump. It was a place, just like any other. If she left her prejudice where it belonged, she'd see that this pleasure house held a lot of pleasant memories for her.

"Petronilla?" a sleepy voice emerged from the doorway. The door opened, light pouring in. Acelina peered in, dressed in her white satin nightgown. She took another step, a large smile on her face, then stopped at the sight of neatly folded clothes on the bed and an open bag. She closed the door behind her and approached Petronilla.

"What are you doing?"

A tense silence hung in the air. Acelina had already seen the guilt stamped on her face.

"We caught my father last night." Petronilla's voice broke through layers of guilt.

"Really? That's wonderful!" Acelina's eyes lit up.

"Yes. I'm going to meet the king and hand over the letters today. Then..." Petronilla dragged out her next sentence with a long pause. Acelina's eyes opened wide, her mouth puckering. "Then, I'll have to leave."

"Leave?"

"Leave Duality," she said. As they both grew silent, she heard the chatter of Duality staff and the clanking of utensils from the kitchen.

"Why?" Acelina remained standing, her eyes fixed on Petronilla.

"What do you mean, why?" Petronilla asked. "I have a house in the city. You've been generous and let me stay, but now that the mission is over, I can't impose on your hospitality—"

"You can."

"What?"

"Impose on my hospitality." Petronilla noticed that Acelina was playing with her fingers with uncharacteristic nervousness.

"What?" It was Petronilla's turn to blink.

"I know you don't like it here, but..." Acelina exhaled. "I thought you might want to live here a little longer...maybe a lot longer..."

"Hmmm?" Petronilla didn't know what she was hearing.

"You could continue staying here and..." Acelina paused, coming to stand before her. When their eyes met, Acelina looped her arms around Petronilla's neck. "I want you to stay with me. I've been thinking about it a lot and..." She took a deep breath. "I've never known anyone like you. I can't stop thinking about you. If you don't mind living here with me, I want to keep you."

Petronilla was too stunned to reply. The ramifications of that statement ran through her mind. If they stayed together, then they were—

"Do you not like it here?" Acelina looked down at her. When she was quiet, she continued, "Of course you don't. It reminds you of your past, doesn't it?"

"No, I like it here," she said quickly, holding Acelina's hands. "I'd love to stay. But I hope you know what that means."

"It means we're in a relationship," Acelina finished for her.

Petronilla had never been in a relationship before. This was all new, uncharted territory for her, and she didn't have a blueprint. What if things died down between them? She'd have nowhere to go. And where would she sleep on days they fought?

The storage, most likely.

"What're you thinking about?" Acelina moved closer, concerned. Petronilla hated to be the one who put that frown on her face.

"I have no idea how this would work. What if it doesn't work out?"

Her mind was racing. She could go to work from here, of course. She'd been here more than a week, and it'd worked out well. But there was something that bothered her more— Acelina's profession. If she lived here, she wouldn't be able to turn a blind eye to the customers she took in.

"We'll figure it out together," Acelina said. "And you always have your house in the city."

"I don't know where this is going and sometimes it terri- fies me," Petronilla says. "But it terrifies me more to let you go without trying."

"Letting you go wasn't an option for me," Acelina said. "I'm too into you. You know how possessive I can be."

"I know." Petronilla frowned.

"What is it?" Acelina asked, kneeling on the floor. "I can tell something's on your mind."

"If we're going to be in a relationship..." she hesitated. "I'd like it if we were...exclusive. I can't bear the thought of you sleeping with somebody else after last night." She paused. "I know it's your job but...please think about it."

"You're asking me to retire? That's a lot." Acelina's voice was teasing, but there was a gravity underlying her words.

"Looking at you with my father drove me crazy. I don't

like you with anyone but me," Petronilla confessed, still not meeting her eye. "I guess we're both possessive." They were close enough now for their arms to brush.

"And I can't offer you anything but my loyalty in return." Petronilla's voice dropped. "I know what your profession means to you. You're always looking out for others, and I don't want to be the person to take that away from you. But it's going to be hard for me to accept I'm not the only one, especially if I live here. So, even if it's temporary—"

Acelina silenced her with a kiss.

"I should be offended," she said, tearing her mouth away. "What?"

"I haven't accepted clients since the first night we spent together," she explained. "You think I could sleep with someone else after what we did?"

The thoughtfulness made her heart warm. What was she thinking? Acelina would never do that to her.

"No, I didn't think—" Petronilla raked a hand through her hair. "I didn't know what to expect. I've never been in a relationship before."

"I should stop forgiving you so easily." Acelina frowned. "You're beginning to take me for granted."

"I didn't mean to. I'll have to work harder on being nice to you," Petronilla said.

"So, what's your answer?" Doubt flickered over Acelina's onyx eyes. Petronilla swallowed, desperately trying to drown out her father's words. Was she ready to close her last exit route? If she said yes, there'd be no going back.

"You know, before you asked me to stay, I was planning to beg you to let me stay," Petronilla said, her voice serious.

"Really?" Acelina's eyes twinkled with amusement. She inched closer, her fingers curling around Petronilla's upper arm. "That would have been fun to watch."

They both stood up together, glad the issue was sorted. "You should move to my room now that you've finished

packing," Acelina said, pulling at her bag. "If you want anything else moved, let me know."

Petronilla leaned in to kiss her. What started as a peck turned into a passionate kiss. They explored each other, tongues clashing and exploring.

"I love you," Acelina said when their lips parted, swollen with morning kisses. Petronilla didn't stiffen this time, embracing her instead.

"Thank you."

And that was that. She was going to take a risk and see where this road would lead.

PETRONILLA WALKED to court a week later, wearing a happy smile. In the preceding week, Felix, Darius, and the secret service had gotten her father to talk. The good news was that they had three of the four stolen letters. The bad news was the missing one was gone for good. Despite the secret service's fervent efforts to trace the whereabouts of Ifer, they had found nothing. For all they knew, Ifer was in Skera. But she remembered her father's words,

"Why does Ifer want to start a revolution in Skera?" Felix had asked her father last week. To that, his reply had been,

"If Ifer helps Skera, they will become allies in fighting for Escayton's freedom."

Escayton had always been a controversial territory of Inferno. They'd had an independent royal family before King Delton married Princess Xara of Escayton. His marriage had helped annex the small kingdom that bordered Elysium to the north and Inferno to the south, but the king and queen hadn't stayed together after the wedding. As far as royal marriages went, theirs was a typical one. Though no children had come out of the marriage, it had advanced King Delton's ambition of owning more land. He would take over all three kingdoms if he could. The queen lived in Snakefront, a town that was halfway between Inferno City and Escayton, and led a generally quiet life. Though Petronilla had never seen her, she'd heard about her from Darius. But if there was a whiff of revolution in Escayton, the king would use the queen to quash it. In his mind, Escayton would always belong to him.

As Petronilla entered the palace in the afternoon, darkness became bright spots of light. The chandeliers on the palace ceiling provided ample light, though, to her dismay, they also made the palace warmer.

"Petronilla!" she heard the pet parrot's voice as she passed through the corridor filled with hissing snakes caged in bones. It smelled of wax and smoke. The gilded walls were spotless, and she caught herself in the mirror once again. For some reason, she thought her face looked softer than before. Her brown hair was tied up, and her face appeared more reddish than usual, but the dark circles under her brown eyes were gone. Instead, her eyes reflected the warmth of the gold framing the mirror. It was as though she was looking at herself through brand new eyes, and she liked what she saw. Petronilla had never thought herself beautiful, but her face glowed with a blinding radiance.

"Hello," she told the pet parrot in the cage of bones. "Petronilla!" the parrot's discordant voice pronounced. "Petronilla." This voice was warmer, with the rich texture of wine.

"General Darius."

"The king wants to see you." Darius wore a frown, indicating something was amiss. "Follow me."

They crossed a range of weird artifacts, emerging outside the golden door to the throne room. The door was open today, the chamber conspicuously empty. As Petronilla approached General Darius, she saw Felix standing next to the king. He wore his grey hair in a small ponytail, his black coat and red eyes giving him a demonic experience.

King Delton rarely looked pleased but today he was especially grumpy. Dressed in a robe of purple velvet embedded with golden finery, he had the superhuman ability to not sweat. The mirrored walls spread all around him. Dark blue curtains tied with golden ribbons framed the window and were reflected in the glass chamber. Sixteen seats made of white bone and decorated with black velvet cushions lined the way to the throne. Petronilla followed the ramp made of black granite to the throne and bowed.

"Your majesty." She got down on her knees with General Darius kneeling beside her.

"I knew you could do it," he said, drinking wine in the middle of the day. His fingers lined with silver rings curved around a glass goblet. "However, I'm disappointed we retrieved only three of the four letters."

"Yes, your majesty," Felix spoke in her stead. "Unfortunately, the final one is in Ifer's hands, and we haven't been able to gauge his whereabouts."

King Delton's forehead creased. "Let's send the letters we have to the king of Terra and inform him of the situation," he announced. "In the meanwhile, I want you looking for Ifer. The revolution in Escayton must be quashed at any cost." His hand gripped the goblet so hard, the glass shattered in his strong fingers. Petronilla saw veins bulging on his forehead and forearms. "Whoever thinks they can take land away from me must be set right."

Felix nodded. "I understand."

"In the meantime, we'll be delivering the three letters we have to the King of Terra." The king's eyes lazily moved over the broken glass pieces and the drops of blood that were beginning to form in his palm. "Petronilla, you will deliver them personally."

Darius and Felix narrowed their gaze on her. Petronilla's skin prickled, her eyes enlarging. The first thought that crossed her mind was that she'd have to leave Acelina. In the week that she'd been living at Duality, they'd forged a deeper bond. Her mornings had been spent trying to get her father to talk about the letters. By the evening, she was so drained, she wanted to do nothing but fall into Acelina's arms. Some nights they made love, some nights they spoke, and some nights they merely slept. But she looked forward to seeing Acelina's face every day. Petronilla was new to relationships, but she knew they weren't supposed to progress this fast. However, it was as if Acelina and her souls had met somewhere in the fabric of time and recognized each other from a lifetime ago. Nothing else could explain this deep connection they shared.

"This is our chance to convince the King of Terra to join us," the king droned on. "I've done my duty. Now it's up to the king to crush the rebellion in Skera."

Darius nodded. They all felt the anger that radiated from King Delton. In her entire life, Petronilla had never seen anyone as hungry for power as him. But no matter how much land he acquired, he was never happy.

His expectant gaze turned to her. "Petronilla will deliver the letters to the king personally and deliver the message. We must assure him our army is on his side should he need us."

"Y-yes." She didn't know what she was agreeing to because her mind had been woolgathering.

"Splendid!" the king's resonant voice echoed like a clap of thunder. "You'll begin the journey tomorrow."

"Tomorrow?"

So soon.

"The sooner we deliver the letters, the better," the king said. His hands twitched. Petronilla knew the news of the rebellion in Escayton bugged him. His feet tapped on their own accord, echoing the restlessness of the rest of him. "I trust you'll protect them."

"Yes, your majesty." Petronilla would do her job, no matter what.

"I'll ask the ministers to make preparations for Lieutenant General Petronilla to leave. She'll be accompanied by four royal guards, just in case." He turned the other way to a servant. "Bring me the royal jewel from the locker. We'll present it to the king as a token of our friendship."

"That's a wonderful idea," Darius said.

"You'll deliver the jewel along with the letters," the king instructed her. "Let him know we're on his side."

"Of course." Petronilla bowed, thoughts buzzing in her head. She didn't want to go to Terra but in light of the current situation, she knew she must.

Now she had to tell Acelina.

TWENTY-FIVE

ACELINA

ACELINA COUNTED OFF THE DAYS ON THE CALENDAR that she'd thrown up. In the past three weeks, she'd been sick almost every morning. Petronilla had been there twice and asked her to see a healer, but with work piling up, she hadn't had the time to visit one. She'd stopped drinking a week ago in an attempt to calm her stomach, but she kept throwing up every morning.

Today was no exception. Acelina had woken up alone in her bed that smelled of her beloved lieutenant general. She'd stared at the covers, breathing in the scent before nausea overtook her, and she had to throw up. When she returned to her room, a stab of loneliness penetrated her heart. Petronilla's clothes were crammed into the closet with hers, and her scent lingered. Everywhere she looked, there was something to remind her of her lover.

"Are you up?" Lily asked, knocking at the door. She emerged wearing a white silk dress, which made her look like a normal person rather than a courtesan. It had full sleeves, a round neck, and provided no provocation.

"Y-yes." Acelina straightened and slid the door open to find a fully dressed Lily standing on the other side. "Good morning."

"Morning. You look a little pale today," Lily said, a ledger clutched between her fingers. Her eyes reflected concern.

"I'm fine. Whatever I ate last night didn't agree with my stomach," she said. "You're up early."

"Yes...I had a few questions," she said, holding up the ledger. "I don't understand how accounting for wines works." Acelina felt pride bubble in her heart, as she invited her first employee in. She'd never thought Lily could shed her vanity and study numbers seriously. But in the past two weeks, she'd been proved wrong. Lily was quickly surpassing her as the manager of Duality, dealing with patrons efficiently and handling deliveries. Soon, she'd be able to manage the entire place without Acelina's guidance.

"Which numbers didn't you understand?" she asked, clearing the desk. Petronilla's correspondence with two pots of ink and feathers filled her desk.

Lily glanced around the room and smiled. "We all like Petronilla, you know," she said. "I thought she was rude in the beginning, but I've come around."

Acelina cleared the table and placed the ledger on it. She attempted to turn the pages, but her face swam with images of Petronilla. Her heartbeat loudly, and she was almost on the verge of tears, just thinking of Petronilla. Who knew people in love were so emotional?

"It's clear as day that you're in love," Lily said, turning to Acelina's eyes absorbed in the figures.

Acelina remained silent, but she also stopped turning pages. "I don't deny it."

Lily took her hands and faced her. "You've had a hard life, Acelina. You deserve happiness."

"Lily..."

"Petronilla might not be the most ideal candidate, but she is loyal and steadfast. She cares for you, and you can count on her to always do the right thing. You need someone like that to stand by you."

"Okay, what's going on here?" Acelina broke her hand free of Lily's.

"Look at this place." Lily pointed to the room. "She's everywhere."

"So?" Acelina placed her hands on her hips. "Why don't you get married?"

"What!?"

"You're getting sick because of living in this place. The smell of smoke and liquor cannot be good for you."

"That applies to you too," Acelina said. "You're older than me."

"I know, but I've adapted to it."

"So have I. Duality is my home. I'm not going to leave."

"I noticed you haven't taken customers for a while now."

Acelina was silent.

"Good for you," Lily said. "You know it's every courtesan's fantasy to settle down, but only some of us are lucky enough to find love.

"We've only known each other for two weeks," was Acelina's answer. "It's too early to think of anything permanent."

"Time is insignificant when it comes to matters of the heart," Lily said, resting a palm on her chest. "What matters is what's here. Two weeks, two years, two centuries...it doesn't matter. It's the connection you share that's important, not time."

"For someone who has never been in love, you give good advice," Acelina sneered.

"We all care about you," Lily said. "You think I don't know how you puke in the gutter behind the house or how you used to skip meals so that we could have more?"

"You knew." Acelina's stomach felt queasy once again.

"Yes," Lily nodded. "I know you think of us as family. We do too. I've never met someone stronger than you, but even you need someone to lean on sometimes. I just never thought someone like that existed until now."

"I couldn't leave Duality—"

"I'll take care of it for you," Lily assured her.

Acelina blinked, clasping her fingers. "I don't know if this could work."

"Give her a chance," Lily said. "Just like you gave me one. She might surprise you."

Acelina inhaled slowly. "Fine. I'll think about it."

Lily's face lit up.

"Now can we talk about the ledger?"

"Yes," Lily said, smiling slyly.

TWENTY-SIX

PETRONILLA

PETRONILLA ARRIVED HOME AT NIGHT. THE FLASHY RED-light district was preparing for another wild night, lanterns and shouts competing. Amidst this chaotic landscape, Duality's garden was an oasis of calm. She'd made a habit of using the back garden to get in, since it was closer to her room, and didn't disrupt business. She'd gone to her house in the city and packed clothes for tomorrow's journey. Felix would have them transported to Terra with her. After that, she'd spent time wandering around the marketplace.

She had no idea how to break the news of her departure to Acelina. Acelina would probably receive it better than she thought, but she was apprehensive, nevertheless. This was the first time they'd been apart for more than a day since the beginning of their relationship. She swallowed and walked, window shopping. Petronilla wondered if she should get Acelina something. She'd never gotten her a gift, but she didn't know what would be appropriate.

"Women like flowers," she'd heard a flower girl say to a hapless male customer, shoving him a bouquet of roses. "Red roses for love."

"Really?" The man had reluctantly paid her a coin, taking the bouquet from her.

"Works like magic," she'd said.

Petronilla agreed because she knew Acelina liked roses. She had never liked flowers before but since moving to Duality, she'd developed a newfound love for lilies. The corridors of Duality were decorated with them. Convinced that this was the way to lessen the blow, she'd bought a bouquet of roses, along with some fine wine. She balanced it all, looking like a clueless, lovesick fool, and stood before Duality several hours later.

As she made her way through the back garden, however, she felt her mind waver again. She didn't want to leave Acelina, but if they were going to stay in this relationship, she should know that Petronilla's job involved traveling sometimes. It wasn't unusual for her to be called away to far-off locations for months. So far, she'd been able to avoid them because there was no war, but considering the situation in Skera or Escayton, the prospect of one was never far away.

"You're back."

While she was spacing out, Acelina had walked into the garden and was now surveying the flowers and bottle of wine Petronilla held with a suspicious glance.

"For you," she said, extending the bouquet. "And this is something for your wine collection."

Sometime during her stay at Duality, Petronilla had heard from the cook that Acelina liked collecting fine wine.

She hoarded them like they were her kids and opened them only on special occasions. Though she didn't want Acelina drinking when she was having digestive issues, she couldn't resist buying the overpriced wine to soften the blow of her announcement.

"Oh, this wine...I've been wanting to collect it." Acelina looked up. "What's the occasion?"

Petronilla shrugged. "I thought of you." The real reason abraded her throat, making it heat with guilt. If she were being honest, it wasn't that Acelina wouldn't let her go, but that she didn't want to leave. She hadn't been to Terra since General Darius had brought her to Inferno two decades ago.

"I love roses," she said, smelling the bouquet. "Thank you."

Petronilla clasped her hands behind her back and shifted her weight from side to side.

"Is there something you want to say?" Acelina narrowed her eyes.

"I wanted to get something for you..." No, this wasn't going the way Petronilla had imagined. "I've never gotten you anything."

"You're a generous lover," Acelina said. "But you don't need to get me things. You're the only thing I need."

The flowers were slipping as her hold on the bottle loosened.

"Want me to hold them for you?"

"Yes, please." Acelina handed her the bouquet, which Petronilla carried in.

"You don't have to bribe me to sleep with you. I'm into you already," Acelina said, crossing their room.

"I'm not bribing you," Petronilla said, straightening. Damn, how did people start difficult conversations? She had no idea.

"And don't feel obliged to get me gifts either," she said. "I don't want anything except your..."

Love.

She coughed. "You."

"I know."

"So, are you going to tell me or not?" Acelina said, cradling the bottle of wine.

They stopped outside the kitchen from where several voices echoed. Petronilla felt the pressure, clearing her throat. "I...I..."

The kitchen door burst open, and Lily came out, laughing. She still wore her courtesan's ensemble of bright-colored silk kimonos and golden hairpins sans makeup. Behind her, the other escorts were gathered for dinner, waving at them. Petronilla waved back, tamping down a wave of disappointment. She'd been so close to telling Acelina about her impending departure. Well, it'd have to wait.

Petronilla smelled the savory scent of potatoes, garlic, roasted meats, and butter as soon as she entered. Her stomach took precedence over her brain. She picked up a plate and began filling it with food. The dinner table was a flurry of activity as everyone laughed, talked, and ate. All the staff was there.

Lily's eyes moved from the wine bottle to the roses. "What's the occasion?"

"Petronilla was feeling generous," Acelina said, passing on the bottle of wine. "Another one for my collection."

"Only one bottle?" Lily pretended to be hurt, her hand dramatically covering her chest. "What about the rest of us?"

"I'm sorry. I'll buy more next time." Petronilla lowered her head.

"She's teasing you," Acelina said, placing a hand on her shoulder. Their eyes met, and the words pushed against her throat. She became lost in the black depths of Acelina's eyes, her eyes caressing the slope of her straight nose, down to her chin that ended in a dot.

"This must've been expensive." Lily cut her a sharp look, studying the label.

Petronilla coughed, cheeks going red. Acelina moved away, knowing nothing would come out of this moment of connection except more speculation.

"The roses smell nice too." She went on, each word laced with meaning.

"Uh...yeah...I passed by the marketplace this afternoon." "I'll put them in a vase." As she crossed over, she whispered, "Acelina got Rose to make pudding for you." "What?"

"You like pudding, don't you?" Lily asked. Petronilla nodded. "Good, because nobody else does."

"You got Rose to make my pudding? That's a lot of work," Petronilla said, walking over to Acelina's side.

"I have my charms too," Acelina teased, dropping a quick peck on her cheek. The rest of the staff cheered at the sight, some hooting, some whistling. Petronilla's face went red, while Acelina merely smiled and brushed the intimate gesture away. "And she was dying to bake today."

"How did you know I liked pudding?"

"Darius told me."

"You went through the trouble of asking him?" Petronilla was touched and surprised.

"He's our only mutual acquaintance," Acelina said, holding the door open for her. "Now, go eat your pudding."

"Aren't you eating?"

"I can't seem to digest anything these days," she grumbled, following Petronilla in. "But I'm hungry."

"Have you seen a healer?" Petronilla's finger brushed hers, concerned.

"I plan to. Soon," she said, squeezing her hand. Throughout the dinner, Petronilla was tense, eating little.

She ate pudding, though, losing herself in the sweet scent of vanilla. Usually, sweets revived her mood, but even pudding couldn't pierce through her anxiety. Petronilla was the first to finish and they parted ways soon after. Acelina stayed back to make sure everyone was doing their job, while Petronilla retired to their room.

She spent some time preparing for the journey but since her clothes were packed and all the documents procured, she was bored. Laying on the soft satin bed covers, she looked at the ceiling wondering if she'd be able to say goodbye before she left the next morning. Words seemed to flow so much easier when you didn't have to worry about other people's feelings. When her thoughts finished going in circles, she fell asleep.

Six hours passed before the door opened again. They were well into the wee hours of the morning now, and a stab of light from the corridor woke Petronilla.

"I'm sorry," Acelina whispered, trying to shut the door as quietly as possible. "Go back to sleep."

"I was going to wake up," Petronilla said, rubbing her eyes. She sat up in bed, the blurry scene condensing to Acelina's face illuminated by a lamp that she was carrying. "What time is it?"

"Four."

"Are you done for today?"

"Yes. Lily said she'd take care of the rest," Acelina said, letting her hair loose. It fell over her shoulders in charcoal waves. Next, she untied her sash and removed her silk kimono, all in the dark. Underneath two layers, she was stark naked. Petronilla's body prickled to attention, but the spark was smothered by Acelina putting on her nightgown immediately. She slipped next to Petronilla on the bed before her reaction died down.

"How was your day?" Petronilla asked, pulling the covers to tuck in Acelina.

"Good. Lily's getting on well," she said. "Thanks for the idea. How was yours?" Acelina looked up at her, exhausted but curious.

Petronilla smiled. An uncomfortable pause followed their small talk.

"I have something to tell you," she said, their gazes meeting in the dark.

"I knew it," Acelina said, finding Petronilla's arm under the blankets.

"I'm nervous," Petronilla said, edging closer. They looked at each other and burst out laughing.

"Is what you're going to say that life-changing?" Acelina said, laughter fading to a smile.

Petronilla nodded. "Not really."

"So, what is it?" she asked, cuddling into the crook of her shoulder.

"I like you," Petronilla began, a prelude to the disappointment that was to follow.

"Just like?" Acelina touched the tip of her nose with a finger. She looked up, their gazes meeting again. "I thought we'd made it past 'like'."

They had, but Petronilla didn't dare to admit her feelings yet.

"I like how things are going," she went on, her stomach shaking.

"Mmm-hmmm." Acelina pressed a kiss onto the tip of her nose. Petronilla blinked. "I've always wanted to do that."

"So..." she went on. "I have to go away for a few days."

Acelina's hands continued caressing her jaw. "Where are you going?"

"To Terra. It's for work. I need to personally deliver the letters we found to the king," Petronilla blurted.

"That sounds important," Acelina said. "How long will you be gone?"

"Just a few days. I'll be back by the end of the week." "Have a nice trip," she said, pressing a kiss on her cheek.

"I'll miss you, though."

"Me too." Then, in a lower voice, "I'm sorry."

Acelina cupped her jaw and pressed a light kiss to her lips. "What for?"

"You aren't disappointed?" Petronilla asked.

"No. I know the responsibilities that come with being a lieutenant general. Darius has been my customer for years and he's goes away for long periods of time. I'm used to sleeping alone, you know," she said. "You didn't have to buy me flowers for that."

"I didn't know how to tell you. I wanted to lessen the blow," she said, kissing her back. For a minute, their lips were locked in a passionate kiss. Acelina's hands pulled her face in, as Petronilla held her petite body closer, feeling the brush of her silk nightgown and aroused nipples. "This relationship is so new. I didn't know if you'd be able to take it."

"A relationship is made of two people," she said, stroking Petronilla's collarbone, and working her way down. "If you and I think we can make it work, it'll work."

Petronilla's lips crushed hers, kissing her with a desire so intense, it made them both weak. Tears stung her eyes, but she shoved them away. There was no calming her heart, no placating the euphoria that tore through her being.

In her life, nobody had understood her as much as Acelina did. Nobody had wanted her. Nobody had loved her. Her father, the madame, and even her mother all wanted to be rid of her the moment they saw her. With every kiss, every hot stroke of their tongues, and every press of their skin, Petronilla sought to incinerate those unpleasant memories.

"Sometimes I think I don't deserve you," Petronilla said. "I have so many faults."

"Your faults are what make you." Acelina nibbled her lower lip. "I wouldn't want you any other way."

"Thank you." Petronilla's throat was tight. Acelina lay back, her head resting against Petronilla's heart. Petronilla wrapped her arms around her, cradling her. She closed her eyes and felt bliss wash through her.

That was when she knew that she'd completely and

utterly fallen for Acelina. It hit her like a ton of bricks. Acelina had slowly wormed her way into Petronilla's heart and she hadn't realized how much she loved the courtesan until now. It was a strange realization to have at four in the morning. She didn't know what to do with it.

"So, when are you leaving?" Acelina asked. "In an hour." Petronilla glanced at the time.

"An hour!?" Acelina sat up straight, head bumping Petronilla's chin.

Her attempts to land a kiss were rebuffed. "There's still time, darling," she protested.

"Stop lazing around and get moving." Acelina was in 'work mode'.

"Calm down."

"I won't be responsible for our country's relationship with Terra breaking down." She gave Petronilla's shoulders a shove.

Petronilla sighed, getting off the bed. "I guess I should start getting dressed." She threw open the wardrobe where her clothes were squeezed alongside Acelina's. It was yet another example of how inextricably entwined their lives were now.

"Don't you have to pack?" Acelina was sorting through her clothes.

"I sent a few clothes from my house in the city," she said, throwing on a shirt.

"Do you need anything else?"

"Nothing. Go to sleep." Petronilla pulled on her pants.

"Are you sure?"

Acelina didn't listen to her, however. She stood at the

door, waving goodbye when she left forty minutes later with bloodshot eyes.

"Don't forget to eat," she called out, rubbing her eyes. "Go to sleep," Petronilla said, embracing Acelina one last time. They kissed, slow and languorous.

"I love you," she said to herself once Acelina left.

TWENTY-SEVEN

ACELINA

THE NEXT DAY, ACELINA DECIDED TO GO INTO TOWN AND finally visit the healer. Her indigestion had gotten worse, and she felt the cause ran deeper than she suspected. Passing by several shops, she caught a glimpse of her grinning face on a window. Her cheeks were flushed, and her eyes were bright. Was that what they called 'the look of love'?

Acelina remembered Petronilla's words and barely suppressed the wave of joy that ran through her body. She'd heard the low, 'I love you,' Petronilla uttered when she retreated. Last night had been special, and she wanted to treasure it forever. She lingered at the window a little longer, fancying herself in love with the unexpectedly kind lieutenant general who made her body quake with pleasure.

She passed by a particularly dark area and found herself wanting to puke, suddenly sensitive to the smell of garbage, stagnant water, and the sweaty bodies that brushed hers. Nausea tugged at her food pipe. Her feet carried her faster to the healer's home down the square. There were several houses made of wood and stone surrounding it. The healer's house was a Tudor-style house with flower pots filled with peonies decorating the door. A creaky wooden board hung from the roof: Healer. The other houses in the line had similar flowers outside, and away from the gutter, she felt her breathing returning thanks to the sweet-smelling flowers.

She knocked, waiting for a reply. A matronly woman with greying red hair opened the door, shooting her a questioning look.

"I am here to see the healer," Acelina said.

"Come in." The door opened wider. She walked into a reception area that had several wooden chairs for waiting. The walls were white with two paintings hung on the walls. They were portraits of people. One was of the healer and his family. The other was of an older woman, his mother, she guessed. The house was pleasantly cool. A clean, citrus smell filled the air.

"He'll be with you shortly," the woman said, disappearing into a room adjacent to the row of chairs. Acelina's belly had calmed down a little, the smell of lemon making her nausea subside. She took in more aspects of the unadorned room, a vase of withering flowers lying on the table.

"You may go in." The middle-aged woman opened the door wider, letting her in. A white bed occupied one side of the room, while the healer sat on the other, mixing potions over a long wooden table.

"Good morning." The healer, clad in a brown kaftan, turned. His hair was gray, the same color as his eyes, which were covered with spectacles.

Acelina sat on the chair meant for patients. The healer sat opposite her.

"I've been feeling sick all week," she explained. "I have become sensitive to seafood and meat and can't manage to keep anything in my stomach. Especially alcohol."

"Hmmm...sounds like a fairly common complaint married women have," he said, adjusting his spectacles.

"I'm not married," she said. For some reason, that made the doctor uncomfortable.

"You're a courtesan," he remarked, taking in her flamboyant sense of fashion. She didn't reply. "When was the last time you had your monthly courses?"

"My courses?" The question put her on edge. To be honest, she couldn't even remember having them last month or the month before that, but that wasn't abnormal for her. She usually had erratic courses. "It's been over a month...or maybe two. Why?"

The healer checked her pulse, and then looked at her again, sighing, "I believe you're pregnant."

Time stopped for a second. His grey eyes held hers, searching for a reaction, but she was too dumbstruck to summon one.

"What!?" Acelina found her voice after a few seconds, feeling like a rock had fallen on her head. Her entire body jerked forward, stunned with shock.

Pregnant?

It was ridiculous. She was a courtesan and always made sure to take measures to prevent conception.

But she'd become lax over time....

And there was no way to completely prevent the consequences...

And, she hadn't gotten her monthly courses last month... That would also explain why she was suddenly sensitive to certain foods, sick quite often, and feeling emotional about aging and a certain lieutenant general's leaving town....

"Eight weeks," he confirmed, his gray eyes probing. "Eight weeks...." She trailed off, recollecting how her

nipples felt sensitive, and her emotions volatile. She had gained a bit of weight over time, but nothing dramatic. "I..." she placed a hand over her stomach. "Are you sure?"

"Yes. It takes around twelve to sixteen weeks to show," he said. "Especially if it's your first time." He quirked his eyebrow in the end, indicating it was a question.

"Yes, it's my first time."

And what terrible timing it was.

"Do you have any idea who the father is?" he went on.

"No." The possibilities were endless. She'd slept with

three men after the bet with Petronilla to quell her frustration. But before that, she'd been taking in two men a week until she stopped two weeks ago. Looking for her child's father was like looking for a needle in a haystack. Her stomach churned, tears threatening to spill.

"Are you sure I'm pregnant?" she asked, the words going over her numb mind. The short-lived happiness she found was already disintegrating. Fate was being far too cruel to her this time. "It couldn't be something else...like...indigestion?"

She sounded desperate, even to her ears.

Worry lines appeared on his forehead. "No. I'm sure you're pregnant. I could conduct additional examinations—"

"It's...unexpected..." she confessed.

Why did this have to happen now when things were going so well?

Burying her face in her palms, she took a moment to process the shocking bit of information. Tears of frustration stung her eyes. She'd seen many women leave the profession after getting pregnant, but she'd always thought herself above that. She'd always been so careful. Acelina's palms filled with tears, the sound of distant sobs filling her ears. The healer's blurry face came into view, his features softening to portray concern.

"Sometimes, one can find joy in unexpected places," he went on, trying to put a positive spin on the situation. "Maybe it'll all work out for the best."

She couldn't believe she was going to be a mother. She'd never expected to become one, and right now, she didn't feel prepared for the responsibility. She was financially secure but that was the only virtue she had as a parent. Acelina didn't know the first thing about caring for children and she didn't want to know. She'd never expected something like this to happen. Which was stupid considering her profession.

"I need time to think," Acelina said, thinking of last night, her face flushed with anxiety. After what they'd shared last night, she didn't want Petronilla to hate her. Having her child was one thing, but burdening someone else with it, was entirely different. Petronilla lived and died by honor, and to discover her lover was carrying someone else's child would break her heart. Sure, she'd do the right thing and stick around, but did Acelina want to burden her with this?

And then there was the incident with Maddie. Acelina

remembered how heartbroken Petronilla had been when she told her about her past. She considered carrying another man's child the ultimate form of betrayal. Knowing what Petronilla had been through, how could Acelina do something like this to her?

"How long before it starts showing?" she asked, dreading the answer.

"Four more weeks," he said.

Four weeks to say goodbye. It was a long time, yet not enough.

"Thank you." She rose and walked back home through a blur of tears. She'd never know how her knees didn't give out.

TWENTY-EIGHT

PETRONILLA

The familiar scenery of Terra filled Petronilla with a mix of longing and disgust. After decades of living in the darkness, she finally felt sunshine on her face. Her cells lit up, absorbing every last ray of light. The gilded royal carriage bounced along the uneven road, carrying her to the palace. There were trees with lush green foliage, unlike the barren brown ones that grew in Inferno City. Sunlight glinted like diamonds on a clear blue brook that flowed down the fertile plains. There were small brick houses, with grey cement showing through the red brick. Houses with roofs lined with hay to keep them cooler followed. A lifetime ago, Petronilla had lived in a house like that.

As they neared the palace, the scenery became one of dense civilization. The half-finished brick houses transitioned into ones decorated with designs outside. The city's market bustled with common folk who flowed through the sides of the carriage like water. Petronilla smelled grilling meats, the savory scent of spices, and a faint whiff of caramel. Patrons consumed delicious-looking food sitting in chairs outside crowded establishments. Steam rose from the pots and pans, and the sizzling sounds of vegetables hitting oil made her stomach growl. Embarrassed, she turned her face away from the four royal guards sitting with her inside the carriage.

They passed a boulevard of neatly manicured trees that led to the large golden gates to Terra's palace. Unlike Inferno's gothic palace with black iron gates, Terra's palace was a patchwork of bright colors. The main palace was made of brown sandstone that sparkled in the sunlight. The buildings behind the main structure were painted blue, yellow, red, and pink. Petronilla guessed those were the queen's quarters, the ministers' quarters, and various offices. A large fountain stood at the entrance of the palace, with several smaller ones populating the lush green gardens. Fragrant, sweet-smelling flowers bloomed all around them, encompassing all the colors of a rainbow.

The carriage stopped in front of marble sandstone steps leading inside. Petronilla and the guards climbed down, carefully holding the letters. King Delton has also sent a selection of wines and foods native to Inferno. Wearing her red uniform with golden buttons closed to her neck, Petronilla felt a cool breeze hit her face. Her skin reacted instantly, welcoming the refreshingly pleasant air devoid of smoke and heat.

Petronilla and the royal guards were escorted by men in light blue and green livery. It was a strange combination of colors that, though aesthetic, appeared casual. The interior of the palace was the grandest thing Petronilla had seen.

Intricate miniatures filled the entire space, climbing over arched doorways, and gilded pillars. It must've taken a lot of artisans and time to create something so opulent. The overall feel was red and gold, though there was a multitude of colors and intricate patterns to break the monotony. Tiny mirrors were embedded in the designs, reflecting a million Petronillas.

The door to the king's chamber was opened by two royal guards standing outside. The structure of the king's chamber was similar to Inferno's. Ministers sat on plush red velvet chairs that lined both sides of the golden marble pathway to the throne. Terra's throne was made of gold, embedded with a rich mixture of rubies, emeralds, amethysts, diamonds, and sapphires. Like the rest of the palace, it was opulent and regal.

"Welcome," the king's voice echoed in the large chamber. He had a deep, resonant voice. The king was small in stature and Petronilla suspected he'd only reached her shoulder if he stood. What he lacked in height, he made up for in weight. The king's belly protruded under his cerulean loose shirt that reached his knees. The garment was embroidered with glass and blue beads, and even some precious stones. Under it, Petronilla saw loose white pants made of silk. His eyes were brown like hers, and his beard and hair were almost white. Humans aged, unlike other immortal creatures.

"Your majesty." Petronilla got to her knees, the four royal guards following suit. Reaching into her pocket, she brought out the three letters and handed them to the king along with a letter King Delton had written. The king received it, his brows eyes shifting like a pendulum as he digested the contents of the letter.

"This is..." He swallowed his words. "A revolution in Skera." His words threw the ministers into disarray. "The king writes that the rebels in Skera plan to use the missing letter as leverage to negotiate independence. He will send the thief back at our request."

The court burst out into chaos. Petronilla and the royal guards glanced at each other.

"King Delton sent me to assure you that should you require military strength, he'd be happy to provide it," Petronilla said. "The rebels plan to use Skera as an example to free Escayton and the king won't have it."

"I owe Delton one," King Ives said, leaning forward. He clicked his fingers, and a servant rushed forward with a royal blue box. "Here's a small token of my appreciation." Petronilla received it. "Tell him if he needs any favors in the future, he has an ally in Terra. Here's a gift for your efforts."

Petronilla bowed, gratefully. A wooden box was thrust into her hands.

"We must prepare for the worst. Summon the army commander," he ordered. Two of the ministers bowed and left. He looked at her, squinting his eyes.

"You look like you're from here," he said, examining her with deep brown eyes.

"I was born in Terra," Petronilla confessed, keeping her eyes on the red carpet.

"A woman for a lieutenant general." He appeared hesitant. "Things are different in Inferno. Does the king know who your father is?"

Petronilla's heart sped up, fingers tightening on the box. "Yes."

"And he entrusted this mission to you?"

"That's why he entrusted the mission to me." Petronilla's eyes met the king's defiantly.

"King Delton is strange but his ways work." King Ives shrugged. "Here are some souvenirs from Terra."

The servant brought forth a crate filled with wine bottles. "Terra's finest wine," the king announced. "I'll have a crate packed for you too."

"Thank you, your majesty." Petronilla bowed, glad she'd found another wine for Acelina to collect. This time, Lily wouldn't complain about it either. She could already imagine the gleeful expressions on the escorts' faces upon seeing the wine. And for some reason, the prospect of their happiness brought her happiness too.

"We also have a precious vase made by our master potter for the king," King Ives went on. "As well as an emergency seal he can use to write to me if he requires an urgent favor."

"You're very generous, your majesty." Petronilla bowed.

After exchanging a few more pleasantries, she was done with the diplomatic visit. She was invited to stay the night at the palace, which she accepted. A royal servant guided her to an ornate golden door that opened to reveal a room as large as her house in the city. At the center was a bed laid with buttercream silk sheets and fluffy pillows. Truth be told, she was exhausted after a three-day journey and wanted nothing more than to place her head on that soft pillow and drift off. However, at the back of her mind, she knew she couldn't return tomorrow morning without visiting one last place in Terra.

After dinner, she called for a carriage. As she sat in her room, her heart was filled with trepidation. She recalled the night she'd told Acelina about her past. Though she still dreaded that part of her life, telling her lover about it had lightened Petronilla's load.

"I'm going out," she told the maid who had been appointed to serve her for the duration of her visit. "I'll be back late in the night."

"Our guards will accompany you."

"No need." She brushed the maid away. "I only need a means of transportation."

"We can't send a guest of the crown alone!"

Petronilla finally gave in to the maid's protests, allowing one guard to accompany her on her errand.

The maid bowed and walked off, leaving her alone in her room. Petronilla caressed the silk sheets, reminded of Acelina. Her bewitching courtesan liked to wear silk. Maybe she should get one of these silk sheets for her. Petronilla lay back on the bed and wondered how nice it would be if Acelina could come with her and see this place. She liked luxury and would've enjoyed the twenty-six-course feast they'd had that evening. Not to mention the assortment of wines in Terra. She'd only drunk a sip of each but knew from one taste that it was the finest stuff in Terra. Twilight, the brothel she'd worked for, served cheap stuff, and she'd always hated that smell. To think now, several years later, she'd risen from a mediocre prostitute to a lieutenant general who met with kings; the thought filled her with pride.

A knock resounded on the door, followed by a smooth opening.

"Your carriage is ready," the maid called out, without peeking. Petronilla rolled off the bed and followed her to the stables. She passed through the gilded hallways, finding her way out the front entrance.

Looking at Terra in the dead of night, Petronilla was reminded of her childhood. Though Terra experienced sunlight during the day, being a prostitute, her existence was confined to the night. The city streets lined with sandy paths were eerily silent save for the sputtering street lamps, and a random dog's howl. The moon in Terra was white, unlike Inferno. Passing the trails of her distant past, Petronilla remembered the time when she'd been a young girl and run out into those streets. At six, the world had seemed such a promising place, devoid of suffering and obligation. At six, she'd believed anything was possible, and that she could never be hurt.

The carriage lurched to an abrupt halt several streets over, in front of a destroyed three-story building illuminated by the streetlight. She vaguely remembered the stony exterior. However, no patrons filled the lonely street outside. Nor was there any light spilling out of the windows. The red-light district was completely different from what it'd been several years ago. There was nothing there except broken buildings outlined by moonlight. In the place of Twilight, the brothel she'd worked at, were ruins of what had been.

Petronilla stepped out of the carriage, asking the driver, "Are you sure this is the right place?"

"Yes," he said. "The brothel you mentioned closed down

years ago. The red-light district moved to the city. This area hasn't been used for a while."

As Petronilla saw the ruins, she found a tendril of laughter escaping her throat. She'd come here, thinking she'd be able to see some shadow of Maddie again, or at least the madame, but it was like they never existed. The uneven roads were replaced with sandy ones when the brothels went. Where there were once sewers and weeds, now weeds and wildflowers grew. In twenty years, the red-light street had disappeared. Just like her past. It was nothing but an old memory. It couldn't hurt her anymore because it didn't exist.

Petronilla's throat closed. She'd come all this way to face her demons. Only, there were no demons to face. Just like her trauma, it had transformed and faded away. Sure, there was a lamppost or building here and there that reminded her of the past, but the ugliness and sorrow that penetrated these quarters had faded to tranquility. Maddie was long gone, and so was the madame. Being humans, their lifespan was a fraction of immortals. All the things that caused her grief had died, leaving behind only the choices she'd made herself. She'd created a future, and in doing so, she'd erased the past.

Petronilla stared at the house for a long time, filled with the realization that the past had no hold on her anymore. Through years of hard work, she'd transformed the ugliness of her youth into a thing of pride and beauty. And now, none of the scars existed except in her mind. She was free to live and love again. Truth be told, she'd been freed several days ago but it had taken her this long to realize.

Turning back with a smile, she told the driver. "I'm done."

He appeared a little surprised, but nodded professionally, driving away once she was inside. She wasn't imprisoned here anymore. Petronilla might've been born in Terra, but she belonged to Inferno now, where the people who loved her would be waiting for her.

Including Acelina.

She knew without a doubt that she loved Acelina. She'd known it for some time now but hadn't felt free to love again. After tonight, she was done with letting her past chain her. As soon as she got back, she was going to tell Acelina how she felt.

TWENTY-NINE

ACELINA

It was the day Petronilla was supposed to return. Acelina hadn't slept all night, her mind filled with disturbing thoughts. She knew what she had to do but the weak part of her didn't want to let go of Petronilla. Their love was so new and still shone with that elusive golden glow. The selfish part of her didn't want to concede that feeling. But she hadn't gotten to this age without realizing that all her actions had consequences.

The baby was growing inside her belly every day, and it scared her more and more. One thing, she knew for sure- she couldn't burden Petronilla with someone else's child. Ever since her visit to the healer, Acelina had been thinking about ways to break off their relationship. They'd been together for only three weeks, but the connection they shared was much deeper than anything time could induce. She'd begun to dream of them growing old together in this home she'd made for herself. She imagined the passionate nights of lovemaking fading into a quiet companionship and a mature love. When the time left her helpless, she'd have Petronilla at her side, still looking at her with those sincere eyes. And she knew she'd give her the same sincerity.

A knock broke the train of Acelina's thoughts. Lily entered without waiting for an answer, staring down at Acelina still lying in bed, staring at the ceiling.

"You're lethargic for a woman in love," she said. "Doesn't Petronilla come home today?"

She didn't want to think about it. The less she thought of Petronilla, the easier this would go. She'd spent the entire last week crying herself to sleep, but today, she was finally ready to move on. She was going to do the right thing for both of them.

"I heard Petronilla's carriage crossed the border," Lily went on. She circled her way to Acelina's bed and stood to overlook her.

"She'll go to the court before coming here," Acelina said, getting to her feet. "How're the preparations for the opening?"

"Fine." Lily crossed her arms over her chest. "I heard you went to the healer."

Acelina stopped abruptly. "It was nothing. He gave me some medicine for indigestion."

He'd told her the morning sickness would stop soon. In the meantime, she was to stay off alcohol and take a digestion tonic.

"You've been having indigestion for some time now," Lily said, walking side-by-side. Her eyes narrowed. "Are you sure that's all it is?"

"Yes." Acelina's voice trailed off. "There's no need to worry."

Acelina opened the drawer on her nightstand and produced a piece of paper.

"Lily, do you think you could manage this place alone for some time?" Her voice was small but filled with resolve.

"What? Why? Are you going somewhere?" Lily leaned forward.

"I want to take a few days off," Acelina indicated. "I haven't taken a day off since I started this place."

"Of course, you deserve a holiday," Lily said. "Will Petronilla be joining you?"

Acelina sighed. "No. She's got work to do," she said. "Please look after her while I'm gone."

"How long will you be gone for?"

"I don't know."

"Acelina-"

Acelina shoved the piece of paper at her. "Give this to her when she arrives."

"You're not going to meet her?"

"No. I have to leave soon."

"But...I thought you'd be excited about meeting her again."

She wasn't excited. Her heart was frozen with trepidation. If she saw Petronilla, she'd never find the courage to turn her away. She had to leave before Petronilla found out. Petronilla would do the honorable thing, and she wasn't sure it'd be good for her in the long run. It was her time to be honorable now.

"At my age, love isn't about excitement," Acelina said,

swallowing another lump of guilt. Soon her condition would become apparent, and word would spread through Duality. She wasn't looking forward to her employees' reactions, but at least they would stand by her. They'd stuck together through the worst, so what was another surprise?

"Is there something you're not telling me?" Lily looked down at the folded piece of paper.

"Lily, please don't ask me anything." Acelina was on the verge of breaking down.

"Why?"

"When you came to me, I didn't ask about your past. I want you to do the same for me."

"You know we'll all love you no matter what mess you're in, don't you?" Lily placed a comforting hand on Acelina's shoulder. Acelina felt a tear run down her cheek.

"Thank you."

"I know you thought about this," Lily rambled on. "But I can't help but feel you're making the wrong decision."

Acelina didn't say anything. She couldn't think anymore. "It's time for dinner!" they heard Rose's voice call out.

Lily and Acelina appeared in the kitchen where the girls were ready for a meal. Acelina took her seat at the head of the table, noticing a vacant chair to her right. Her heart constricted, remembering who that chair belonged to. The members of Duality had added an extra chair to the table for Petronilla. Acelina rang the bell, getting the dinner started, but she couldn't taste the food sliding down her stomach.

"This casserole is amazing," one of the girls complimented Rose.

Acelina felt dizzy, her heart tightening at the memory of

the last dinner she and Petronilla had together. If she'd known things would turn out this way, she'd have stayed awake all those nights to spend more time with Petronilla. She'd have awoken early in the morning and kissed her before work. More potatoes went down her throat as her mind traced every last memory of her and the lieutenant general. After tonight, they'd become strangers, no, enemies, just like they were when they began. Only this time, there'd be no falling in love again.

THIRTY

PETRONILLA

As Petronilla's carriage crossed the border, a flutter of anticipation crossed her chest. She had missed Acelina in the past week and wanted to see her again. Now that she'd put a name to her feelings, she couldn't wait to tell her. She'd missed the enchanting proprietress, the darkness of Inferno, and everybody at Duality.

Duality was beginning to grow on her. It reflected Acelina's personality better than any other house because she'd built it through her blood, sweat, and tears. Every room of the pleasure house held fond memories for her. When she walked into the kitchen, she'd always remember the first kiss she and Acelina had shared. The storage held fond memories of the time they'd been enemies, and Acelina had let her rot with bugs. Acelina's room was stamped with memories of their lovemaking, every surface, and angle reminding her of a time they'd done something dirty on it.

It wasn't only Acelina she wondered about. She wanted

to see Turstin mature into an attractive man and watch Lily turn into an efficient manager. As the carriage rocked past the border security, Petronilla realized she'd begun to think of those at Duality as her family, and she was invested in their growth now. Those strangers were part of her world, and in their little ways, made sure it stayed bright.

After several minutes, the carriage stopped at the palace, where she was welcomed by the guards. Sifting through familiar rooms, she arrived at the king's court where only King Delton sat today. The ministers' chairs with velvet cushions were empty.

"Petronilla!" his voice ricocheted through the high-ceilinged room, echoing several times before dying.

Petronilla's footsteps echoed too as she transversed the space between them, carrying a velvet square box. She bowed at the base of the stairs that led to the king's throne and got on her knees.

"How was your visit?" he asked, narrowing dark eyes. "Very eventful," she said. "The king was pleased with our efforts. He sent you gifts. He will ask for help if Terra's army can't manage the rebellion in Skera."

The king's resonant laughter erupted, washing the walls in mirth. "Very good."

"He also sent a gift." Petronilla held up a square box covered in blue velvet. The king received it from her and opened it. A golden tablet embossed with Terra's coat of arms gleamed in the chandelier light.

"Exquisite," he said, holding it up against the light.

"He also sent a crate of Terra's finest wines and a vase

made by a master potter. They've been delivered to the palace."

"You've done a good job," the king said, laying the golden tablet aside. It was swept up by a royal servant to be taken to the storage. "I want to reward you with a new posting."

"A new posting?" Dread gripped Petronilla's heart.

"How do you feel about spending six months in the border training our new military recruits?" he asked, eyeing her with his gleaming black eyes. Petronilla swallowed. Several years ago, she'd told the king it was her dream to mentor future recruits so that more women would feel motivated to stay in the army. Back then, she hadn't even been a captain.

"It's too early for me to retire," she said, attempting humor.

"I want you to assess the situation at the border if we're going to go to war with Skera," the king said. "Once the six months are up," he paused, "you'll be promoted to general."

"What!?"

"You've done very well and I believe you have what it takes to win should we wage a war against Skera or Escayton," he said.

"But...General Darius—"

"Won't mind sharing his responsibilities," the king said, "I'm planning on a promotion for him too."

Petronilla's throat tightened. This was everything she wanted. It was a huge step, and she was grateful for his generosity. However, she now had Acelina to think about. She didn't want to live apart. A denial lingered at the edge of

Petronilla's lips, but she inhaled deeply, choosing to be more diplomatic.

"That's very generous of you, but it's very sudden," she said smoothly, not wanting to disappoint the king with an instant refusal. She'd find a way to tell him later in the week. "I need time to think."

The king nodded, moving to examine the porcelain vase King Ivan had sent, along with the crate of alcohol.

"He gave me a crate too," Petronilla said. "And some souvenirs."

"Good. Share it with your friends," the king said and then signaled to his servant. "Yolen, send for General Darius and Felix."

"Yes, your majesty." The servant disappeared with light footsteps, leaving Petronilla alone with the king.

"Thank you, Lieutenant General. You're done for today. Take some time off, and I'll see you once you've made your decision."

"Thank you, your majesty." Petronilla bowed and walked out into the dark.

THE CARRIAGE RATTLED its way through the city. Petronilla's mind was occupied with her imminent promotion and the sacrifices it would take. But she'd think about it another time. For today, she wanted to spend time with Acelina. As the long trail of red lanterns leading to Duality appeared, her excitement grew. Not too long ago, she'd thought them cheap and gaudy, but tonight, they illuminated the way to her love. Petronilla held the crate of wine in the seat next to her to keep them from breaking, wondering how everybody at Duality would react to having her back. About now, the staff would be having dinner together, an hour before Duality's opening.

After a torturous five minutes, the carriage stopped at the back door of Duality. Petronilla thanked the driver and got off with the crate of wine. The back gate was open, and the wind blew through the artfully cut trees, casting ripples in the goldfish pond. A shadow stood at the edge of the garden, waving to Petronilla. The carriage driver stopped at the gate with Petronilla's luggage.

"You're back," Turstin said, stepping forward to take the luggage off the carriage driver. He appeared happy but there was a hollowness in his eyes.

"Turstin." Petronilla gazed down at the crate of wine.

"We were all waiting for you," he said, trying to infuse more enthusiasm into his voice, but it shook. "Welcome back."

Petronilla blinked, feeling a strange emotion tightening her throat. So this was what it felt like to come back home. To know the familiar warmth of love.

"Thank you."

Turstin went ahead with carrying her single piece of luggage while she followed with the crate of wine.

Petronilla stopped outside the kitchen, hearing loud laughs and voices echoing in the corridor. Duality was quiet now that the day had ended but everyone was waiting for her. She kicked the door open with her foot and was enveloped by sound. Several escorts waved to her, and Lily stood up.

"Our lieutenant general's back," one of them said. "Did you have a good trip?"

"Yes. Here's something for you," Petronilla said, placing the crate of wine bottles on the table.

"What's this?" Lily picked out a bottle of wine and examined the label. Uncorking it, she sniffed. "Looks like fine stuff."

"The king gave it to me," Petronilla said, scanning the room for Acelina. She was nowhere to be seen. The smell of wine filled her nostrils. Lily was pouring the wine she'd brought into glasses, bringing one to her lips. "This tastes heavenly," she said, taking a sip. "You're forgiven for last time."

"Thank you," Petronilla said, plucking a glass of wine from the tray of glasses Lily and Rose were pouring. "Save one for Acelina's collection."

"Sure," Lily said, looking unsure. Petronilla sensed something was up but nobody was telling her what. The escorts gathered around the new wine bottles, eager to taste the finest wine in Terra.

"Where's Acelina?" she asked. That seemed to suck all the air in the room. They all looked at her, with a mixture of emotions from doubt to sympathy to concern. Lily stepped forward.

"She's taking a holiday."

"A holiday?" Petronilla didn't know how to process that information. On the surface, it seemed harmless, but her intuition told her there were layers to it. "She's never taken a holiday."

"That's why she's finally decided to take one."

"When did she decide to go?"

"Yesterday, actually," Lily said. "She left yesterday."

At that, Petronilla's hands froze over her glass. She convinced herself that there was nothing wrong with Acelina taking a holiday. She had been gone for a week, and if Acelina wanted some time off, she should let her have it. If only someone could explain that to her heart.

"Oh," she said. She'd looked forward to seeing Acelina all week; to professing her love. "When will she be back?"

"I don't know," Lily said. "She didn't say."

"Do you know where she went?" Petronilla asked, the doubt in her mind transitioning to panic.

"No."

"Does anybody know?" she asked the room at large.

They were back to sampling the wine and didn't have anything to say.

"Petronilla," Lily said, meeting her eyes. "I have something for you." She motioned to the door and walked out. Petronilla followed her to the end of the corridor where Acelina's room was. Throwing the door open, Lily told her to step inside.

"What's going on, Lily?" Petronilla asked, as soon as the door closed.

"I don't know myself," Lily said. Producing a scrap of paper from her dress, she handed it to Petronilla. "Acelina left this for you."

Raising an eyebrow, Petronilla took the piece of paper from her. Unfolding the note, she read it.

I'm sorry.

I won't be coming back.

Please forget me.

It was Acelina's handwriting, all right. If it weren't, Petronilla wouldn't have believed what she just read. Neat, cursive lines curved around each other, plunging her into an abyss of despair.

"What's the meaning of this?" Her eyes became unfocused. Lily took the note from her and read through it. "Is she all right?"

"Oh my god," Lily gasped, placing a hand before her mouth. "I was afraid she'd do something stupid like this."

"What do you mean?" Petronilla's entire body vibrated with fear. What if Acelina was in danger? What if she wanted to—

"She'd been acting strange since she returned from the healer a week ago," she explained, pacing. "I asked her about it so many times, but she refused to reply. I think he said something that got her worked up."

"What?"

"I don't know, but I suspect..." Lily trailed off. "It's not my place to say this."

"Say it anyway," Petronilla said.

"It's only a suspicion, but do you remember how Acelina used to be sick often?"

Petronilla knew that all too well. She'd held up her hair when Acelina puked that first morning.

"Yes. That's why she visited the healer, right?" At that, both Lily and Petronilla grew still. Her eyes widened, color draining out of her face. "Do you think she—"

"It's only speculation," Lily said. "But she's been showing all the signs."

"She is pregnant?" Petronilla's eyes were hollow, not knowing how to process the information. If Lily's suspicions were true—

She sank to the floor on her knees, holding her face in her hands. "That's why she left?"

"She didn't tell me anything but yes, it would make sense," Lily said. "And if she's made up her mind not to see you, you can't find her."

"I've got to find her. If she's pregnant, it's an even worse idea for her to be missing." Petronilla went to Acelina's desk and began going through the papers, desperate for a lead. "I know she can take care of herself." She paused, her face losing color again. Petronilla sat on the floor, all the facts running through her mind. "I don't know what I'm going to do."

"You're not going to forget her as she advised?" Lily asked.

"I don't think I can," Petronilla said, pausing. "I love her." Her declaration was followed by silence. When she turned around, she saw Lily's face soften. Brushing her tear away, she straightened her face. "Then there's only one thing you can do," Lily advised. "Wait for her." "Huh? But—"

"If she loves you, she'll return." Her tone was final. "That's the worst advice I've ever received. I'm going to go after her—"

"She needs time to process her emotions," Lily suggested. "Your going to her won't help."

Petronilla hated what Lily implied but she knew she was right. She had no idea where Acelina was and pushing her to make a decision when her feelings were in disarray wasn't the best way to deal with the situation. Acelina and Petronilla had never been apart before. Perhaps she should get used to these weeks of separation. It would do her some good. If they were going to be together, she'd eventually have to learn to give Acelina her space. So, she decided to wait. Acelina was smart. And she said she loved her. It wouldn't take her long to return.

THIRTY-ONE

PETRONILLA

Acelina didn't return the next day.

Or the next.

Or the next.

Leaves changed color outside the window, withered, and turned orange. Still, she didn't return. One week became two, and two became three. Petronilla had to decide on her promotion, but she couldn't bring herself to do it. Today, again, she was looking outside the window, waiting for the night to pass.

Today, again, she hadn't come. General Darius, however, had come around to visit. His eyes were alert, his usual rakish self, smiling happily at the sight of food and escorts, he asked Lily to see her. When she appeared, however, all his glee seemed to vanish, his green eyes filled with concern. She went to sit next to him, the air weighing down on her.

He'd chosen the VIP room once again. Instead of a life-less room, however, Petronilla saw her fondest memories in the neutral flower arrangement. She saw Acelina's face in the lamps that sat in all four corners. When the window opened, she smelled the flowers outside and was reminded of when Turstin left the room once she came in. Darius lifted a ceramic glass of rice wine to his lips, reminding her of the time when he'd dropped the glass, and her arms had brushed Acelina's. She turned her face away, praying the burn in her eyes would go away.

"The king told me he offered you a promotion," Darius began unceremoniously. His eyes penetrated her deepest thoughts, though his words were light. He'd always had the ability to read people's minds.

"Yes." Petronilla thought talking about work would help take her mind off Acelina's departure. She'd been attending to her daily duties and training, but she knew she was at a standstill.

"He wants you to assess the situation from the border," Darius went on, leading her into revealing the source of her indecision through indirect means. "You'll have to move there."

"I know."

"You still haven't given him an answer." Darius' voice was gentle. When she didn't say anything, he went on, "Don't worry about me. I'll be fine by myself."

"I know." Her voice was devoid of any cheer. "Are you going to tell me what happened, or should I continue talking in circles?" he asked, exasperated. Petronilla looked up, feeling a tad light-hearted.

"Continue talking in circles," was her reply. He smiled. "This is frustrating," Darius said. "I can't believe I'm losing my best lieutenant general to Acelina. Where is she, anyway?"

"I don't know." Petronilla's voice became smaller. "She left."

"Left?" Darius' eyes widened.

"Left without saying anything," Petronilla said. "I don't know where she is. Nobody knows. I tried to find her—" She shook her head. "Lily says she doesn't want to be found."

"People are stupid in love," Darius said. "They do things they wouldn't otherwise do...make sacrifices they don't need to make."

It sounded as though he was speaking from experience. The wistful expression she was used to seeing occasionally entered his eyes.

"Are you speaking from experience?" She'd never dared to ask him about the person he'd given his heart to.

He smiled. "The situation in Skera is under control for now," he said. "The king suppressed the rebellion. It turns out the letter was a love letter from the king to a courtesan. The usual fare." He waved his hand. "There was hue and cry, but it's all under control now."

"That's good."

"In light of the political situation, King Delton might reconsider your transfer," he hinted. "If you want to continue staying here, you can."

"I don't know if I should," Petronilla said. "I don't think Acelina plans to come back. Lily said I should wait for her, but I'm tired of waiting. If only..." She saw her own tortured expression mirrored in Darius' eyes.

"If only you could let her go," Darius expanded. "If only you could find her and tell her you loved her..." He laughed. "But all you can do is wait, no matter how frustrating it is." His breath turned ragged. "Because you don't want to force her feelings. You want her to love you back of her own free will."

Petronilla blinked, her gaze misty. Whatever General Darius had gone through hadn't been easy. She knew that now. He'd always been by her side, supporting her, but she wondered if he was lonely. No happy person would spend all their evenings at a pleasure house, sleeping with nameless strangers. Perhaps, Darius was trying to fill the hole in his heart by numbing his senses.

"Who was it?" she asked, now that they seemed to be trading confidences. Darius looked up. "The person you loved."

Darius shook his head, smiling ruefully. She was beginning to recognize that expression. It filled his face every time she brought up the past.

"It's all in the past." He stood up. "You should drop by the palace tomorrow and tell the king you want to stay in the city."

He reached for the door without turning back. "General—"

He turned around.

"Thank you for always looking out for me," Petronilla said. "I don't know what I'd have done if you hadn't taken me away from Twilight all those years ago."

"You'd still have made something of yourself," he said. "I merely facilitated your destiny."

Petronilla returned to her room, not sure she'd made any

breakthroughs in her relationship. When Duality wound up for the day, she closed the sliding door and reached for a bottle of liquor, desperate to drown her sorrows in the amber liquid. But she couldn't drink it. Weeks ago, Acelina had told her that alcohol was a courtesan's constant companion. But she didn't like its company much.

She let herself unravel in the dark, remembering every gentle touch, lick, and moan with which Acelina had made her come. With her eyes closed, she sometimes believed those touches were real, as if Acelina stood here, her melting onyx eyes hazy with desire. She remembered her lips and the feel of her tongue.

It wasn't just the sex she thought of. The gentler moments, like when Acelina had kissed her nose, and her cheek, squeezed her hand through the nightmares and held her as she slept, were the ones that proved to be her undoing. Her vision blurred, and ugly sobs racked her body.

She wanted to hold Acelina again, cry into her warmth of her, and know that she'd be by her side, no matter what. She wanted to tell her how sorry she was to have let her go, and that she'd do anything for another chance.

If only wishes came true...

At her age, she knew better than to hope.

So, she waited another day.

THIRTY-TWO

ACELINA

ACELINA FELT THE SEA BREEZE ON HER FACE, TASTING the saltiness on her tongue. The ocean blurred in front of her eyes. That's when realization dawned. The saltiness on her tongue wasn't sea breeze but tears. She was in love, and her plan had miserably failed. Three weeks of rusticating in a quaint seaside town had done nothing to smother her feelings for Petronilla.

She watched the ships come and go. It had been three weeks since she'd left Inferno City and come to Aquarine. In the beginning, the sea breeze, the rural scenery, and the food had soothed her. But over the weeks, the appeal of fresh air had worn off. There was nothing to anchor her here. Now that the fog of dread had cleared, she saw her mistakes. Over the weeks, she'd become determined to change the course of her life, to reverse the rotten hand fate had played her.

She had no defenses against Petronilla's sincerity. To be loved was a courtesan's deepest desire, and as the years embraced her, that desire only grew. With Petronilla, she'd had companionship and understanding, and those things were worth more than her pride. She couldn't let that opportunity go in exchange for a miserable life in a seaside town.

She knew she should have given Petronilla the right to choose. Maybe then, she'd have chosen her. No, Acelina knew she would've chosen her, with or without a child. It was Petronilla's strong sense of duty that she was drawn to. And that was the reason she hadn't asked. She couldn't be like Maddie and break her heart by carrying someone else's child. It would've been cruel to be subjected to that twice. So, she'd taken the easy way out. This way, only one of them would suffer. But she'd been wrong. Both of them were suffering thanks to her impulse decision.

Acelina walked back to her inn, not looking forward to another sleepless night in the hard bed. She missed lying in her bed. She missed Petronilla lying next to her. She missed Lily, Turstin, and Rose; she missed Duality. It had been ages since she'd seen General Darius. She wondered how he was doing. Over the years, she'd never had a chance to ask him about the person who held his heart. Now, she never would. It was difficult to accept that this would be her reality. All her belongings were still at Duality. She wondered if Petronilla had returned safely from Terra. She was tired of wondering. It was time to see for herself.

"I am leaving today," she said, barging into the inn. Her mind calculated the fastest way to get her clothes packed. "Is there a carriage going to Inferno City?"

"Yes, in two hours, as a matter of fact," the innkeeper, a

silver-haired man with red eyes said. "Do you want me to reserve a place for you?"

"Yes, please."

The ride took six hours. Just as they approached Inferno City, it started to rain. At first, Acelina thought it'd go away, but forceful raindrops shook the windows of their carriage, exacerbating her discomfort. A man sighed on the seat opposite hers, looking out at the rain falling in sheets. The constant pitter-patter of raindrops on the carriage's roof was intensifying. Abruptly, the carriage stopped in the middle of the road, and the driver got off.

"What happened?" she came off her seat, glancing at the pouring rain outside. It never rained in Inferno City.

"We can't go on in this weather," he said, putting out his thick neck. His hair was limp, drenched in rainwater.

"Let's stop and rest," the other passenger said. They weren't even at the city gate. At this rate, Acelina would never make it to Duality. It was almost time to open. She needed to be there.

"No. Let's keep going," Acelina said, swallowing her discomfort.

"It's not possible to go on in this weather," the driver reasoned. "Let's wait for the rain to stop."

Acelina didn't want to stop and wait. If she didn't do this now, her willpower might disappear tomorrow. But going on in this weather was impossible, so she nodded.

The rain poured and poured, as violent and endless as her thoughts.

. . .

THE CARRIAGE PASSED through the gates when the rain slowed down for a few minutes but hadn't made any progress after that. The roads had turned to sludge. At this rate, she'd have to sleep in the carriage. It was past nine. Duality would be open by now.

The man next to her had spent all day reading a book, while the driver watched on restlessly. She, on the other hand, had nothing to do. She'd only dreamt of Petronilla all day, trying to hide her emotions behind a veil of normalcy. Pregnancy had made her emotional and the fact that all she thought of was Petronilla didn't do much to improve her mood. Acelina had eaten nothing since morning. She was so hungry she could eat the carriage walls.

Unable to hold it in any longer, Acelina stood up. Even if it was going to kill her, she'd walk through the rain and go home, where at least there was food. Some things needed to be said before she lost her nerve.

"I'm leaving," she announced, stepping out of the carriage. In the misty rain, she saw a distant silhouette of the palace. The red-light district would be a good thirty-minute walk from here, but she was prepared.

"You're crazy," the driver said. "The rain won't be stopping anytime soon. You'll catch your death out there."

"I don't care," she said, boldly marching down the pavement. She had no idea where she was, but she'd figure it out. There were few people out in the streets at this time, and all of them carried umbrellas. The wet rain drenched her, making her clothes dark, but she didn't feel the dampness or the heaviness. She felt alive for the first time in a long while. She stood under the open skies, embracing the feeling of being alive. Flowers of hope sprouted inside her heart, filling her tired eyes with renewed optimism.

"Acelina—" she heard a familiar voice and stopped five minutes down the road. She saw a carriage roll past her and come to a stop. A face peeked out. Those familiar green eyes stuck on her.

"General Darius." Acelina found her breath. She walked to the carriage door. The royal crest was embossed on it.

"What are you doing out in the rain?" He took in her wet, disheveled form. "Never mind, just get in."

Acelina couldn't have been more grateful. She took the opportunity and brought her soaking self into the carriage. Sitting opposite Darius, she bled water onto the floor. "I'm sorry, I'm dripping water everywhere."

"It's the king's carriage. I couldn't care less," Darius said. To the driver, he said, "To Duality." His perceptive eyes gazed at her. "Lily told me you were taking a holiday. Where have you been?"

The horses began moving instantly as she leaned against the wooden seat, drenched in rainwater and bursting with anticipation. They couldn't move fast enough.

"Aquarine," she sneezed.

"The air in Aquarine is so refreshing," he nodded his head. "So, how did you get from Aquarine to walking in the rain?"

"I decided to return," she paused, "On impulse. It was raining, but I had to get to Duality. How is Lieutenant General Petronilla doing?"

Darius tilted his head as if amused.

"She got a promotion." He crossed one leg over the other.

"Really?" Acelina's eyes lit up.

"She spoke to the king this morning," he said. "He wanted her to move to the border, but she's decided to stay in the city."

Acelina was secretly relieved. "How nice. Were the letters delivered to Terra?"

"Yes. Thanks to our efforts, the political situation in Skera has become more stable," he said. "I never got to thank you for allowing Petronilla to stay."

Her stomach constricted, pain tightening at the back of her eyes.

"You don't have to thank me," Acelina resorted to politeness, but she couldn't maintain her veneer.

Looking away, she began to cry. Darius abandoned her to silence, serenely watching the rain fall on fogged glass.

THIRTY-THREE

PETRONILLA

Petronilla stood at the door of Duality, shaking like a leaf. The blood moon was hidden by clouds, the string of red lanterns lining Duality's walls a blurry picture. The goldfish pond she'd walked over the first time cooled the air; the fishes adjusted to autumn's slower pace. It was still humid, but the heat had waned, thanks to the rain.

Her visit to the palace had been eventful. Just as Darius had suggested, the king was amenable to her idea of staying in the city. She was to be promoted in three months, once Darius took up another position. She thought about her new position on the way back, deriving comfort from the fact that her increased responsibilities would occupy more of her time.

Petronilla pushed through the rain to the main door, joining a line of customers spilling out to the door. Even on rainy days, Duality was full. The gaudy silk and gold interiors now made her heart light up with warmth. Men with breaths already stinking of drink populated the sofas. When she stepped in, their gazes raked over her, making her skin prickle.

Amidst the cloud of moving escorts, she spotted Lily overlooking the process. She'd stopped wearing makeup somewhere along the line so men would know she was the manager, not one of the girls. Without the paint, her face showed age, fine lines creeping up near her eyes and lips. Petronilla cut a direct path to her. On seeing her, Lily smiled, her voice cut off.

"Good evening," she said, surveying her from top to bottom.

"You're soaked."

"It rained. Can you believe it?" she asked, wringing water from her hair. Rains were rare in Inferno and Petronilla enjoyed the coolness. "I'll go get changed."

Lily nodded, busying herself with attending to customer requests.

Petronilla walked out of the main building and into the workers' quarters. As she stood outside Acelina's room, she remembered that four weeks ago, she'd stood outside this very room, shaking with trepidation. Now, she was glad she'd risked her fears, and her insecurities, because even if for a moment, she'd been able to glimpse love beyond them. Petronilla closed her eyes, feeling tears push through her eyes. She entered in a swift movement and drifted to the window, watching the barrage of raindrops clatter on the windowsill. With a sigh, she sunk back on Acelina's bed, smelling her everywhere. Her heart ached with longing as the ceaseless rain fell.

It was going to be another long night.

. . .

PETRONILLA AWOKE an hour later to footsteps. Her back was numb. She'd fallen asleep on the floor, reading Acelina's accounts, of all things. Chattering followed the loud footsteps, waking up her mind. Sleepily, she glanced at the door, expecting Lily to knock.

But it wasn't Lily who slid the door open.

And it wasn't her who seared Petronilla's soul with her dark, penetrating gaze.

Acelina stood on the other side, her hand holding the sliding door open, panting and soaked to the bone. She wore a modest crimson dress today which clung to her body, droplets dripping down its heavy surface. Her face was wet, but her eyes were fixed on Petronilla.

She rubbed her eyes.

The scent of rain and mud was as real as anything could be. Petronilla came off the floor, standing in attention. Acelina had put on weight since the last time they'd met and now looked even more beautiful if that was even possible. Her stomach was beginning to increase but it was still hard to tell.

Even as a realization dawned on her, Petronilla's eyes absorbed every scent and color that made Acelina, like water falling on the parched earth. Her senses came to life. Their eyes met across the room, droplets of water sliding down Acelina's face. Her makeup was smudged, creating haunting dark lines around her eyes, and her breast heaved. If she couldn't have another moment with Acelina, she'd always remember this.

They stood transfixed for a long moment at opposite sides of the room, all words dissolving to nothingness. In moments like these, silence said more than words.

"I saw someone sneak in—" Lily emerged from behind her and stopped short. "Oh. My—"

"Give me a minute," Acelina said, sliding the door shut and locking Lily outside. Silence permeated the room as their gazes remained locked. They waited until Lily's footsteps faded away. Petronilla's hands were shaking but she clasped them at her back and began talking.

"I waited for you," she said. "I wished you'd come back, but I...I was afraid you might not." Acelina wrung her dress, making puddles of water collect on the floor. Petronilla swallowed but Acelina didn't say anything. Instead, she took a step forward, approaching Petronilla with slow steps, blinking the entire way. "I..." Petronilla's throat constricted, but she had to keep going. "You don't have to explain if you don't want to—" Acelina moved another step, and awareness consumed Petronilla. Her heart stirred up in recognition of the familiar scent of lilies. It was faint, muffled by the smell of wet clothes, but it was there. "I'm so glad you're back."

Acelina was standing in front of her now, her nose inches from Petronilla's chin. Never once did she break eye contact. Her pink rosebud lips parted.

"I missed you." Her right hand reached up to cup Petronilla's cheek. Petronilla felt the sensation down to her toes. "I'm sorry."

Without hesitation, Acelina got on her toes and kissed her. The minute their lips met, all the words she wanted to say died away, and heat drowned her. Fireworks exploded in her heart, and tears, unbidden, ran down her closed eyes.

Acelina's hands slid up her back, pulling her down to deepen the kiss. Petronilla wanted to give all of herself until they became one and nothing remained of her sorrow and weakness. At this moment, she felt infinite, as if with their love, they'd transcended time and space.

Their tongues met, re-acclimating. It was like they'd parted last night and met again today. Despite a four-week separation, there was no watering down the intensity of emotion she felt. Their bodies, though altered, still recognized each other. Acelina broke the kiss abruptly, but her palms remained on Petronilla's cheeks.

"I'm sorry," Acelina said again. "I never should've left you without a word. I was scared...and...I didn't know what to do." Acelina's hands slid to her shirt, grasping handfuls of fabric, and drowning her face in it. Her shoulders shook with sobs. "You're too good for me, Petronilla." Acelina held on tighter. "It's selfish of me, but I want you even though you deserve better—"

This time, Petronilla kissed her, making her forget all the excuses. They couldn't get back the time they'd lost, but the future was theirs. And she intended for it to start as soon as possible. Acelina's tears pressed into her cheek as their mouths met again, nuzzling and coaxing. Acelina shifted angles so that they could get even closer.

"There's something I must tell you," Acelina said when they broke apart. She took a step back, finding the courage to put distance between them. Then, she was looking at Petronilla again in a way that shot straight to her heart. "I can't touch you and find the courage to say this." She closed her eyes, a stream of tears running down her cheek. "You're free to hate me but...I thought I should let you know..." Acelina wiped her tears and stepped back.

"I'm pregnant." She held a hand up, choking on her sobs. Petronilla longed to reach for her, but Acelina backed away from her touch. "I don't know whose child I'm carrying. I don't care to find out. I went to the healer and found out while you were away...the first thing I thought was..." She took a deep breath. "Maddie. I thought of you and how Maddie's betrayal hurt you...And here I was, in the same situation...." Acelina leaned against the door, finding the strength to go on. "I didn't want to do that to you. I knew if I told you, you'd do the right thing and stay with me."

"Acelina..."

Acelina shook her head. Petronilla let her speak. Acelina's lips were trembling, her eyes pouring. "This is much worse. She...You..." Acelina swallowed. "She didn't love you...but I do..." Acelina's throat was hoarse. "I...did not want to break your heart...but I didn't know how to tell you." Petronilla didn't want to hear anymore. She wanted Acelina to stop crying, to wipe the sorrow from her being by embracing her, but she had to let her finish. "I knew you would do the right thing, but I couldn't bring myself to burden you."

"You're not a burden to me," Petronilla said. "Never."

"I thought about it so many times in my head...What I'd do when I saw you again...if I saw you again...." She inhaled hurriedly. She was gasping for air, torn between crying and breathing. "I regret having taken away your power to choose...I regret running away. I knew you'd never leave me and...I was scared because I loved you so much. I pushed you away because I was afraid." Her voice broke. "But..."

"Stop crying..." Petronilla's voice coaxed gently. "I hate to see you cry."

"I was a fool for thinking I could go on without you. Call me selfish if you will...I'm so sorry for breaking your heart... for running away." She brushed more tears away, straining her neck up to meet Petronilla's gaze. "If you decide that you can't forgive me, that's okay. But please..." Acelina swallowed, closing her eyes again. "Don't forget me."

"Darling—"

"I'm never going to find someone as good as you," her words caught on each other. "I hurt your pride."

"I don't care about pride."

"I betrayed you without meaning to." Acelina's words tumbled out like a flood. "I wanted to tell you that you had all of my heart...You've had it for some time now."

Acelina's eyes flooded with tears, unable to form any more words. She looked up at Petronilla, waiting for her to speak.

Petronilla closed the distance between them and took Acelina in her arms. Acelina's wetness seeped through her clothes, her hands clasping behind her back. She felt whole with her lover in her arms again. Yes, she loved Acelina and would do anything for her. Though the news of her carrying a child had come as a shock to her, she'd never hated Acelina for it. Perhaps, it was a blessing in disguise, a new start to their life together. Petronilla would love any child that was Acelina's. It would be theirs.

"I love you. I love every part of you," she said, holding

Acelina tighter. "There's nothing you can do to turn me away," Petronilla said, bending down to kiss her hair. "I'd wait as long as it took you to return to me."

"I don't...deserve you..." Acelina said, crying into her shoulder. "But I want you anyway. I can't believe you waited for me."

"If you'd told me the truth, I wouldn't have run away, you know," she said. "I wouldn't have stayed with you out of obligation either. How could you think that after all we shared? I love you and I cannot live without you. These past few weeks have confirmed that. You'll never be a burden to me. On the contrary, you've lifted my burdens...and given me a place to call home. You took in my bruised heart and made it whole. My heart belongs to you just as yours belongs to me. I'll love this child because they will carry a piece of you."

Acelina smiled a feeble smile. "You say the nicest things," she said.

Then, their lips met once again, this time in a sweeter, but more intense kiss. No matter how much Petronilla tasted her, it was never enough. It never would be. Somehow, against all odds, she'd found somebody like her and had no intention of letting go. Acelina was the first to pull away, gasping for breath. She brushed away a tear and looked at Petronilla with her lips curved up in a smile.

"I haven't felt this good in days. I couldn't do anything but cry since I found out about the child," she said.

"Let's change that," Petronilla said, holding her tighter, never wanting to let her go. "We're together in this. We'll figure it out together."

Acelina hugged her tighter. "Together...I like the sound of that."

They kissed once more and Petronilla let herself go completely this time. She drank Acelina in like air. She cherished all that they shared and looked forward to the future. Finally, her heart was home. Petronilla never thought she'd fall in love but now that she had, she knew it would last forever.

As if reading her thoughts, Acelina said, "I want to love you forever. I want to grow old with you until all our teeth and hair fall out, and my eyes can't see you anymore. Even then, I will love you."

"You're painting a very grim picture of our future," Petronilla said, but she couldn't laugh, because her eyes were misted with emotion. She too, wanted to be with Acelina forever, knowing she had someone as strong and caring as Acelina by her side. Someone who'd share her joys and sorrows, never judge her and see all her flaws as strengths. With her, she could be better than herself. And she wanted to be better.

Long ago, a man who visited the brothel had told her that love forgives and forgets, and love absorbs all sorrow and pain. He'd been heartbroken over his wife's death and cried all night while she'd watched on with mute sympathy. Now, all these years later, she understood what he meant.

"It's not grim," Acelina said, resting her head on Petronilla's chest. "We're both humans...at least half-human. We'll make mistakes. We'll age, we'll get sick, we'll hurt each other...but knowing you're by my side makes the experience better." Lifting her head up, she trailed a wet kiss on Petronilla's cheek. "Thank you for loving me. And thank you for taking me back."

Petronilla hugged her. "Let's get you out of those clothes before you get sick."

"I don't want to let you go," Acelina said, holding on even tighter.

"I'm not going anywhere," Petronilla whispered into Acelina's ear. "For a very, very long time."

ACKNOWLEDGMENTS

The idea for Silk and Sword came to me five years ago. I wrote the entire book in a frenzy and forgot about it. I never thought I'd ever publish this book. But this year, I finally gathered the courage to share it with the world. Silk and Sword was the first romance novel I ever wrote and it will always have a special place it my heart.

That being said, this book wouldn't have been possible without the help and support of some amazing people.

I would like to thank Kenna Young, who went above and beyond my expectations and helped breathe new life into this book. Your feedback and comments were invaluable in polishing Silk and Sword and making it shine.

I'd also like to thank my beta reader Gabrielle Finney for her support and feedback. Thank you for giving this book your love and attention.

Thank you Gennifer Ulman for proofreading this mess and doing your best to make it error-free.

I am also grateful to my sister for being there for me throughout this journey and for pushing me to be better everyday.

Finally, I'd like to thank all the readers for giving this book a place in their hearts.

If you liked Silk and Sword, please leave a review. Thank you so much!

ABOUT THE AUTHOR

P.S. Scott first started writing at seven and hasn't looked back. An unabashed optimist, manga lover and true believer in the power of chocolate, P.S. now writes books that transport her to faraway lands of imagination and shares them with other dreamers.

Subscribe to the P.S. Scott newsletter for updates: eepurl.com/hmhgAz

ALSO BY P.S. SCOTT

The Prince and the Thief

From author P.S. Scott comes the new Ambrosia Royals series, a high fantasy with a slow-burn M/M romance and plenty of action and political intrigue.

"The Prince and the Thief is an entertaining read with an intriguing plot and realistic dialogues." —*Reader's Favorite Reviews*

"It's scary how much I'm loving this book right now." —*Renee, Goodreads Reviewer*

"A great book with a great plot and suspense." — *Danial, Goodreads Reviewer*

Eighteen-year-old Will is a jewel thief with only one goal in life — to be rich. That's why when he spots Aidan, the second prince of Ambrosia saving a peasant girl from royal guards, he steals the prince's ruby bracelet. A few days later, Aidan stumbles into Will during a robbery, and the two strike a bargain.

Aidan is a prince torn between duty and desire. In a world where same-sex relationships are forbidden in the royal family, he is attracted to men. To make matters worse, his uncle is in possession of love letters that Aidan exchanged with his old lover. To save himself from becoming a pawn in his uncle's power games, Aidan hires Will to steal the letters.

Navigating a world full of thievery, magic, and jewels, Aidan and Will stumble upon secrets that could change the face of Ambrosia. As the unlikely partnership blossoms into something more, political tensions escalate. Will's loyalty lies with the rebels who want to overthrow the king, and Aidan is honor-bound to protect his family. Will they end up together or be torn apart by the hands of fate?

Made in the USA
Las Vegas, NV
05 May 2023

71611951R00188